Stolen Hearts on the Sound

On the Sound Book Three

Gemma Christina

Jpenname Publishing, LLC

Contents

Chapter One

Detective Jefferson Hughes ducked out of the rain and through the door of Callie B's Cafe. The scent of freshly baked bread, cinnamon, and coffee immediately took some of the chill from his bones.

And he needed it. West Sound and the entire Puget Sound area had been in a constant state of drizzle or downpour since November. They were now well into December, a fact made all too clear by the constant strains of Michael Bublé Christmas music playing all over town.

"You're bright and early this morning, Detective." The owner of the cafe, Callie Brown, stood at the counter, carefully adding muffins to the display case while Bublé's rendition of "White Christmas" played in the background. Her shoulder-length brown hair was in a springy ponytail.

"I bet you're here for one of these." She motioned with her head to the freshly placed muffins, grinning so that her eyes smiled too. Callie's place had become incredibly popular lately, and Jefferson suspected it was due in part to the owner's knack for making each customer feel like they were her favorite.

"How'd you guess?" He gazed longingly at the muffins as he ran a hand through his blond hair, dispersing the raindrops gathered there.

"Oh, I think you can smell the muffins from the station, because you always seem to show up when they are fresh from the oven," she teased. "But this is a little earlier than usual."

"Station training today," he said flatly. "I need something to get me through it," he added with a sigh. "How about that coconut chocolate chip?"

"Ooh, excellent choice," said a bubbly voice next to him.

Surprised, he turned to see MJ's friend, the cute blonde school counselor.

"I love that flavor," she said. "I think I snagged the first one." She held up a Callie B's bag as proof.

When he didn't say anything, she grinned at him with sparkling brown eyes. "You probably don't remember me. I'm Shannon Davis. I'm—"

"Sorry. Of course, I remember," he cut in. "You work at the middle school."

She was even more attractive than he remembered. They met earlier in the year when she and teacher MJ Brooks came to check on a missing student at the home of a dead man. MJ's presence there had surprised and somewhat agitated Jefferson. He didn't really see Shannon that day, except to notice how it irked MJ when her friend flirted with him.

"Yeah, I'm headed there now, but I didn't want to miss my chance to say hello," she said, her smile bright for such a cold, dreary day.

With a thud, Callie closed the display case and set his bagged muffin on the counter. Jefferson flicked his eyes at her just in time to see her raised eyebrows and encouraging wink. Then she turned to help another customer at the register.

Shannon had suddenly started digging in her enormous purse, either out of need or because she also saw Callie's facial signals.

Jefferson grabbed the muffin. "It was nice to see you," he said.

She raised her eyes back to his, holding a gaggle of keys and putting the bag back on her shoulder. "You too."

"I'm really sorry about your uncle," Jefferson added, lowering his voice.

She nodded. "I appreciate that. My aunt is doing much better." Her pretty features stilled as she reflected on the events of a few months ago. "I'm afraid that the holidays are going to be quite difficult, though."

The case involving the missing student also involved Shannon's uncle, who died at the hands of a ruthless drug trafficker.

"Hey," she said, shaking her head to recapture her sunny attitude. "I hope I'm not being too forward. I really have to get to work, but I'd love to see you again." She gave him a side-eye out of her long lashes. "I'm pretty sure MJ told me you're single. That's true, right? Because if not, I will feel really stupid."

Her brilliant smile lit up her face, and Jefferson found himself smiling back at her.

"I'd like that," he said, shocking himself. Why shouldn't he say yes? From what he'd seen so far, Shannon was both beautiful and intelligent.

Their eyes locked. She blushed slightly before saying. "Can I see your phone?"

He wasn't sure what to make of that, but he put in his password and handed it to her with an amused version of his crooked smile.

With fingers flying at top speed, she typed something into it. "There. I sent me a message from you. Now you have my number, and you can call me."

"Well, okay," he said with a light laugh. Was she *really* afraid of being forward?

"Okay," she repeated, her eyes locked on his. "I hope to hear from you soon. Goodbye, Detective." She pulled the hood of her raincoat over her golden blonde hair and headed out the door and into the downpour.

Jefferson looked at his phone to see what she'd typed.

"I'm free Saturday."

He stared at the screen of his phone before stashing it in his pocket. A mixture of competing emotions washed over him, namely anticipation and dread. He knew MJ caused the dread. There'd been a fleeting moment in the fall when he felt a spark of something deeper between them.

When they first met, he viewed her as an annoyance, a nosy teacher who intruded on his cases and didn't like being told what to do. He knew her better now. She still didn't like being told what to do, but he couldn't deny that he solved cases faster with her help. MJ's curiosity often got her into trouble, but it also meant she had an unconventional way of getting information, a unique lens through which she viewed evidence. She saved his life with that gift of hers, and perhaps that connection led him into mistakenly believing she felt something for him.

He rubbed his eyes against a memory—that moment on the shore of the sound, when he almost told her about his own feelings. Even he couldn't be sure what words would have come out of his mouth, but he knew now that saying anything would've been a mistake.

Since then, he'd done his best to put MJ Brooks out of his mind. Now she was back, taking up space and conjuring up this uncertainty about taking Shannon out, or letting her take him out. He wasn't sure which it was.

Jefferson closed his eyes and pushed thoughts of MJ back into the deep where they belonged. Get over it, he told himself, and get on with life.

Callie was still helping the other customer, so he grabbed his muffin and laid some cash on the counter with a wave. As he turned to go, she caught his eye with a knowing grin.

"Enjoy your weekend, Detective."

Chapter Two

MJ Brooks's windshield wipers flew back and forth, barely able to clear the glass before it became a mass of broken raindrops again. She loved her Bronco, but the restored 1987 rig, red with a broad white stripe, didn't have the fancy windshield sensors of modern cars. She had to flip manually between faster and slower wiper speeds as the storm ebbed and then surged again with renewed energy and more moisture.

The winding road away from the middle school where she taught eighth grade didn't need help to be treacherous. The blind curves and evergreen shadows made sure of that, but this downpour, oblivious to the danger it created, would not let up.

Gripping the steering wheel with white knuckles, MJ wished they'd canceled the class at the senior center tonight. Nobody canceled events in Washington because of the rain. They'd laugh her back to her hometown of Las Vegas if she suggested it.

Since October, MJ and Shannon had been advisors for a club started by one of MJ's students, Loralee Whitmore. Loralee helped her grandmother with technology, like using apps on her phone and laptop. Her grandmother suggested Loralee extend her skills to helping other citizens at the West Sound Senior Center.

That is how the club "Tech Bridge" was born. Loralee brought her idea to the school's technology teacher, Wade Simms. Wade loved the idea, but with three kids under seven years old, he couldn't spend one night a week at the senior center while also running the robotics club. The school district added a further difficulty by requiring at least two school advisors to be present at every class.

When Wade put out a call for volunteers, MJ agreed to take on the club, dragging Shannon along with her because Shannon couldn't say no to her best friend.

Tonight would be their fourth class. The student volunteers included kids from Mariner Middle School and Orca High School. It wouldn't surprise MJ if their numbers were fewer tonight. She couldn't imagine letting a high school student drive in this weather.

There I go again, she thought, thinking like a dry lander. They'll probably all be there.

Whoever showed up would beat her there. MJ called Shannon earlier to warn her that she might be late. With only two days left until winter break, MJ had some essay grading to finish, giving her language arts students time to do rewrites over the two-weeks off. Only the highly committed students, or those with highly committed parents, would improve their grades, but she offered the chance to everyone.

Unfortunately, she did not have time to change out of her elf shirt or the striped leggings she wore under her skirt and stuffed into boots. Today had been "Santa's Helpers" day, and MJ never missed dressing up for a spirit day. The outfit looked slightly ridiculous, but she considered it part of middle school teacher life.

When she finally sailed into the parking lot on what felt like an ocean of water, she saw Meredith Hamblin dropping off her daughter Diana, one of their volunteers. Diana was a freshman at the high school now, but she'd been one of MJ's students last year, as had her siblings in previous years.

MJ waved to Meredith as she drove past in her whale of a pickup truck. The family owned a farm near the middle school, and MJ often dropped by to visit and purchase fresh eggs.

Meredith waved back through the mad wipers of her massive windshield.

When MJ finally made it inside, she pulled off the hood of her sapphire Columbia jacket and attempted to shake some of the rain from her arms. Diana was hanging her jacket up on a coat rack by the main desk.

"Hi, Ms. Brooks. That rain was like driving through a waterfall."

MJ smiled. "Mm, yes. It was also like your windshield constantly getting licked by a Saint Bernard."

The girl wrinkled her nose. "That's a gross one." Then she touched her chin with a thoughtful look. "It's gross, but I think you win for creativity."

After hanging up her coat, MJ turned and bowed slightly. "Thank you for your kind words. They are the like a warm wind for my soggy hair."

They both laughed as they signed in at the front desk. MJ and Diana started their simile battles last year and continued them whenever they had the chance.

"Thank you for signing in," said the young attendant as he eyed MJ's get up. She didn't recognize him, though she was far from knowing everyone who worked or volunteered at the senior center. His name tag read Ned. "Santa and the rest of his elves are in classroom number three this evening," he deadpanned in a hard southern accent.

Diana snickered and MJ smiled in appreciation of his humor.

"Have you bought your ticket to the Christmas ball yet?" Ned asked. "It's a chance to get fancy." He said the last word with a flourish of his hand. "Sorry, honey," he said to Diana. "It's only for adults cause we have some spicy beverages, if you know what I mean."

"Ball?" asked MJ, wondering if Ned himself was old enough for "spicy" beverages. With his wispy strawberry blond hair and nose full of freckles, he looked little older than Diana

Ned pointed to a small poster on a countertop easel. "Yes, it's the biggest fundraiser of the year, and it's Saturday. All the who's who will be here."

"I'll think about it," said MJ, knowing she had no plans to attend. "Maybe I'll just buy a ticket on the way out . . . to support the cause."

"Sure, but you'll miss out if you don't come. I hear they've hired a live band and everything."

MJ winked at him. "You're a good salesman, Ned. But we better get in there."

"Sure thing, hon. Enjoy your class."

They thanked him and headed to join the group. As they entered, the class was already in full swing. All the students were there and engaged in helping the senior attendees, including Loralee, sitting with her own grandmother and another woman. Loralee wore a headband of reindeer antlers.

The senior center staff had decorated the room with a Christmas tree in the corner and white icicle lights dangling from the ceiling.

Diana pointed to a table where a teenage boy helped a woman with gray hair that hung down her back in a perfect French braid. "I'm going to go where Landon is, helping Mrs. Van Buren."

MJ nodded. "Go get 'em."

The girl floated away with a graceful step. MJ remembered how the Diana of last year would have skipped there, her blonde ponytail swinging with her.

"Oh, you made it," said Shannon, coming over with a lopsided grin. "I know how much you love driving in such heavy rain, especially after going full blast today, like a good little elf. I didn't see you around the school building at all."

"Where's *your* Santa's helper outfit?"

Shannon crinkled her face in an apology. "Sorry, I forgot."

MJ glared with pretend hurt. Then she shrugged. "Anyway, I was deep into hibernation grading. And we had a language arts team meeting after school about our upcoming short-story unit." She sighed, feeling more tired than she would ever admit. "I knew it would be a long day, so Claire is taking care of Edgar for me."

Claire owned a beautiful house on Stanton Inlet, and MJ rented the back side of it, giving her an amazing view of the Puget Sound. It also gave her beach access where she usually walked her dog Edgar after school.

Shannon glanced around the room. "At least you can relax here. The kids are doing all the work. They seem to enjoy it, which gives us a little time to catch up."

She said the last part with a noticeably higher pitch in her voice. MJ gave her a side eye. How did Shannon look like she'd just stepped out of a photo shoot? Did the rain just skip around her blonde head as she dashed inside the building?

"Why are you looking so happy and put together on this dreary day?"

Shannon's eyes dropped to the floor as a smile forced its way onto her lips. "What do you mean?" She glanced up through her eyelashes, a slight blush on her cheeks.

MJ's eyes narrowed. Her friend had some news, but she couldn't fathom what it could be. "Okay. Spill it. You obviously can't hide whatever it is. You are dying to tell me."

Biting her bottom lip to contain her grin, Shannon cast her eyes around the room. Seeing all the kids were busy, she pulled MJ off to a quiet corner.

"I did something," Shannon said, her nervous excitement about to boil over. "Even I can't believe I did it. You'll be shocked; it was so unlike me, but I couldn't help it. He was just there, and then—"

"Shannon," MJ said, with a light laugh and a hand on her shoulder. "What the devil are you talking about?"

She cast her eyes down again and took a deep breath. "I asked him out. Jefferson Hughes, that hot detective." She put her hands on MJ's shoulders, meeting her gaze with a wild gleam in her brown eyes. "Can you believe it? I basically asked him out at Callie B's this morning."

MJ froze. She may have even stopped breathing. Jefferson?

That name sent her mind reeling, and she missed the next words Shannon spoke. She couldn't move. Her mind seemed disconnected from her body as she tried to make sense of what her friend had just told her.

Jefferson?

Shannon was staring at her, and MJ knew she had to snap out of it. Shannon would expect her to be happy. And shouldn't she be?

With forced mirth, MJ plastered a smile on her face. Swallowing hard, she tried her voice. "What . . . what did he say?"

Covering her cheeks with her hands, Shannon's next words came out in an embarrassed whisper. "He was definitely flirting back, and he let me put my number in his phone. Oh my gosh, MJ. He is so freaking gorgeous. It was like fate or something, seeing him this morning. I really hope he calls."

"Wow," said MJ. "That really isn't like you. Way to go for it."

Suddenly Shannon's face turned serious. "I know you two don't always see eye-to-eye, so I hope it doesn't bother you if we go out."

MJ waved a hand to dismiss the idea. "No, not at all. In fact, we get along better than we used to."

Unbidden, Jefferson's face entered MJ's mind. Just a few months ago, he stood close to her, taking her hand as they stood on the sand. She could almost feel the warmth of his touch again, seeping into her heart as the cold water of the sound lapped at their feet. There seemed to be something he wanted to say, but before he could speak, her ex-husband Justin had appeared, and she'd dropped the detective's hand like a hot stone.

It was obvious now what that moment had signaled to Jefferson, even if she didn't understand it herself.

"Who knows if he'll even call," Shannon said, tamping down her earlier enthusiasm.

MJ smirked. "I don't think he would take your number if he wasn't interested." She tried to ignore the pang her own words caused. "He doesn't mess around like that. He's a pretty straight arrow."

"I know," Shannon said, getting animated again. "He seems like such a great guy. So many other men are so . . ." She glanced away as she hunted for the words. "Self-absorbed. I think that's it. He doesn't seem like that."

MJ pictured Jefferson again, his expensive shoes covered in sand. The memory made her chuckle. "He's a *little* self-absorbed, but you're right, he's a good guy."

"You know him better than I do," Shannon said, her eyes sparkling. "But I hope that will change soon."

MJ smiled, but inside, her heart felt anything but light. In fact, it seemed tied to a sinking anchor.

Chapter Three

MJ and Shannon took opposite sides of the room, checking in with the volunteers and their senior students. Distraction continued to follow MJ as she mulled over the counselor's news. With a sigh meant to heave the whole thing to the back of her mind, she turned her attention outward. She needed to focus on the students.

Checking in with Loralee sounded like a good idea. She was working with her grandmother, who brought a friend along.

"Hi Ms. Brooks," said Loralee, looking up from her grandmother's computer as MJ approached.

"Hello Loralee, and hello again, Mrs. Whitmore. I see our PNW monsoon didn't keep you away."

Loralee's grandmother grinned, her piercing blue eyes a contrast to her fair skin. Her sleek salt-and-pepper hair rested on her shoulders, one side behind her ear. "Please, call me Pam. Let me pretend we are the same age."

Her friend, whose stark white hair hung in a straight bob at her chin, nodded with an approving chuckle.

"And," continued Pam, "I wouldn't miss being here with this amazing granddaughter of mine." She took in MJ's outfit with a wide grin and a wink. "At least someone here has some holiday spirit."

She opened her arms wide to show off her own ode to the season—a Christmas sweater featuring Santa riding a motorcycle.

"Oh, and this lovely woman," Pam continued, gesturing toward her friend, who wore a green and red plaid sweater with a smiling Rudolph, complete with a blazing red bulb for his nose. "This is Fanny Boice. She's my bestie. Loralee is teaching us to use the city's transit website and app. We don't like to drive much anymore. Too many crazies out there. But we still have places to go and people to see." She patted Fanny's arm, and they shared a conspiratorial giggle.

Loralee rolled her eyes. "You mean like watching hot guys at the gym?"

They giggled again. "Don't be silly, honey," her grandmother said. "We go for the hot yoga, not the hot guys. You misunderstood." Her wink at Fanny told a different story.

"Sure," said Loralee with a smirk. "But that's not what you told my mom."

"How else are we supposed to get dates to the Christmas ball?" Pam teased.

"Oh, Grandma."

MJ chuckled. "It's nice to meet you, Fanny. I'm glad you could join us."

"Oh, I'd follow this crazy lady just about anywhere," said Fanny, flicking her hand toward Pam. "Even on public transit. She knows how to have an adventure."

"Whatever the reason for your travels, I'm sure Loralee has you covered. So, I'll let you ladies continue before our time is up."

Shaking her head as she walked away, MJ wondered whether Mrs. Whitmore really needed help. Probably not, but she always showed up to support her granddaughter.

Those two ladies looked like they could get into some trouble together, mused MJ.

Most members of their group had lost a spouse, and Pam Whitmore was no different. According to Loralee, her grandfather died five years ago after a marriage of forty-five years.

As she surveyed the room, MJ's thoughts unwillingly returned to the detective, his changeable blue eyes staring at her from the back of her mind, forcing their way into her consciousness.

Despite her own confusion about Jefferson, MJ owed it to her friend to be happy, or at least pretend to be. Her own relationship with Jefferson couldn't even be called a friendship, much less anything more.

Had she been wanting more?

She shook her head. It didn't matter now.

If MJ thought worse of him, she might warn Shannon off, but she knew the truth. Jefferson Hughes had earned her admiration, something she didn't give freely.

Just a few months ago, they had worked together when a student went missing. During a long drive together, Jefferson opened up to her about his brother's drug addiction. How it had motivated him to become a police officer. And how Jefferson spent much of his early career trying to save him.

Before that day, she'd sensed that the detective carried some sorrow, some burden that made him seem stiff or too controlled. Now she knew it was the drive to do the right thing, in the right way, and to save people who didn't think they needed saving.

She sucked in a breath as she imagined seeing him with Shannon. Seeing them together as a couple. Just the thought filled her with awkwardness and, if she was honest, something like regret.

"Ms. Brooks?"

MJ came back to reality. Diana Hamblin stood in front of her with a worried crease in her young brow.

"What is it, Diana?"

The girl looked over her shoulder to where Landon sat with Mrs. Van Buren. "I'm not sure it's anything," she whispered. "But I'm worried that Mrs. Van Buren is getting scammed."

"Oh? What makes you think that?" MJ asked, also keeping her voice down.

Diana's brows came together as she tried to explain. "She keeps asking us to help her set up a GreenShare account, one of those apps that people use to send money. We aren't supposed to help with money stuff. That's part of the club rules Mr. Simms wrote. I told her that, but she is upset that we won't help her."

MJ glanced over at the woman and Landon. Mrs. Van Buren sat against the back of her chair with her arms folded, her laptop open on the table in front of her. Landon wore the same concerned look as Diana.

"Hm. Did she say where she needs to send money?"

"She said her grandkids, but . . ." Diana shrugged. "I don't know. She seems too, well, almost panicky for that."

"Okay. I'll go talk to her. You and Landon can take a break for now."

Diana sighed with relief. "Thanks, Ms. Brooks."

"Thank you for taking the rules seriously."

The girl nodded and then went to take Landon with her to the snack table.

Internet safety was the first topic the kids covered with the citizens they tutored. The club members did weeks of research to create the lesson with direction from the technology teacher. When the students discovered how often criminals targeted senior citizens, it shocked them. Diana and Landon were likely just being extra vigilant.

***

"Hello, Mrs. Van Buren," MJ said, taking a seat next to the woman. "How are you tonight?"

The woman sat up and unfolded her arms. "Please, dear, call me Millie. And things were going just fine until the young lady told me they can't help me with some financial matters. Can you do that?"

MJ shook her head. "I'm sorry, Millie. It's a condition of the club that none of us have access to your financial accounts. It's protecting you and us from any potential issues."

"I see," she said, sounding very much like she did not agree. "I just feel so bad because I want to send my grandchild some birthday money. You know, I don't have any idea what else I could buy, so I thought sending money would be best."

"How many grandchildren do you have?"

The older woman's face melted into a smile. "I have five in all. I've been using that Keep in Touch social media program or site, whatever it's called, to see what they're all up to. Your students showed me how to do that. See here," she said, pulling up a screen on her laptop. "This is my grandson Braden's page. He just started college." She pointed at the screen. "He looks a lot like his dad, my son Christopher."

MJ leaned forward. Braden's profile picture showed a handsome, tan young man with a wide, toothy grin. The other pictures showed him in various outdoor locations, posing in front of canyons, cliffs, and mountain lakes.

"He seems to love the outdoors. Is Braden the one having the birthday?" MJ asked.

"What?" asked Millie, confusion clouding her gray eyes. She cleared her throat. "Oh. No, no, not Braden. It's . . . um . . . it's one of the girls, one of . . . one of my granddaughters. Yes . . . that's it." For a few seconds, Millie stared ahead, her fingers tapping restlessly on the tabletop.

Then the woman suddenly slapped her hands on her lap. "You know what? I think I'm going to get a drink of water." Avoiding eye contact, Millie raised herself from the chair, using the table for assistance. Then her hand drifted slowly to her laptop. With undue force, she closed the lid. "Please excuse me, dear."

Still not looking at MJ, Millie shuffled toward the snack table the senior center had provided. They'd even decorated it with a holly print tablecloth and a group of lighted elves, Santa, and reindeer figurines.

With narrowed eyes, MJ watched her go. That was a weird inter-action. Diana's concern might be justified. Millie seemed less than honest about her motivation for sending money.

It's a good thing we didn't show her how to use GreenShare, thought MJ, grateful for Wade Simms's foresight in creating the club regulations.

She watched Millie fill a plastic cup from a water pitcher. This was an adult woman who had the right to send money to whomever she chose. But MJ couldn't help feeling like she needed to find out more, just to be sure Diana wasn't right. Maybe asking Millie directly was the best course.

Just as MJ stood to do that, Mr. Newman, another of their senior citizen students, joined Millie at the snack table and engaged her in conversation.

Noticing Shannon conferring with Luis Lopez, a middle schooler, MJ made her way over to see what her friend thought about Millie's situation.

"He's so excited to play games," Luis was saying as MJ approached. "I thought older people don't like gaming, but Mr. Newman is all over it. We only had to go over a few things about the game he brought. I've never played it, but it's not much different from the stuff I like."

"What game is it?" Shannon asked, biting a frosted snowflake cookie.

"Rise of Rome," he said. "It's the Romans battling for territory over and over. But it has tons of information about the history. I think that's why Mr. Newman likes it so much. Maybe because he was in the army for a long time. I think he was in the police, too. He also said his son plays it."

"Ah, that's so awesome," said Shannon, sharing a fist bump with Luis. "I bet he'll get to play with his son now because of your help."

Luis's face lit up with a sheepish grin. "I know. It feels good to help people." He glanced at MJ, a rosy hue coloring his cheeks. "I'm going to go get a cookie."

"Of course," said Shannon. "You've earned it."

As the boy hurried away, MJ said, "I need your opinion about something."

"Sure. What is it?"

MJ repeated what Diana said, as well as her own interaction with Millie Van Buren.

Shannon put a manicured finger to her chin, her mouth twisting to the side as she considered the information. "Do you think she just feels embarrassed? Maybe she's already tried to figure it out herself and couldn't do it."

MJ considered this. "You could be right. I think sometimes those app builders purposely confuse people." She absently watched Millie and Mr. Newman chat between cookie bites, her mind still chewing on the matter. After a while, something in their interaction cleared her mind and brought them into focus. Neither of them was smiling. In fact, their stiff body language suggested a terse conversation.

"What do you make of that?" MJ asked, pushing her eyes toward Millie and Mr. Newman to direct Shannon's attention. "Do those two know each other outside of class?"

"I suppose it's possible. The senior center has all kinds of meetups and activities. They could be neighbors. Who knows?" she said without moving her eyes away from the couple. Then she tilted her head to inspect her friend. "MJ," she said, drawing out the name in a warning. "I can see your mind working. We are not here to solve adult financial or social problems. Whatever is going on, I'm sure they can handle it."

Suddenly, Mr. Newman balled his eating hand into a fist, his cookie crumbling to the ground. His next words were loud enough for everyone to hear.

"Fine," he said, his face flushed. "I won't bother you any longer, Millie. You just remember what I said. I meant it."

With the sharp about-face of a military man, he turned his back to Millie, forcefully throwing what remained of his cookie into the garbage can near the refreshment table.

Then he marched to his station where Luis sat eating a cookie. "I'm sorry, young man," he said as he began gathering up his laptop. "I appreciate your help, but I need to be done for tonight." Mr. Newman seemed to reach for a smile but only managed a grimace.

"That's okay, Mr. Newman. We'll play more next time."

With a brisk nod of agreement, the old man gave Luis's shoulder a reassuring pat before briskly exiting the room.

Luis watched him go, confusion clouding his brow.

Millie grabbed another cookie and nibbled it. Then she padded back to her computer, not seeming to notice as every eye in the room followed her in stunned silence.

With her brows almost into her hairline, MJ stared at Shannon.

"Okay. That was weird," Shannon admitted. "But you still shouldn't get involved. You don't have to fix everything, you know."

"I know," MJ said with a grin, looking away to hide the curiosity growing in her eyes. Her friend knew her too well. She was indeed wondering why this entire night had been so weird, and why it all seemed to center on Mrs. Van Buren. "I'll just make sure Millie is okay. You should have a chat with Luis. Mr. Newman's abrupt exit seems to have burst his bubble."

The boy sat in a metal folding chair next to the spot vacated by the older man. Sitting with hunched shoulders, his earlier exuberance seemed to have leaked out of him.

"I'll do that, but don't you go searching for a mystery here. Remember, just another week and you are off to Vegas for a well-deserved break and visit with your parents, and I will be on a cruise to Cozumel with my family."

"I don't see how checking in with Millie is going to ruin our vacations. So don't worry."

Shannon sighed. "Easy for you to say. You're not MJ Brooks's best friend."

MJ rolled her smiling eyes at her. True, her curiosity sometimes caused trouble, but it also helped to solve problems. Whatever was going on with Millie was not likely to need any intervention from MJ. She just wanted to make sure the woman wasn't upset after Mr. Newman's response to her.

As she made her way toward Millie, MJ mused that Jefferson also found her innate curiosity annoying. He was not a happy camper the first time she dragged him to a clue following some unsanctioned nosing around.

Maybe Shannon and he are a perfect match, she thought.

"Hey, Millie," she said, once again seating herself next to Mrs. Van Buren. "Is everything okay?"

"What? What do you mean?" She didn't look at MJ, but focused on reopening the KIT website.

"I mean, your conversation with Mr. Newman?" she clarified, leaning in closer to keep her voice low while ensuring the woman could hear her. "He seemed kind of angry."

With a wave of her hand, Millie dismissed her concern. "Oh, that's nothing. I've known Ira for a long time. We're old friends. In fact," she said, finally turning to face MJ, "he and my husband were poker buddies before Walter passed." Her mouth turned up in a sad smile, but her eyes grew heavy and she glanced away.

Going back to her computer, she continued. "Ira always thinks he has to look out for me now that Walter is gone." She shook her head. "I suppose it frustrates him when I make my own decisions."

MJ nodded. That was something she could understand. She had the same issue with her ex-husband, Justin. It was the main reason for their split. It felt so suffocating.

She had to accept Millie's explanation. If she went any further with questions, she would definitely pry into the lady's business.

"I see," MJ said. Noticing a pad of sticky notes behind Millie's computer, she grabbed one along with a pen lying nearby. "Here's my phone number. If you need anything, I'd be willing to help; just call me."

With a slow turn of her head, Millie scrutinized MJ like she was a riddle.

"That's very kind of you. Unnecessary, I'm sure, but kind all the same." With a slow move of her hand, she took the number, and just as slowly, stuck it on the top of her computer.

Chapter Four

D etective Sergeant Greg Larson felt the splash at the same time he heard it.

Gritting his teeth, he glared at his partner, Detective Jaime Mendez, who watched him from the driver's side of their unmarked Ford Explorer.

"What?" Mendez asked, too innocently. "You should look before you step out of the car, amigo. It's been raining for days. I thought you were pure PNW? Related to Big Foot or something." He made a tsking sound and waved his finger. "You should know better."

"Don't think I'm going to forget this," Larson growled at the younger detective as he pulled himself out of the car, stepping wide to avoid hitting the puddle with his other foot.

Unaffected by Larson's distemper, Mendez grinned as he closed his door.

The damp morning air exerted a heaviness that made Larson's bones groan as he stretched to his full height. His wife, Trina, wanted to move to Florida when they retired, which could be as soon as two years from now. He'd resisted but today it didn't sound too bad.

At least the sky had stopped dumping buckets of water on them, as it had been doing nonstop since November.

He shook his foot like a dog trying to clear rain from its back. While it was an effective method for the animal, it did nothing for Larson's soaked shoe and sock.

Mendez pulled up the collar of his overcoat. "It's gotten colder. And darker."

"I think you're turning into more of a Pacific Northwesterner than me—always jawing about the weather."

"If I didn't, you'd be lost. But I won't bother you anymore. I won't tell you that there may be snow soon."

With a snort, Larson walked toward the yellow crime scene tape where dark shapes of uniform officers gathered near the bobbing fishing boats of the Shopside Docks. "They always say that. I'll believe it when I see it."

A flock of early-rising seagulls cackled overhead, seeming to agree with the detective.

Officer Evie Hanson met them at the entrance to the dock, holding a clipboard. "Good morning, detectives," she said as she handed the clipboard to Larson.

"Good morning, Hanson." Larson signed his name, then handed it to Mendez. "What do we know so far?"

Her dark eyes flew open as if this was the most unexpected question. "Sir?"

He gestured toward the water. "You and Officer Fogarty were the first on scene?"

She nodded, keeping her eyes trained on him.

"Tell me what you know. We hear Fogarty's voice most of the time, which we all know he loves, but I'd like you to do the honors today. You almost have a year under your belt, so I'm sure you took excellent notes."

Officer Hanson glanced at Mendez, who nodded encouragingly.

"Yes, sir." She pulled a small notebook from the pocket of her ballistic vest, flipping it open while clearing her throat. She squinted to make out the words in the dark morning. "Dispatch put out a call at 6:15 a.m. to Shopside Docks for a potential. We arrived at 6:25 and spoke to a fisherman who saw a man's boots stuck under his boat at slip number fifteen. That's a Mr. . . . ." She shuffled to the next page, "or, I mean, Captain Chase Bell. Captain Bell realized it was a person and jumped in, thinking he could pull the person out, but he said he soon saw the victim was deceased. He left the water and called 911. Claims he did not touch the victim while in the water. EMTs arrived and declared the victim deceased. Forensic divers are taking underwater photos now, and the fire department and Underhill's team are just waiting on your word to retrieve the body from the water. We've closed down this part of the dock. So far, we only know what the fisherman reported—that the victim is male." She returned her notebook to the pocket and grinned. "How'd I do?"

Larson nodded his approval. "Not too shabby. Was the body damaged at all by the boat?"

Hanson shook her head. "Not as far as I know. Bell said he hasn't turned his boat on at all."

"The feet are still attached? With boots on?" Mendez pulled his collar tighter as a sea-soaked breeze swept over them. "He must be recently dead or recently in the water."

Larson shoved his hands into his coat pockets. He should have worn a hat. The ice-water mist clung to his bald head, draining the heat from his body with unusual speed. "Let's go check it out. Thanks, Hanson."

"Yes, sir."

The weathered planks of the decking tugged at the detectives' shoes as they trod the steep gangway. The dock itself formed the shape of a capital letter E, with three smaller sections branching off. Five or six boats dotted the sides of each section, their hulls bobbing gently in the water.

Even with all the police activity, the morning was eerily quiet, only disrupted by the squeaking protestations of the dock against the movement of the water and the heavy steps of the detectives.

"These docks need some love," said Mendez as the boards groaned under their feet.

"They're old," said Larson. "Shopside used to be the only dock in the area, until the city built West Sound Marina. People offloaded seafood and all kinds of stuff here to sell in shops up there." He shoved his hands deeper in his pockets. "It's mostly tours now . . . deep-sea fishing or sailing."

"Ah, I'm so much smarter now," Mendez joked.

"Keep hanging with me, kid. The sky's the limit."

As they approached the last prong of the E, a variety of emergency personnel, either working or waiting, separated from the darkness to come more clearly into view. The forensics team moved like ghosts in the fading night, seeming to float in and around what Larson guessed to be a thirty or forty-foot sport fisher of some kind, probably used for fishing tours. The flat-roofed center console created the illusion that the boat itself wore a captain's hat.

As the detectives approached, Bud Lochlann, the lead forensics officer, watched them from the boat's bow. He stood under the one floodlight like the star of the show.

"Huzzah! They're finally here!" he yelled to the rest of the group.

Another figure in white, who had been staring over the dock railing into the water, straightened to watch them approach. It was Dr. Stacey Underhill, the Rainier County medical examiner.

Larson shrugged, his hands still trying to gather warmth from his jacket pockets. All the surrounding faces were shadows of themselves in the low light. "This makes up for all the times we waited for your crew," Larson shouted back. He glanced at his phone. Ten minutes after seven. The December sun wouldn't show itself fully for another forty-five minutes.

"Oh, give him a break, Bud," Stacey called out. "We all know Larson needs his beauty sleep." She tilted her blonde head thoughtfully. She wore the white protective suit of the others, but her hood still hung back on her shoulders. "Mendez, not so much, though. Maybe you should tell your boss what night moisturizer you're using."

Larson waved off the chuckles that followed. "I'm happy to provide your entertainment on this crappy morning."

Stacey grinned as the two men approached. "You're a good sport, Larson. So I'll just get down to business. The divers will be up soon. We need your approval before we extricate this poor guy."

"Can they see anything down there?" asked Mendez, peering over the railing to the watery blackness below. "Oh," he said, leaning further over the railing and gazing toward the bow of the fishing boat. "I see the boots. They are a type of hiking boot, maybe? Not a work boot?"

"From here, I'd agree. And yes, the divers have lights on their equipment, but the pictures will be murky. I don't even know how important they'll be in the long run," said Underhill. "He probably washed down here on the tide. But, as usual, without an examination, we're guessing."

Larson shivered, ready to get moving. "If you are ready, then I see no reason to wait. Pull him out as soon as the divers are done. I trust you to make sure he comes out with everything as intact as possible. Where's the captain?"

Stacey tilted her head toward the boat. "I believe he's in the cabin with Fogarty."

A snort escaped the older detective. "Of course. Send Evie to stand guard and then sit in the warm spot. That's Fogarty."

"Don't act like you wouldn't do the same thing," said Stacey.

Before Larson could respond, a rustle of water sent their attention back over the railing. Two divers had broken through the inky surface, only distinguishable from the water by light glinting off their masks.

Larson stepped away. "Mendez. Stay and oversee the removal. I'll go talk to the fisherman."

"See?" said Underhill. "You prove my point."

Larson hunched his shoulders against the cold, smirking at the two of them as he walked away.

Chapter Five

As Larson stepped down the narrow stairs into the boat's cabin, he instinctively crouched to avoid hitting his head.

Fogarty sat on one end of a U-shaped seating area with another man sitting on the other side, facing away from Larson. They both glanced up as the detective entered.

The cabin, though cramped, had an impressive number of features, including a heater. It smelled of warm coffee. Larson glanced to his right where a tiny kitchen had miniature versions of the essentials: stove top, dishwasher, microwave, fridge, and a coffee pot. Rich, dark wood covered the cabin floor, contrasting with the tan leather where the men sat, and a flat-screen TV hung in the back.

"Good morning, Detective Larson," said Fogarty, his boyish face still boasting red cheeks from the cold.

"Fogarty." He gave a nod in the officer's direction. "And you must be Captain Bell," Larson said to the other man as he took a seat next to the officer. "This is quite the rig you've got here."

"Thank you. She's pretty much all I got," he said with a faint smile that vanished before it could gain any strength. Larson sensed the man really meant it.

"Would you like some coffee?" Bell asked, getting up.

"No. I'm fine."

"You sure? I made an entire pot, and no one seems to want it. Don't drink it myself, but I keep it around for clients. I've been told I make great coffee."

Larson had to admit that a warm cup sounded perfect right now. "In that case, I'd love one. No point in wasting it."

"Do you live here on the boat?" the detective asked, glancing around for clues that might answer his own question. It was clean, but there were blankets and pillows thrown to the back of the seating.

This must be where he sleeps, thought Larson, which was mildly off-putting.

"Yeah," said Bell, carrying a steaming mug and a container holding individual creamers and sweeteners. He handed them to Larson and returned to his spot. "My parents live in town, so I stay with them if the weather gets too bad." He tugged at the bottom of his wiry, golden-oak beard as he gazed around the cabin. He seemed to analyze how the detective might view it.

Larson nodded while stirring his coffee. It was warmish in the cabin right now, but he could see how a prolonged winter storm might make it intolerably cold or unstable. "I'm sure you've already told Officer Fogarty how you came to discover the body this morning," he said, setting his coffee on a tiny counter next to him and taking a notebook from his jacket pocket. "But it would be a great help if you could go over it again with me."

Bell glanced at Fogarty, pulling his black beanie down further over his ears. Larson pegged him for early thirties, but he could be younger. He seemed nervous, but not guiltily so, more like someone unacquainted with being caught behind crime scene tape.

"Sure, if it will help."

The front of his hat boasted the words "Bell Reel Adventures" with a fishing hook looped through the A, a trailing line connecting it to the B and the R.

Larson sipped his coffee, which he had to admit tasted good. It slid down and warmed his bones. He pointed at the hat. "Is that your company?"

Bell ran a finger over the stitching. "Yeah. I was supposed to take a few people out today, but I've already canceled."

"Sorry about that."

Bell waved it off. "I'm glad for the break, for a little time to process. It's not every day you find a dead body."

"True," piped up Fogarty. "Not even for us."

Ignoring Fogarty's comment, Larson asked, "What were your first movements this morning, starting from the beginning?"

Bell ran a hand over his beard, which fell a couple of inches past his chin. "My alarm went off at five. I got up and took a quick shower. I did a little reading before I looked over the itinerary for today to see what gear I needed to set up." He blew out a breath as he continued. "Uh, then I went out on the deck—"

"Sorry," Larson asked, his writing hand suspended above his notebook, "but what kind of reading?"

"What?"

"You said you did a little reading. What was it?"

"Oh." He seemed flummoxed by the question. "Just some scriptures."

"Like the Bible?" asked Fogarty.

The young man tilted his head to the side with a gentle smile. "Yeah, like the Bible."

The detective stared at the man. Larson didn't have a religious bone in his body, but he knew enough to appreciate the biblical poetry of a scripture-reading fisherman.

"Okay, sorry. Go ahead. You were going out on the deck."

Bell looked ahead toward the stairs. "So I went out there and started pulling poles and such from the gear boxes. I kept noticing an extra little bumping sound under the boat. It's always super quiet out here, so every little sound gets amplified. And when you live out here like I do, you get to know what it should sound like. The water hitting the boat, the creaking and squeaking of the moors, you know. I can't really explain it, but after about fifteen minutes, I finally stopped what I was doing to look. My floodlight was already on, so it only took a few seconds for me to see the boots under the bow."

He shivered with the memory of it. "Then I regretted waiting so long. I grabbed a dive light, took off my boots and jumped in." Bell shook his head, a soft sheen coming into his eyes. "I wish I hadn't. His face . . ." He stopped and looked away, emotion taking his voice.

Larson sat against the back of the leather seat, glancing at Fogarty, surprised to see a shine in the officer's eyes as well.

"I'm sorry you had to see that," Larson said with as much patience as he could muster. Sometimes he found it hard to remember that the public at large didn't encounter death on the regular. "I see you are in dry clothes. Where are your wet ones?"

Fogarty answered for him. "I bagged them for evidence, sir. Bud Lochlann has them."

"Good work." He turned back to Bell. "Did you see anyone else out this morning, on other boats, walking the dock, on the shore?"

"No, no one. And that's not unusual. I'm the only one who lives out here, and this time of year, the other boaters don't roll in until seven or eight, after the sun comes up."

I don't blame them, Larson thought.

"Police and forensics will need to be here most of the day, I'm sorry to say. I'd appreciate it if you could stick around to answer questions that might come up. Officer Fogarty can stay here for a while longer."

Bell nodded, wiping his eyes with the sleeve of his blue plaid shirt. "Sorry for losing it."

"Not a problem." Larson said as he stood. "Just make sure you take care of yourself. This is a traumatic event. If you don't already have someone to talk to, there are people and services in place to help. Officer Fogarty can give you those numbers."

Bell offered a weak smile. "Thanks. I'll probably just call my mom and dad."

"Good. Alright, here is my card. Call if you think of anything else that might be important."

Before Larson took a step toward the stairs, Mendez's heavy steps thudded down, and he poked his head into the cabin. "He's out of the water and Underhill wants you."

"She knows I'm married, right?"

Mendez rolled his eyes. "You sound just like her."

"I'm coming." Before reaching the stairs, he turned back. "Captain Bell, do you have any people who work for you, have access to your boat?"

He shook his head. "It's just me. My brother used to help, but he's on a two-year church mission in Spain."

"Spain?"

"Yeah. But we plan on being business partners when he gets back. He's got a year to go."

"That's cool," Fogarty said.

Larson thanked the young man again and climbed the steps, emerging onto the deck like a man reaching a glacial mountain top.

The freezing morning mist assaulted his bald head, and the detective gritted his teeth against the shiver it sent down his spine. Spain sounded pretty darn good right now.

***

The body lay on a sheet of plastic, ready to be wrapped and placed in a body bag. Mud, seaweed, or some other organic material clung to the victim's clothes and short, black hair.

Larson stared down at him, suddenly grateful for the cold air and even colder water keeping the usual putrid smells at bay. All he could smell was the same salty, fishy odor that always clung to this dock.

"Any ID?" he asked.

Underhill shook her head. "Nope. We've checked all his pockets, socks, everywhere. There's nothing on him but clothes. Not even a watch or other jewelry. And the divers found no personal effects in this area."

"Ugh. Poor hombre looks like a balloon." Mendez said, his face bunched in a sickened expression. "Do you think he drowned?"

Looking up from a squatting position, the medical examiner tapped something into her computer tablet. "I can't say for sure, but I don't think so. Usually drowning victims sink pretty fast, and this guy seems to have floated for a while. All these contusions on his face," she said, pointing with her gloved hand. "He probably came into contact with debris in the water, possibly even some marine life. It's hard to say without an exam."

"No obvious causes of death?" Larson asked.

She tilted her head and considered the dead man again. "I don't like all this bruising around his neck. It seems to stand out more than the rest, but you can see why I'm going to remain non-committal. His whole body is likely one massive, marbled bruise under this t-shirt and jeans. I saw what could be a head wound on the back, but there's too much debris to know for sure."

"But," she said, standing up and holding the tablet out to Larson. "I need to you sign so we can get him moved. Once exposed to air, decomposition speeds up, making my job harder. We need to take him to the lab."

Larson signed. "When can we expect more information?"

"Soon."

"Soon? Thanks for being precise."

"He'll be top priority. How's that?"

"That'll do."

Chapter Six

J efferson turned his phone aimlessly in his hand, his mind caught in a similar internal rotation. Call her . . . Don't call her . . . Call her . . . Don't call her.

To his right, Detective Rory Jackson munched on a pumpkin chocolate chip muffin the chief had provided. Jefferson saw the offering as an apology for the second day of training the detectives had to endure. His own muffin sat untouched on the table in front of him. It wasn't Callie B's, and he knew it would be disappointing.

"So, Jeffy," said Rory in between chews. "I want to try out this new interrogation technique we are learning, since our state lawmakers felt the need to purchase some new books and hire this talking head. But," he said, raising his pointer finger in the air, "I'm skipping to step two because who has time for step one?"

After ten years of working in the same department as patrol officers and now as partners and detectives, they knew each other well. Perceiving Jefferson's preoccupation, Rory would poke him until he gave up the reason.

Jefferson cringed at the idea of his partner knowing anything about his romantic life. He'd never hear the end of it. "No. Just eat your muffin like a good boy."

"Now wait. I need the practice." Rory sat back with a foot on the opposite knee. "I will explain the purpose of this interview, which is to learn why you are incessantly staring at your blank phone. The procedure? I will continue peppering you with questions. Do you feel that you have any relevant information to share?" He sipped his coffee and stared at Jefferson with forced sternness in his eyes, humor hidden in his ginger beard.

Focusing on the front of the room, Jefferson dropped his phone on the table, ignoring Rory's attempt at extracting information. Instead, he studied the conference room door. So far, only he and Rory were in attendance. Even their training instructor, Allen Valencia, a retired detective from Minnesota, hadn't made an appearance.

"Why do I sense that Larson and Mendez will be skipping class today?"

"Probably because they got called out to Shopside Docks this morning to investigate a dead body."

"I know that," Jefferson said, looking at his watch, a Patek Philippe Calatrava that had been his father's. His mother gave it to him on his recent trip home to Redding, California. He'd had to deliver some news about his brother Alex that would both elate and devastate her. Overall, the good news outweighed the bad, and he'd enjoyed the time away. "That's why we delayed an hour. They should be back now."

"Would you rush back here?" Rory murmured.

"Nope. I see your point."

What a wasted morning, he thought. They didn't have any major cases at the moment, but there were plenty of reports that needed follow up. If nothing else, they could have gone out to the docks with Larson and Mendez.

Rory, his muffin gone, slouched down in his seat and closed his eyes. Jefferson watched him with envy. Knowing Rory, he was already asleep.

The conference room door suddenly swung open and Chief Keith Carlson stepped in, followed by Valencia. The chief was a couple inches taller than the other man, but they both had full heads of silver hair cut with military precision.

"Sorry to keep you waiting, gentlemen," boomed the chief. "Glad to see you made good use of time, Jackson."

Rory sat up, stretching his arms overhead. "I dreamed Jefferson let me have his pumpkin muffin."

Without a word, Jefferson pushed it in front of him.

"Dreams do come true." Rory rubbed his hands together before taking a gigantic bite.

"Cute," said the chief. "But I'm afraid this case at the docks is anything but. Doesn't appear to be a drowning, although we will know precious little else until Underhill does her examination. Larson and Mendez are going to be busy attempting to identify the victim." He motioned toward Valencia. "Allen says he doesn't mind postponing the rest of the training for a few days."

Valencia gave one firm nod. "Absolutely," he said. "The work comes first." He spoke with a staccato beat, making each word seem of the utmost importance. "Your department will benefit the most if all detectives receive the final module of training together. In the meantime, we can practice the techniques you've learned during any interviews that need to be conducted this week."

The chief cleared his throat. The detectives knew he didn't like this state-mandated training any more than they did. "Anyway, you two meet in my office in five minutes. Something else has come up."

Jefferson immediately pushed his chair back and stood, relieved to avoid another day of sit-and-get instruction. "We can meet now," he said, smoothing down his Kiton paisley silk tie.

The chief gave a heavy, slow shake of his head. "I have to make an announcement in the hub first." He sighed like he would rather jump into a lake of venomous snakes. "Let's go."

The chief marched toward the door with Valencia right behind.

Jefferson raised a brow at Rory, who simply shrugged and said, "Guess we have to follow to find out." The muffin was already gone.

***

The Hub, an expansive room full of desks and people, was the heart of the West Sound Police Station. Almost everyone worked in this room. The chief had an office, and a few other specialty services operated elsewhere, but all other officers and detectives used this space.

Most worked wherever they could find an unoccupied seat. Detectives, however, had assigned desks. They were all near each other, close to the station's interview rooms.

"Listen up, everyone," Chief Carlson bellowed. Though he was still his loud self, Jefferson noticed a heaviness in the man's expression as all eyes turned to him.

Whatever was eating the chief was about to take a bite out of all of them.

"I know some of you will remember Ira Newman."

A murmur floated around the room. The youngest officers wouldn't remember, but Jefferson did. Ira retired from the detective ranks about three years after Jefferson started as a West Sound patrol officer. He'd been a top-notch detective, and everyone loved him. But after his wife died, the man seemed to lose his passion for the job. He left to spend more time with his kids and grandkids.

"I am sorry to say that I received word this morning from his son that Ira passed away sometime last night. It seems he passed in his sleep."

Those who knew Ira Newman responded with intakes of breath and quiet expressions of surprise.

The chief inhaled, holding the breath in before sending out a long, regretful sigh. "I will let you know about the service and where you can send condolences. Until then, keep the family in your thoughts and prayers."

Kathy, the chief's secretary, stood outside his office with red-rimmed eyes and a tissue. A few other sniffles sounded around the room.

Without warning, the threat of tears assaulted Jefferson with a thousand pinpricks behind his eyeballs. Gratefully, the chief turned abruptly toward his office, motioning for the two detectives to follow.

Once behind his desk, Chief Carlson folded his hands, looking at Jefferson and Rory with a heavy brow.

"You two are about to hear the part of my conversation with Ira's son that I did not share with the rest of the station."

The detectives exchanged confused glances.

Was there more to this story? "Does it have something to do with the 'seems he passed in his sleep' part?" asked Jefferson.

The chief closed his eyes momentarily and then nodded. "I don't know what to think. This could just be a grieving son not wanting to accept his father's death, wanting to blame someone or something. But . . ."

"But there could be more to the story," finished Rory.

"Let me be clear," said the chief, his flinty eyes boring into them. "I am not saying there is any credibility to the son's claims, but Ira was a friend. He gave a lot of good years to this department, and so did his family. We all understand the sacrifice it takes sometimes. We owe him the respect of at least checking it out."

"Of course," said Jefferson, as Rory nodded his agreement. "If I remember right, he had a son named Robbie, and a daughter named Laurel?"

The chief eyed him. "Good memory, except he goes by Rob now."

"Thanks. So what exactly are his son's claims? And is it just Rob, or does Laurel also think their father's death is suspicious?"

"Laurel lives in Texas, but according to Rob, she'll be here later today. I'm not sure where she stands, but they've ordered an autopsy." He sat back with another deep breath. Somehow, this did not relax the man's posture. He still sat straight as a police themed nutcracker.

"Rob says his father was religious about his regular medical checkups, and the only condition he was being treated for was toe fungus."

"I can understand that," said Rory, holding his foot up.

"They don't call you swamp foot for nothing," Jefferson added.

Rory dropped his foot to the floor. "You're making that up."

Jefferson shrugged innocently.

"Are you two done?" snapped the chief.

They went silent.

"Anyway, Rob can't point to any specific evidence or reason someone would want to hurt his father, but he reminded me, rightly so, that Newman put away some nasty criminals. He believes it could be a grudge killing."

"Does Rob live in town?" Rory asked.

"Yes. He and his family live near the marina, just as you start up Stanton Inlet. Here's his address and phone number." He reached across his desk with a sticky note, which Jefferson took. "I told him you'd be over to see him today so get in touch ASAP."

"Any idea when the autopsy will be done?" Jefferson asked as he read the sticky note.

"None. And it's likely to take a back seat to the guy out at Shopside this morning. But don't wait for it. As much as I appreciate Rob's concerns, he seems to have a . . . how shall I put it? A, um, a conspiracy mindset." He pressed his lips together, a large breath escaping out of his nose. "The last thing I need is for him to think we're ignoring him because of some imagined cover-up."

Rory raised his eyebrows. "Okay. Noted."

The chief pointed at the two of them. "And nothing about this case, though I hesitate to call it that, gets out for now. Got it?"

"Got it." They said in unison.

"Jinx," said Rory.

Jefferson gave him a side-eye as he stood. "Whatever."

The chief turned his steely eyes to the ceiling. "Get out."

Chapter Seven

R ob Newman's house had the low-pitch roof of 1970s con-
struction. Despite its obvious age, it appeared well-maintained
with fresh paint and a trimmed, orderly yard.

The oatmeal-colored house boasted a center column of rust brick
that flowed from ground to roof. On the left side of the column, an
above-ground deck perched in front of a sliding-glass door. On the
other side, a partial rectangle of glass rose almost to the top of the brick
and an off-center red door completing the shape.

Jefferson was sure the two-story house had views of Stanton Inlet,
even though it sat three blocks from the shore. That didn't keep the
freezing salty air from grabbing their skin with an uncomfortable
sharpness.

Rory raised a hand, red with cold, to knock just as the door opened,
his fist almost flying into a man's face.

There stood a younger version of Ira Newman, although he was
easily two times his father's girth.

"Detectives Hughes and Jackson?" He spoke briskly, as if they
couldn't waste time with hellos.

"That's us," said Rory.

"I'm Rob Newman. You better come in," he said as he glanced
behind them and down the street.

A groan almost escaped Jefferson. The chief had definitely down-played the "conspiracy theorist" part of Rob Newman. The man seemed as jittery as a caffeinated squirrel.

"We're very sorry for your loss," Jefferson said as Newman led them to a sunken family room with surprisingly new shag carpet the color of cornbread.

"Thank you," he said, walking with rapid steps and motioning for them to sit on a retro 1970s black leather sofa. "I've taken the next few days off to deal with all of dad's things." He shook his head. "I shouldn't have to be doing this, you know? There was nothing wrong with him."

The big man, eyes bloodshot from either exhaustion or crying, sat on the edge of a beige armchair that reminded Jefferson of one his grandmother had.

Ira Newman had been a tall man, as Jefferson remembered, but he was wiry and fit. His son seemed to have only inherited the tall part.

"Where do you work, Mr. Newman?" he asked.

"Call me Rob, and I teach online history classes for a couple of universities, and I write books. Science fiction, mostly." He waved a hand to bat those things away. "But I want to talk about my dad. I know he didn't die in his sleep."

Jefferson pulled off his overcoat and laid it over the arm of the couch, trying not to react to the man's insistent demeanor. The guy just lost his dad, and Jefferson knew all too well how that felt. It took a while for the truth of it to sink into your bones. And then it never left.

"Let's go back to yesterday. What can you tell us about your father's movements?" he asked as Rory pulled out his notebook.

Newman rubbed his face. "I don't know." He raked both hands through his graying blond hair. "My wife and I have been at his house all morning, trying to figure that out." His head dipped as he took a deep breath. "She ... she took the kids to her mom's place. They didn't want to go to school, but they shouldn't see me like this."

"Were you the one that found him?" Rory asked.

He shook his head without looking at them. "No. His housekeeper comes early because Dad was usually at the gym by six. She has a key ..." Eyes closed tight, he seemed to fight against the next words. "She called me this morning, crying. Just sobbing."

Without warning, he shot out of his chair. "Don't worry," he said, pacing the room. "The only people that have been in the house are me, my wife, the paramedics, and the housekeeper. We aren't going to take anything out. I know a little something about preserving a crime scene."

Jefferson could feel Rory shift. He didn't dare look at him. "That's expected as the son of one of our best detectives. We both worked with your dad for a few years. He was a good man."

This seemed to calm the beast threatening to escape from Rob Newman. Nodding, he returned to his chair.

"So, do you know anything about where your father went yesterday—people he may have had contact with?" Jefferson tried again.

Looking past them, he rubbed his hands on his thighs as if trying to push out the pain. "I can't say he went anywhere for sure, but I can tell you what he usually did. He kept a routine schedule," he said, a slight tremble in his lips. Pressing them together, he looked down at his hands.

"That'll work," Jefferson assured him. "It gives us a few things to check into."

The man stood again, but this time he walked slowly, his head low and a hand on his forehead. "He would've gone to the gym. He sees a personal trainer there named Forrest. Sorry," he said, glancing up, "I don't know his last name."

"Name of the gym," asked Rory, taking notes.

"Uh, Senior Strength. They only take older clients. He loved it there, and sometimes, after his workout, he went to breakfast with other seniors from there, but I don't know . . ."

"We can find out. What else can you remember?" asked Jefferson.

"Well, unless he had a doctor's appointment or other errands to run, he usually just stayed home and worked in his yard, read books, napped—you know, normal stuff. Sometimes he would go to the senior center to play pool or cards."

"This is good information," encouraged Jefferson. "Did he go out at night?"

The man snapped his fingers. "That computer class. I almost forgot. For the past few weeks, he went to a computer class put on by some students from the high school, I think, or maybe it's the middle school. I don't remember, but that's the only night thing I can think of."

"And you're sure it was last night?" asked Rory.

"Yes. I'm pretty sure it's on Tuesday nights."

Jefferson tensed as he always did at the mention of Mariner Middle School during an investigation. But computer classes? No. There's no way MJ could wriggle herself into this case—if it turned into a case. She likely had nothing to do with this class. While she could research like nobody's business, he didn't remember her being unusually skilled or interested in technology.

He pushed the thought aside. "Did you talk to your dad yesterday?"

At this question, Rob Newman's face crumpled into a broken mess. Tears welled in his eyes, and he attempted to squash them by pushing his thumb and forefinger into them. "No." It was barely a whisper. "I had a busy day. And now it all feels so stupid and worthless." He spat out.

Jefferson winced. It was like having his own guilt and remorse thrown back in his face. Why hadn't he gone home more often to see his parents? He'd taken for granted that they'd always be there. His dad was gone, and the missed opportunities to see him still had the power to make Jefferson feel sick with regret.

He understood the pain racking Rob Newman.

"Sorry," muttered Newman as he mopped his face with his shirtsleeve.

"Don't be," said Jefferson. "I lost my dad recently, too. At least it still feels recent to me. Don't apologize for missing him."

His watery eyes met Jefferson's. "I'm sorry, man."

Jefferson gave a weak smile, not able to speak, a wave of emotion hitting him for the second time that day.

Thankfully, Rory bailed him out. "You said that you are certain your dad didn't die in his sleep, that he was in excellent shape. Is there any other reason you think there could be foul play here?"

He threw his eyes open. "Just look at the guys he put away. He used to keep track of them, you know, the ones that got released. He told me about some of the bad dudes who got out. I think it's logical to assume one of them might go after Dad."

"If so, it's a sophisticated hit, making it look like he died naturally," said Jefferson, attempting to keep the doubt from his voice.

Newman shrugged, not the least put off by the difficulty of the crime. "That's why my sister and I want an autopsy."

"Do you have any evidence, anything you witnessed, overheard, or saw at his house that would lead you to any specific person?" Rory pressed.

"I only remember one name, and that's because he got out on parole last week. Warren Harris. Dad said he was a psychopath who killed a mom and her kid because she owed him money. Dad couldn't believe they let him out." His jaw tightened and his words next words were cold. "People like that have no right to live."

No one spoke for a moment as Newman seemed to wait for them to agree. Jefferson couldn't deny that the same thoughts crossed his mind with the most ruthless criminals, but he refused to engage in that conversation with a civilian.

Newman folded his arms. "You all should check Dad's computer. I couldn't log onto it, but I'm sure you have people to do that. I bet he tracked all of those guys."

Jefferson stood up, putting his coat back on. "Sure. You'll just have to give permission, as long as you are the executor of his estate."

"My sister and I are meeting with Dad's attorney as soon as she gets here."

"Just let us know as soon as that's worked out. We need that before we can enter his house or examine any of his belongings. Unless the autopsy shows a crime. In the meantime," added Jefferson, "we will follow up on the information you've provided."

Rory put a hand on the man's shoulder. "We are sorry about your dad." Then he patted it twice before following Jefferson to the door.

Chapter Eight

"What do you make of that?" Rory asked, as he steered them out of Newman's neighborhood.

"Like the chief sent us on a wild goose chase."

Rory cocked his head. "True. But I'd rather chase geese than sit for training."

"Oh, I'm with you there." Jefferson grinned. "I think this will take us a very long time." He glanced out the window as they turned onto Cecil Bay Highway. The sky, a patchwork of light and dark grays fell like a quilt onto the boats saddled at West Sound Marina, their long white masts or antennae piercing it uselessly. He'd heard there might be snow this weekend, but that wouldn't happen if Mother Nature kept providing this heavy, atmospheric blanket.

"So, shall we start at the start?" Rory asked. "See if Senior Strength is real or just an oxymoron?"

Jefferson chuckled. "Don't go offending people, Jackson."

"Who, me?"

Senior Strength filled a spot in an old, nondescript strip mall. By tinting the door and front windows, the business concealed its purpose from the casual passersby.

As the detectives entered, a too-happy young man called out a friendly, "Welcome!"

He was filling Dixie cups with milk-like liquid. After taking a second look, he set the container down and regarded them with narrowed his eyes. "Are you here to work out?"

Rory stepped back with his hands up. "I'm sure he's talking to you, bro."

Ignoring him, Jefferson pulled out his badge. "I'm Detective Hughes and this is Detective Jackson with the West Sound Police. We have some questions about one of your members."

The young man's eyes widened to saucers. "Oh. I better call my manager."

"Sure. You do that."

"First, you should try our new Senior Strength Protein Plus drink mix," he offered, gesturing toward a row of cups on the counter. "This is strawberry vanilla. It's the best one, in my opinion." The young man screwed the lid onto the container. "And you don't have to be a senior to drink it. They're good for everybody."

"Thanks, Shane," Jefferson said, reading the man's name tag, "but I'll pass."

Rory stepped forward and grabbed a cup, lifting it into the air. "Cheers." He swallowed the mixture in one gulp. With a smack of his lips, he threw the cup in a nearby trashcan. "Pretty good."

"We also have an entire line of vitamin supplements. And we also are sponsoring the senior center Christmas ba—"

"No." A clenching of Jefferson's jaw and hard eyes sent the young man scurrying.

"Right. Sorry. I'll just make that call."

While Shane called his manager, Jefferson wandered toward a wall of glass, peering through it to the spacious room full of workout equipment. There were a few machines, but most people were working out with free weights and other equipment.

"That looks like a personal trainer," Rory said, motioning with his head toward a muscle-built man who, from the back, appeared to be much younger than the clientele. "Could be Forrest."

Sensing their inspection, the man turned. Jefferson almost choked on his own breath.

Justin Brooks, MJ's ex-husband, squinted at the glass before waving at them, his glowing smile bouncing off Jefferson's retinas.

"Well, well, well," said Rory, as the two of them waved back. "If it isn't Mr. Universe."

Jefferson breathed a sigh of relief when Justin turned back to his client, a wisp of a woman with white hair, grateful to avoid a conversation.

The last time he lay eyes on Justin was also the last time he'd seen MJ. He could still feel how fast she dropped his hand as Justin came down the beach stairs. Jefferson had been just a breath away from telling her . . . Telling her what? He wasn't even sure.

"Detectives?"

They turned to see an attractive woman, red hair pulled up in a long ponytail, looking at them curiously with jade eyes, the color amplified by the green of her sweatshirt.

"Hi, I'm Detective Hughes and this is Detective Jackson. Is there somewhere more private we could talk?"

"Okay," she said, drawing out the word. "I guess we can go to my office." Her eyes became guarded. "Can I ask what this is about?"

"We'd rather not discuss it out here," he said with a brief glance toward the counter.

Her eyes flicked to the young man there, then back. "Follow me."

The three of them squeezed into what was a tiny, utilitarian room with mostly blank white walls. Jefferson took in the limited decoration of a crooked bulletin board behind the desk and two framed diplomas, one for a registered dietician and the other for a certified senior fitness specialist.

The manager closed the door as Rory stepped inside. "I'm Eden Dedman, by the way. I'm the manager here."

"Is that you riding horseback there?" asked Rory, pointing to the bulletin board.

She flashed an impatient half smile. "Yes. My grandmother had a farm once upon a time. It's gone now."

She sat behind the desk, her hands clasped on top as she bored into them with those intense eyes. "So, what's this about?"

Jefferson had to restrain the crooked smile threatening to crawl up his face. Her last name coincided a little too well with their visit.

"Do you know Mr. Ira Newman?" He asked.

She nodded. "Sure, I know Ira. He's here as regular as the sunrise. I didn't see him this morning, though." As soon as she said this, her eyes grew wide, flicking anxiously between them. "Has something happened?"

"We are sorry to report that Mr. Newman died last night," Rory said.

"What?" she said, her brow knit together in shock. "Ira? I can't believe it. That man was our most fit customer. He was strong, in excellent shape." She sat back in disbelief. "He had a lifting competition coming up. No. It can't be true." A shimmer softened her intense eyes.

"I'm afraid it is," said Jefferson quietly.

He waited a minute before continuing, giving her time to compose herself.

"We've been told that he meets with a personal trainer by the name of Forrest?"

"Yes," she said, grabbing a tissue from the top of a filing cabinet behind her. "He's not here today. He's been out for a couple of days."

Rory sat forward with his pen and notebook. "If his trainer was out, did Ira still come in yesterday?"

"He did. We have another trainer who only comes twice a week. He covered for Forrest. His name is Justin." She ran a hand over her ponytail. "He's a great guy—won't even take any pay. A lot of our clients are veterans, so he sees it as a thank you for their service."

Her eyes melted like a green puddle of wax as she described Justin.

Jefferson clenched his jaw. She likely carried a torch for the guy, as did every other woman in West Sound. No surprise.

"Justin Brooks, right?" asked Rory, the amusement in his voice not lost on Jefferson.

"Oh, yeah, I guess he's pretty popular in West Sound." A smile flickered on her lips, but she pressed them together as if remembering why they were there. "Do you want to talk to him?"

No, Jefferson wanted to say. No, I do not want to talk to him. Instead, he let Rory answer the question.

"Yes, we do. We also need contact information for Forrest, if you have it."

She moved to get up, but then stopped. "Wait. Do you need a warrant or something for that? I'm not sure I should give out personal information."

"How about just a last name, then? We can find the information from there."

She tapped her chin, seeming to debate. "His last name is Bernard, and it can't hurt to give you his information. I'm a little worried about him, anyway. It's not like him to skip work."

"So he didn't call out?" Jefferson asked.

"Nope."

"And that's unusual?" he pressed.

She tilted her head back and forth, weighing her answer. "Well, it's unusual for him to not show up at all, but he's definitely careless with time, you know, coming ten, fifteen, thirty minutes late. I tried calling this morning, but he hasn't answered. Maybe you'll have more luck."

She left the office and returned with the trainer's information—and Justin Brooks.

Chapter Nine

"Hey guys," Justin said, reaching out a hand, which the detectives shook.

His grip just about crushed Jefferson's fingers, and he had to wonder if it was intentional.

Justin flashed his magnetic smile. "It's been a while since we were saving the world together."

He wore a black tank top that annoyingly highlighted his solid, world-saving shoulders and arms.

One of Justin's many redeeming qualities to all of womankind was his courage in the face of a maniacal killer in West Sound last year. The fanfare and news coverage had been massive. It was a little much, or a lot much, in Jefferson's opinion, but he couldn't deny that the man had proved himself to be a real-life hero.

Rory chuckled. "True. Good to see you, man."

"Thanks . . . I think. At least until I know what this is about." Confusion wrinkled his otherwise sculpted brow. "Is this about MJ. Did she get herself in some kind of trouble again?"

Jefferson bristled at this characterization of MJ. As if she were a naughty child, and they were coming to him to "tell on" her.

"No," jumped in Eden, with a light laugh before she lowered her voice. "It's about Ira Newman, one of Forrest's guys. You remember."

She laid a hand on his bicep. "But who is MJ? Is she a relative or something?"

Justin had his eyes fixed on Jefferson, not even looking at Eden. "She's my wife." He let that settle in before turning to Rory. "But Ira? He didn't show up this morning. Is something wrong?"

"You mean ex, of course," said Jefferson before Rory could answer.

Justin turned back to him, his smile wide but definitely forced. "Sure. Ex-wife."

"Oh, say no more," said Eden, with a light chuckle. "I know the kind of trouble an ex can cause. I have one of my own."

Tired of this time waste, Jefferson turned to Eden, who was hovering in the doorway. "Do you mind if we use your office while we talk with Justin?"

"Oh, I-I see," she stuttered. "I guess that's fine. I'll just wait at the front desk." She pointed behind her, keeping her eyes on Brooks with the irrepressible grin of a teenager. "Let me know if you need anything else," she said, forcing her face into a more serious aspect.

If Justin noticed the flirtatious way she looked at him, he showed no sign. He'd probably learned to tune out the constant adoration. And it wasn't just women. His ability to charm extended to all without prejudice.

With the door closed, Jefferson motioned for Brooks to take the seat behind Eden's desk.

He did so with a pleasant smile, but his intense blue eyes were cautious, even a little hostile. That could simply be the surprise of being questioned by the police, or it could be more personal.

Though he tried to keep his posture relaxed and friendly, Jefferson felt his own eyes harden. This interview would be interesting.

"We won't take too much of your time," Jefferson started, almost cringing at the wooden tone in his voice. It hinted at his discomfort.

Willing himself to adopt a more casual delivery, he cleared his throat and continued with what he hoped was a friendlier expression. "We appreciate your willingness to talk with us. I'm sure it's unexpected. As Eden said, we are looking for information related to Ira Newman, a member of the gym, so you're not in any kind of trouble or anything."

"That's good to know. Thanks," Brooks said stiffly, his eyes fixed on Jefferson.

"Sure. So . . . I'll just get right to it. We've been told that you did a training session with Ira yesterday?"

Justin watched Jefferson like a hawk waiting for his prey to make a move. "Yes, I trained him. He's a retired army captain and cop. Good guy, strong as an ox."

The two detectives exchanged a somber glance.

"Unfortunately," said Rory, "Mr. Newman passed away last night."

Justin's jaw dropped. "What? No," he said, shaking his head, his guard dropping at the news. "That can't be. Ira was in amazing shape . . . I mean, I didn't work with the guy often, but I've seen him enough to know he was a fitness and health nut. Took fantastic care of himself."

He sat forward, rubbing his hands down his face. "I can't believe it. That's so crazy." He took a breath before fixing narrowed eyes on Jefferson again. "Do you think someone killed him? Is that why you're here?"

Forcing his face into a blank slate, Jefferson responded, "As you stated, Ira is a retired West Sound police officer. A detective. We're doing some inquiries as a matter of course."

The last thing they needed was for Justin or anyone else to spread the idea that someone murdered Ira. So far, other than the unexpectedness of his death, they had no evidence to suggest that was the case.

"How well did you know Ira?" asked Rory, steering the interview away from the question of murder.

Justin blew out a breath. "Like I said, I didn't work out with him often, maybe five or six times. He was Forrest's guy. I only know the few things he told me abot himself. We swapped some military stories, but that's it."

Though his words were relaxed, Justin's movements were slow and tense, suggesting he wasn't any more comfortable with this situation than Jefferson.

"How was he yesterday? Did anything seem off or out of the ordinary?" Rory continued, keeping Justin's attention on him.

Brooks sat back, clasping his hands behind his head, his muscles flaring out in the same way a peacock might spread his feathers.

"Now that you ask," he said. "Ira seemed distracted yesterday . . . like his head was somewhere else. I asked him if everything was okay." He shrugged as he dropped his arms back to his lap. "Everything was fine, according to Ira. We finished the workout, and that was that. If something was going down, he didn't tell me what it was. I chalked his mood up to being out of sorts with Forrest for not showing up."

The emphasis he put on the name Forrest suggested Justin wasn't a fan. There was an expectant darting of his blue eyes between the detectives, as if he would say more on the subject if asked.

Rory bit. "Did Ira mention Forrest?"

"Not in so many words. But clients become attached to their coach, how they work and what they expect. That coach knows how far to push and when the client has had enough. It's like any relationship. You have to know when to expect more from someone, and when it's time to back off."

A stone-like stillness hardened Justin's already chiseled features, and his eyes shot daggers of blue ice at Jefferson.

So there it is, he thought, a not-so-subtle warning.

Jefferson felt Rory watching the two of them in this strange, unspoken showdown. There could be no doubt that MJ's ex meant to send the detective a message. That message? Back off and stay away from her.

Rather than intimidate Jefferson, this created a guttural need to laugh that threatened to explode like an amused volcano. One thing he knew about MJ Brooks was that she did not appreciate Justin's attempts at being her guard dog.

To cover his mirth, the detective looked down at the floor. He knew Justin would interpret this move as a type of concession. Jefferson didn't care. Let Brooks think he'd scored some kind of point. MJ knew her own mind and made her own choices. If this man was it, Jefferson wouldn't let it bother him.

At least that's what he told himself.

Brooks directed his next words to Rory.

"Ira knew Forrest was a flake. The dude likes to have a good time, if you know what I mean. I've seen him doing training sessions with a clear hangover. He comes late, leaves early. The gym won't fire him because his clients love him. There would be a revolt. No joke."

"Have you had any contact with Forrest today?" Rory asked with a quick flick of his eyes toward his partner.

Rory would have questions after this interview, and Jefferson did not look forward to fending off his inquisitiveness.

Justin shrank back, offended. "No man. I don't interact with that dude outside of the gym. I'd fire him if I owned this place. It's only a matter of time before he comes in here under the influence and hurts somebody."

With a chuckle, Rory repeated Justin's earlier phrase. "And yet, his clients love him."

"Yes, they do." Justin folded his arms and sat back against the desk chair. "He's charming, good looking, and he makes people feel good about themselves. They won't be able to get rid of him until he really screws up."

Jefferson recognized the irony of Justin describing himself as he attempted to describe Forrest. Even down to the last sentence. MJ and Justin had divorced, but she still hadn't completely freed herself from his influence. What was it that kept Justin Brooks in MJ's life? And what would it take for him to move on?

Despite telling himself repeatedly that he didn't care, Jefferson knew he wanted an answer to that question.

Chapter Ten

"So . . . partner," Rory said, as he climbed behind the wheel of the car. "I don't want to be too nosy." They both shut their doors. "Well, you know that's a lie. I want to be nosy. What was up with the clash of the titan egos in there?"

"Nothing. Let's go." Jefferson rubbed his hands together to warm them again. The quick trip to the car had been like a walk through an arctic windstorm.

Rory turned to look at him. Concern tempered the amusement that usually crinkled the corners of his brown eyes. "I know you think I just want to razz you, Jeffy, but . . ." He sighed. "I don't know why I keep starting every sentence with a lie. I want to razz you, and I will, but I'm also your friend, so spill it."

"There's nothing to spill."

"You lie about as well as my kids. Come on, let me be your mop bucket for clean up on aisle Jefferson. Just let it out."

He just stared ahead. "Let's go. We need to find Forrest."

"Hm. I'll wager that you went on a date with MJ, and Mr. Universe doesn't approve? Wait. You would definitely tell me if you went on a date with MJ, right? That can't be it."

Shooting a glare at his partner, Jefferson growled, "Stop guessing and start driving."

"So you want to go on a date with MJ, but she said no, and Justin, the dragon slayer, doesn't approve of you asking?"

Jefferson scrolled on his phone, doing his best to tune out Rory's attempt at interrogation.

"Did you and MJ . . . you know, kiss or something? You two spent a lot of 'alone' time together the last time she was around."

That was it. Jefferson could take no more of Rory's incessant babbling and lack of driving. And that he was hitting too close to home.

"I did not kiss MJ. I did not go out with MJ. I did not ask MJ out. I won't be asking MJ out, ever. There is nothing between MJ and me. In fact, the only person I'll be taking on a date is her friend, Shannon, the school counselor. Watch. I'll text her right now." He pulled out his phone, recklessly setting aside the indecision that had kept him from texting her earlier.

"Saturday, at seven?" he said aloud as he typed. "I'll pick you up."

"Whoa, Jeffy. Are you sure this is a good idea?"

Jefferson ignored him as his phone was already pinging a response.

"Sounds great. I'm at 5679 Fern Alley Dr."

Rory started the car, watching Jefferson as he stared at the screen of his phone.

"What?" Jefferson said, turning to look at him, his tone more hostile than he intended.

With a slow shake of his head, Rory backed out of the parking spot. "I just have a feeling your life is about to get very complicated."

Chapter Eleven

The bell rang, sending MJ's fourth period language arts class darting away to lunch. She straightened a few desks before grabbing her own lunch, a left-over chili that her neighbor Claire had brought to her the previous night. The woman always accused MJ of not eating well enough, which was mostly true.

Ten fifty in the morning always felt like an unnatural time to eat lunch, but it made sense when the day started at 5:30 am.

Popping the chili in the microwave next to her desk, MJ set the timer, pushing the start button at the same time someone opened her classroom door.

Shannon popped her head in and smiled. "Is now a good time?"

"Always." She waved her in.

"Cute," said Shannon, surveying MJ's red and white striped pants, red sweater with candy canes, and her dark bun with two actual candy canes crisscrossed through it.

MJ curtsied. "Thank you. But once again, where is your spirit, Ms. Davis?"

"I . . . um . . . forgot."

"Likely story," MJ chided. "But I'm always glad to see you. Is something up, or is this just a lunch visit?"

A shadow fell over Shannon's features. "I'm afraid I have bad news. I just got off the phone with the manager at the senior center. Mr. Newman died last night."

"Mr. Newman?" MJ said, incredulous, leaning against a student desktop. "That's horrible, and completely shocking. His poor family . . . Do you know what happened?"

"No. I think he died in his sleep, but they didn't say anything more than that on the call."

MJ mentally replayed the scene of Mr. Newman storming out of the club meeting. Maybe he wasn't feeling well, and nobody knew.

She narrowed her eyes at Shannon. "Don't you think it's a little odd that he died so soon after his outburst with Millie?"

Her friend wagged a finger at her. "Don't even start. Not everything is shady, MJ."

MJ covered her mouth as she realized what this meant. "Oh no. This will devastate poor Luis."

"I know," Shannon agreed. "That's why I want to meet with our middle school club members here in your room, so we can tell them before they hear it from the news or an obituary or something. I'll call Lucy, the counselor up at the high school, to do the same with the club members up there."

"Good idea. I have planning next period too, so we won't have to rush them out."

"Oh perfect. That gives me time to call parents before we meet with the students. Some of our more tender-hearted kiddos might want to call home, or even go home."

MJ's heart broke for Luis. He'd been so excited about his work with Mr. Newman. But all the kids would be affected. For some of them, this might be their first experience with death.

"Are you going to tell them?" MJ asked, dreading the idea of uttering the words herself.

"Yes, don't worry. And Carrie wants to be here, too. She thinks it's best if we suspend the club for now."

Carrie Chadwick was Mariner Middle School's principal, and MJ agreed with her assessment. They could bring the club back in the spring, or even next year, if the kids were still interested.

Shannon eyed MJ with a slight upturn on her lips. "I know this is horrible timing, and you'll think the worst of me for bringing it up right now, but I have to show you something."

She pulled her phone out, swiped the screen, and then held it out so MJ could read it.

There, on the screen, she saw the name "Jefferson" and then the words "How about seven? I'll pick you up."

MJ swallowed, a sudden lump swelling in her throat.

So, Jefferson followed through.

"I knew he would get in touch," she said, her eyes still on the phone. She didn't trust her expression yet.

It's just the surprise, she thought. That's why she felt this crater yawning inside of her. It was the strangeness of these two people in her world pairing up that confused her emotions, nothing else.

Plastering a grin, she glanced up. "He'd be a fool not to go out with an amazing, gorgeous woman like you."

"You're too much," laughed Shannon. "But I was so blown away when I got his text. You'll have to help me pick out something to wear on Saturday. He always looks so sharp. I don't want to look like a sheep herder next to him."

"Saturday? Maybe he can take you to the Christmas ball?" MJ wriggled her eyebrows.

"Oh, but we just bought those tickets to support the center. You weren't planning to go, were you?"

MJ laughed longer and louder than was necessary. "No, of course not. I was kidding. And, anyway, I'm not sure I'm your best option for clothing advice," she pointed out, motioning head to toe of her current outfit.

"Well, you got me there." Shannon laughed. "Eat your lunch," she added, heading for the door. "I'll let you know when everyone will be down here."

When she was gone, MJ pulled the chili out of the microwave. The thought of eating it made her stomach roil like a pile of rotten tomatoes had plopped there. Instead, she stood at the window watching the wind batter the very tops of the otherwise sturdy fir trees. It looked cold, like stepping outside might freeze the blood in your veins. Though she stood safely inside, she understood the feeling.

Warmth and blue skies. That's what she needed. Two weeks in Las Vegas, visiting her parents would be perfect for wrapping her mind around this shift in her universe. She glared at the gray sky and straightened her spine, mentally flinging her melancholy attitude into the clouds where it belonged.

She had things to do.

Chapter Twelve

"**I**'ve missed you."

Millie took a sip of tea as she waited for a response to pop up on her computer screen. Oloff always responded so quickly, like he couldn't wait to talk with her.

She'd only met him a month ago, when he sent her a friend request on Keep In Touch. Now she couldn't imagine a day without one of their chats.

"We just talked last night, you silly goose," Oloff responded, his words encased with little red hearts. "Supposed to be working right now. What my partner doesn't know won't hurt him, right?"

Millie giggled to herself. She felt like a teenager sneaking out of the house at night, even though Oloff was a world away.

"How is the business?" She rubbed the fingers of her left hand with her right, trying to loosen the tendons that made typing painful. Thank goodness the arthritis hadn't settled its sharp talons in both hands. Yet.

This time, it took him about a minute to respond. Millie knew things had been difficult for Oloff. He and his partner were both doctors from Sweden. The two of them were trying to build a new clinic in Zimbabwe, but money had been tight. Even worse, Oloff suspected his partner spent a good chunk of their investment funds on his girlfriend. He hadn't been able to prove it yet, but he was working on finding a new investment partner.

Things were so bad that her sweet Oloff had to rely on a local church for meals. It kept her up at night to think of him being so destitute when he was trying to do so much good. So, when he asked if Millie could send him a little money, just to help him get by for a month, she didn't hesitate.

She deposited a thousand dollars into his business account. His shock at the amount had made her grin like a schoolgirl. The gratitude he expressed still filled her heart with joy. That much money would last him almost a year, he'd said.

"Oh, you know. I'm getting by, thanks to you. We finally found the perfect building to rent."

Directly following this post, he sent a picture of a run-down cement building that Millie couldn't imagine being used for medical services.

"Will you need to remodel it?" She couldn't think of a more polite way to ask.

"Yes!" He included a row of crying, laughing emojis. "But let's talk about you. How is your latest oil painting? A Christmas scene? I want a picture."

A blush crept across her cheeks even though she was alone. Oloff always showed so much interest in her paintings. When they first started chatting, it didn't take long for them to discover they both loved painting oils.

"It's not much yet."

"So. Here is a picture of mine. It's the African coast."

A partial painting of the ocean crashing against some black and brown rocks entered the feed.

Sucking in a breath, she leaned in and studied the painting. Oloff had so many talents. And he was a wonderful human.

"That's beautiful," she typed.

"Not as beautiful as you."

She blushed harder this time, her eyes watering at the love exploding inside of her. If only Oloff were here, or she had the courage to travel to a place as exotic as Africa.

"I think we should meet. In person." The words were on the screen, but she hadn't hit enter yet. Something stopped her.

It was Ira. That overbearing man thought he knew her better than she knew herself.

Sure, she still loved Ira in a way. He was the first man to show her any attention after her husband died.

Years ago, when their spouses were alive, they were all great friends. Then, Millie and Ira both found themselves alone. They started spending almost every day together. Sometimes going out, sometimes just playing games at the senior center. They even went to church together at the old Methodist building.

While she knew Ira genuinely cared about her, she also knew he was wrong about Oloff.

Millie hadn't meant to tell Ira about him, but the man wouldn't quit showing up at her house, checking in on her, bringing her healthy meals, and trying to convince her to join his stupid gym.

He also never appreciated her paintings, not like Oloff.

The last straw was at that senior center computer club. Ira said he'd checked into Oloff, found his profile on KIT.

She told him to quit trying to pretend he was still a detective. That made him angry, but at least he'd left her alone.

Taking a deep breath, she hit enter. Then she waited.

Nothing.

Five minutes passed with Millie staring at the screen, her hands taut on the keyboard.

The wind made a high-pitched hissing sound as it tried to rush on its course, like her house was an annoying obstacle.

Had she made him mad? Maybe he didn't want to meet her after all.

"Oloff?" Before she could hit enter, his response popped into the stream.

"Sorry. A contractor came by to drop off a bid."

"Oh." She added a smiley face. "I thought you'd left me."

"Never."

"Sooooo. What do you think?"

"Yes! I want to meet. But no money." He added a frowning face. "And I just saw the bid amount," Oloff added. "No investor. No clinic."

Millie chewed her thumbnail. She still had a lot of her husband's life insurance money. Wasn't it worth spending some of it to see Oloff in person? What price wouldn't she pay to feel him hold her and tell her how much he loved her?

"I could buy your ticket to Seattle."

"You've already helped too much."

"Seeing you means more to me than money."

"Are you still having that problem?"

This surprised Millie, and for a minute, she wasn't sure what Oloff meant. Then she remembered.

"Oh, Ira means well. It's fine."

"If you say so."

Oloff worried too much about her living by herself. She'd been doing it for years now. It didn't frighten her at all, but lately, she'd felt more alone than ever. That is until she found Oloff.

"I guess you'll just have to come here and save me." She could feel the goofy love-sick smile on her face, but she didn't care.

The next post contained just an image of a red rose and the words, "I love you, Millie."

"I love you, too."

She waited a few seconds before continuing. "Should I buy the ticket or send the money?"

"Send the money. Weird here about foreigners."

Millie wasn't sure what that meant, but she trusted Oloff knew what he was talking about. "Same account?"

"No. Made a new account. Can't trust my partner. Will send details tomorrow. Sorry, have a meeting. Goodbye, my love."

"I love you. Goodbye."

She couldn't bear to close the chat. Instead, she clicked on Oloff's profile picture and stared at his deep blue eyes, set off so well by his silver hair. She traced his mouth with her finger. She couldn't wait to see that irresistible smile in flesh and blood, to see him smile it just for her.

Chapter Thirteen

F orrest Bernard lived in a moss-laden apartment complex just on the outskirts of downtown. The two detectives arrived with no more discussion of Jefferson's romantic life. Not that Rory didn't try.

"It's building G, apartment number 101," Jefferson said as they rolled into the overcrowded parking lot.

"D, E . . . There she is." Rory turned to the left and parked in the only empty spot, one reserved for apartment G302.

Every building of the complex lay in the shadows of the towering Douglas fir trees that bordered the property. Without enough light penetrating their wing-like branches, the area suffered from a permanent state of damp. The trees seemed determined to reclaim the wood siding of the apartments, covering them in lichen and needles.

Jefferson glanced up at the branches swaying dangerously, his hair mimicking their wild dance as the wind tousled it.

"Brrr," Rory said, closing his car door. "Time to pull out the winter coat and gloves. Darn kids."

"Kids?"

"Yep. They've been praying for a snow day all month."

Jefferson rolled his eyes. "Kids."

At apartment number 101, a bright vine of flowers may have once outlined the welcome mat. Over time and traffic, dirt and other questionable debris had ground it into an almost opaque slab of brown. A peephole stared back at them from the door, which was also marred by dents and scratches in its black paint.

Jefferson knocked, immediately stuffing his hand back into his pocket.

No one came to the door, but they couldn't miss the sudden thumps and rustling coming from inside.

Rory sighed with a disappointed shake of his head. "Does this really have to be hard?"

Jefferson knocked again. "West Sound Police," he called. "We have some questions for Forrest."

Silence greeted them. The sounds from inside had gone quiet.

Then a new sound caught Jefferson's ear. It was coming from the back side of the apartment.

"Did you hear . . . ?"

"Yep," said Rory. "Sliding-glass door."

"Stay here."

Jefferson took off toward the back of the building. As he rounded the corner, he saw the apartment had a tiny cement patio. Standing on it and doing his best to close the sliding-glass door silently was a plaid-shirted, skinny man with black hair. With his back to Jefferson, he threw down a pair of lime crocs and slipped his bare feet inside.

"Going somewhere?"

The man's head jerked around, a move that almost cost him his balance. Without a word, he took off, running along the wet strip of grass bordering the patios of the neighboring apartments.

With a groan, Jefferson followed him.

Wet grass and crocs, he thought, almost feeling sorry for the idiot. If I can't catch this guy, I'll never hear the end.

"Stop!" he bellowed at the plaid figure in front of him. "Police!"

When the man reached the end of building G, he had to negotiate a pine needle and mud-covered slope toward the parking lot.

His gear was not up to the task. One foot and then the other slid from beneath him, sending his bottom slapping onto the wet ground. As he struggled to get up, his hands grasping for a hold in the mud, Jefferson reached out and grabbed the neck of his shirt.

"Just st—"

Thwack! A slimy, mud-coated fist landed on Jefferson's cheek.

The punch surprised him more than it hurt. The detective, however, did not relinquish the man's shirt. Instead, he used it to slam him, stomach first, back to the ground.

"You're lucky you're a lightweight," he said, putting a knee in the man's back and pulling his two arms behind him, securing them with handcuffs.

"What's your name?" Jefferson asked as he pulled him to his feet.

No answer.

"Are you Forrest Bernard?"

The guy snorted as if Jefferson had asked the stupidest question in the world.

"Fine. Have it your way. We'll get it sorted out at the station." He marched the man back to where Rory still waited.

The captive attempted to wriggle free. "You can't arrest me. I ain't done nothing."

"That's what they all say," said Rory, who had come away from the door to meet them. "And all we wanted to do was have a little chat."

"Oh, we're still having a chat," said Jefferson. "Right after I book this guy for assaulting a police officer."

Rory eyed Jefferson's mud-splattered cheek. "Ooh, I see. Man," he said to their detainee, "that was dirty."

This prompted a skyward eye roll from Jefferson. "Not funny. Let's just get him in the car."

Opening the back passenger door with a smug grin, Rory said, "I don't know. I think most people would find that pretty funny."

"What was funny? How I'm gonna sue you for mis-arresting me?" sneered the muddy captive.

"See?" Jefferson said as he planted the man in the backseat. "Mud boy here doesn't even get it."

"Get what?" the man asked, trying to poke his head back out.

"Oh, he's gonna get it," chuckled Rory.

Jefferson nodded. "For sure."

"Get what?"

Chapter Fourteen

J efferson and Rory deposited their runaway at the station in the hands of Officer Meyers. Since the man was still being uncooperative, Meyers would process him, take his fingerprints, and run them through the system. Sitting in a cell for an hour or two might prod the man's desire to cooperate.

After Jefferson cleaned his shoes and the rest of the mud from his face and clothes, he and Rory were headed to the senior center to find out if Ira had been there last night.

The only thing Jefferson knew about the place was that it's not a residential facility. Instead, it served as a type of "club" for the city's seniors. He'd been there once, a long time ago.

The police and fire departments collaborated on a safety fair at the center. Jefferson was new to the department, having just moved from his hometown of Redding, California. Being the new guy, he drew the short straw and spent the day explaining tips on theft prevention.

"Welcome," said the desk attendant as the detectives walked in. "Are you here for tickets to the Christmas ball?"

"Uh, no," said Jefferson, momentarily thrown off.

"Well, you should, because it's our biggest fundraising event of the year. Live band, catered food, open bar . . . Who doesn't love a ball?"

Rory was reading the poster on the counter. "Hmm, and it's this Saturday. Sounds like just the thing for a first date."

Jefferson swallowed his snarky response and ignored Rory's attempt to bait him, calmly pulling out his ID.

A string of white lights and evergreen garland hung from the counter. A banner below it said Happy Holidays in candy cane lettering. An artificial, all-white tree stood in the corner of the small entry.

The smell didn't match the decor. Jefferson fought the urge to wrinkle his nose against the stench of overcooked food. Cafeteria food. He couldn't hear it, but he knew there must be one in the building.

"No, thanks . . . Ned," Jefferson said, reading the man's name tag. "I'm Detective Hughes and this is Detective Jackson. We're with West Sound PD. We have a few questions about one of your regular attendees."

"Questions about someone here?" Ned's eyes flew open with theatrical speed, making his question comical. The southern accent didn't help. "This has to be the most chill place on earth. That's weird, you needing to ask about one of these folks." He flung his hand in a dismissive wave. "They're all so sweet."

"Is there a manager we can speak with?" Jefferson asked, hoping to avoid giving too many details to Ned.

"Nah, sorry. She's at lunch. If you come back in an hour, you'll catch her."

"She's not eating lunch here?" Rory asked, looking around. "It smells like lunchtime."

Ned smirked, pushing his lips out disapprovingly. "There's no way Ms. Sierra is gonna eat the mushy pasta and boiled vegetables they're serving around here." He leaned closer and lowered his voice. "You know what I'm saying?"

Rory likewise lowered his voice. "So, you're saying that she enjoys good food?"

Ned straightened up. "If you want to call it that."

Jefferson had his notepad out. "Ms. Sierra? Is that her first or last name?"

"That's her first name, sweetie. Her last—"

Jefferson's death glare cut him off.

"Sorry," pouted Ned. "It's habit. Like I said, all the people here are so sweet, I just can't help it. My grandma raised me, and she called everyone sweetie even if they weren't so sweet." He gave Jefferson a side eye. "Anyway, Ms. Sierra's last name is Bennington."

The detective vowed there and then to cut out the tongue of any young person who addressed him with such terms of endearment when he got old. As if getting wrinkles and achy joints wasn't hard enough.

"Were you here last night?" Rory asked.

"Yep. I sure was, though the center's not always open at night. But last night, we had that computer class, so Ms. Sierra gave me the chance to get extra hours." He lifted his eyes past them to the entrance.

"Oh, here comes Ms. Kat. That girl is always late for quilting club."

The detectives turned to see a tiny woman shuffling inside, a bright yellow canvas bag on her arm, and bright white hair like a curly snowball atop her head.

"Good morning, sweety," said Ned, emphasizing the last word for Jefferson's sake.

Ms. Kat took in the detectives with sharp blue eyes.

"You have visitors, Ned?" Her words came through an amiable smile, but her voice sounded like her vocal chords were rusty.

"Oh, they're not here for long. Don't bother stopping, dear. Let me just sign you in. You go straight to the room, okay?"

"Thank you, Ned."

She turned left and shuffled down the hallway, which offered access to the rest of the senior center.

"Ned, do you remember seeing Ira Newman last night?" Rory continued once the woman was well on her way.

"Oh, Mr. Newman!" Ned put a hand on his chest. "Ms. Sierra told me this morning that he passed. That shocked me. Really shocked me."

"Did you see him?"

"Yes. Sorry, I just ... I'm still in shock. He was here last night, at the computer class. In fact," he leaned in conspiratorially again. Jefferson imagined Ned used his position to collect senior center gossip. "He left early. You might even say he stormed out." He put his hands up and stood back. "Can't say why, but he was not a happy camper."

Jefferson took his coat off and laid it over his arm. The place was an oven. "You didn't see him have an argument with anyone?"

"Nope. I was at the counter. There's a couple of lady teachers who run the club. They might know what made him stomp on outta here."

With just a hint of humor crinkling his eyes, Rory glanced at Jefferson, watching his reaction as he questioned Ned.

"Lady teachers, huh? Do you have their names?"

Ned bent down and retrieved a clipboard from below the counter. "We got Ms. Davis and Ms. Brooks," he read from the list. "Both of 'em are gorgeous ladies. And sweet as can be with our folks here."

No answer in the world could have perturbed Jefferson more than the one Ned just gave them. This couldn't be happening. What does MJ, or Shannon for that matter, know about computers? Why are an English teacher and school counselor running a tech club?

"Are you sure you have the names right?" he asked, knowing it wouldn't make any difference.

"Uh, yes. We don't have any other student-run clubs here."

A snort escaped Rory as he turned away from the counter, trying but not succeeding in stifling his laughter.

"Is something the matter?" asked Ned, concerned about Rory's ability to breathe.

"No, thank you for your help."

Jefferson couldn't escape the building fast enough. He strode out, leaving the laughing Rory in his dust.

Chapter Fifteen

E ven Rory knew better than to glory in his "I told you so" moment on the ride back to the station. Staring out of the car window, Jefferson tried to focus on questioning the man apprehended at Forrest's apartment, whoever he was. He didn't think it was Forrest himself, based on his skinny, unathletic build.

Despite his best efforts, Jefferson spent most of the ride to the station doing mental gymnastics, each woman's face taking turns flipping through his thoughts.

Of course, this case would involve MJ. As soon as Ira's son mentioned students, Jefferson should have expected it.

But the two of them together? Add to that the interview with Justin, and the detective knew he was living a relationship nightmare. The gods, fate, whatever, had a nasty sense of humor. He almost suspected Rory of casting spells to make comic entertainment for himself.

Ira's death may not be suspicious at all, but he and his family deserved Jefferson's undivided attention. By the time the two detectives walked into the station, Jefferson had successfully disciplined his mind into refocusing on the investigation.

After grabbing drinks, a cup of coffee for Rory and water for Jefferson, they found Meyers sitting at a desk in the hub.

"Any luck?" Jefferson asked, pulling a chair over from an empty desk.

The officer turned his computer screen, showing the detectives a mug shot of the skinny guy they had in lock up. "Leon Albright, twenty-seven. Fifteen priors. Mostly drug related, possession and dealing. One domestic . . . looks like a fight with his brother."

"Did he have this?" asked Rory, picking up an evidence bag next to the computer.

Meyers sat forward, stretching his back. "Nice haul, eh? I'm surprised you didn't see that bulge in his pocket. There's a couple hundred pills in there. Did a test strip on it, and it's definitely got fentanyl in it, some cocaine and other random fillers."

"Yeah, we missed that. Jeffy was too busy trying not to kill him after he swatted his muddy paw at him."

"And you were too busy practicing your comedy routine," Jefferson shot back. Then he added with a lopsided grin, "Don't quit your day job, by the way."

"Well, it's enough to charge him with possession and intent to sell, even more so if there's any equipment at his place. Are you going to request a warrant?" Meyers asked, his eyes wide with interest.

Considering the young officer, Jefferson asked, "Are you working toward detective?"

A smile worked its way up Meyers's cheeks. He nodded without looking at them. "Someday."

"Good," said Jefferson, standing up. "We need guys willing to work."

The officer lit up. "Thanks, and anytime you have something like this . . ." He let the rest go unspoken.

"Got it. And as far as a warrant," Jefferson turned to Rory. "Let's go talk to our friend Leon and see what he knows about Forrest. If the trainer is missing, we'll have a stronger case for a judge to issue the warrant."

"True," said Meyers. "That's smart."

"You're so smart, Jeffy," Rory mocked. "Except when it comes to women."

Meyers's face clouded in confusion. "What?"

"Hurry and make detective," Jefferson told him. "I'm going to need a new partner right after I kill this one."

He turned to leave and almost bumped into Allen Valencia, who had somehow soundlessly walked up behind him.

"I hear you boys have a detainee to question?" He clasped his arms behind his back like a drill sergeant.

The detectives exchanged a glance.

"Uh, sure. That's true," Rory answered.

"Great. I look forward to observing your implementation of the new skills you've learned. But first, what is your purpose here? Is it an interview or an interrogation? Remember, the first step of the KARES process is to . . ."

It took a minute for Jefferson to realize Valencia expected them to finish the sentence. The buds of impatience were just starting to bloom as he pressed his lips together. Not going to happen.

The more amiable Rory took one for the team. With a pointer finger in the air, he said, "Know and explain your purpose."

"Very good. Very good," Valencia said, without changing his expression. "And what is that purpose?"

Rory looked at Jefferson, a gleam in his eye. "I'll let Detective Hughes take that one." He rocked back on his heels, as if enjoying the torture he knew this conversation inflicted on his partner.

The urge to walk away without answering just about caused Jefferson's muscles to visibly twitch. He wondered how Valencia, the detective, would have reacted to the same type of questioning. Not well, he guessed.

Finally, out of respect for his chief and Valencia's service, he gave an answer. "Interview. We need information."

"Okay," said Valencia nodding, his voice less than enthusiastic. "That's a start."

"Great," said Jefferson, moving past the man, not giving him a chance to continue his line of questioning.

Chapter Sixteen

L eon Albright sat bent over with his hands in his hair. His head shot up when the door opened, his face devoid of its earlier bluster.

"Hello, Leon," said Rory.

"Look man, I'm sorry about earlier," he said, his frantic eyes on Jefferson as the detectives pulled out the plastic chairs across the table. Valencia came in behind them.

Upon realizing all the chairs were taken, Jefferson gave his to the older man. Then he stuck his head out of the door, telling the officer outside to bring another chair. He stood against the wall as he waited.

Leon was still apologizing to him. "You know, the punch. I just panicked, you know? My mom just kicked me out," he said, running a hand over his shaggy black hair, "and Forrest let me crash at his place, but I swear I didn't do nothing. Whatever he's got going on, I don't know nothing about it."

"I appreciate the apology," Jefferson said with a slow nod. "We all have bad days."

He caught just a glimpse of Valencia nodding approvingly.

Step two of K.A.R.E.S, thought Jefferson. "Aspire to Relationship." He longed to point out that he would have said the same thing before the training.

The conciliatory tone caused the man to relax, his shoulders slumping as he sat back in the chair.

"Thanks, man. I really am sorry. Sometimes I'm just so stupid."

"You mean like carrying a bowling ball's worth of dope in your pocket?" asked Rory.

This time, Valencia stiffened. Rory was about to get voted off the island.

Leon went instantly bug-eyed, his back straightening as if hit with a cattle prod. "Hey, I told the officer that ain't mine. I was just lazing around, you know, in my underwear."

His eyes darted between them, as if trying to decide who might best appreciate chilling at home in your undies. Of course it would be Rory.

"I didn't have no plans to go anywhere," Leon insisted, locking his pleading eyes on the bearded detective, "so when you all knocked, I just grabbed pants from the floor. They ain't even mine."

Rory folded his arms across his chest. "That's some bad luck. I wouldn't suggest you do any gambling."

"Look, Leon," Jefferson said, sitting forward and resting his hands casually on the table. "It's unfortunate you had those drugs on you, because we weren't even looking for you."

"I know," he said, sitting back again at the softer tone. "You're looking for Forrest."

Jefferson didn't look, but he could guess that Valencia's body language mirrored Leon's.

"That's right. He's the guy we really want to talk to. We need your help with that. When was the last time you saw him?"

Leon sniffed and looked down at his hands. Then he offered a one-sided shoulder shrug.

"Think real hard, Leon," Rory warned. "This doesn't get any better for you if we can't find Forrest."

Valencia folded his arms. Rory's eyes never left Leon. If he knew Valencia disapproved, he didn't care.

Twisting his fingers around each other, the young man seemed to weigh his options. "I don't know where he is," he said after a minute, his eyes on the floor.

"That wasn't the question, although we want to know that," Jefferson said. "When was the last time you saw him?"

"I don't know, man," Leon said, releasing his hands and throwing his eyes up to the ceiling. Drawing in a deep breath, he exhaled loudly before leveling his gaze with Jefferson's. "I think maybe three days ago?"

"He hasn't been home for three days?"

A zing of energy hit Jefferson at this information. Skipping work was one thing. And while they might find a logical reason for Forrest's absence from his apartment for three days, this heightened his sense that something was wrong.

Leon shook his head. "Not that I seen. I been in and out some, but mostly in."

"Did you call or text, or did he try to contact you?"

Jefferson couldn't be sure, but he thought he saw a flash of guilt run across Leon's features.

"No." He suddenly became interested in his fingers again. "I figured the less I reminded him about me crashing at his house, the longer he'd let me stay. If I didn't bug him, you know."

With his arms still crossed, Rory slouched in his chair like he was watching a disappointing football game. "Let's back up. How do you know Forrest? And don't tell us you were in the church choir together."

An amused snicker slipped past Leon's lips. "Church choir."

The room fell silent, the detectives' humorless gazes fixed upon him. Valencia watched quietly. His eyes narrowed as they all waited for an answer.

Leon shifted uncomfortably. "Right. Uh, we just hang with the same people. My friends from high school."

"So Forrest didn't go to school with you?" Jefferson asked.

He shook his head. "No. I think he's from California or something. He was with a girl in the group, but they broke up like . . . something like a year ago."

"What's her name?" Jefferson asked.

"I told you they broke up."

"And I asked you her name."

Leon stared at Jefferson as if the detective smelled like week-old garbage. Then he ran his hand through his unruly dark hair. "She's gonna hate me."

"If it's any consolation," said Rory. "We will find out, anyway. You'd just be helping us out, something that might be to your benefit, if you get my drift."

With a tortured face, Leon conceded. "Fine. It's Emily Simons. She used to work at the gym with Forrest, but she quit. To get away from him, I think. I ain't seen her in a while." He shifted his position in the chair again.

"Do you know her number or where she works now?" asked Jefferson, taking notes.

The man wriggled in his seat while whipping his head back and forth. "No, man. She changed her number and stuff. I think Forrest kind of stalked her; till she got a couple enormous dogs," he snickered. "One of 'em chased his sorry self all the way down the street once."

Bernard sounded shadier and shadier as the interview went on. It seemed he might have a lot of reasons to disappear.

"Do you know where Forrest went the last time you saw him?"

"To work at the gym, I guess. I didn't ask." Leon shifted again. "Can I use the bathroom?"

Jefferson dropped his pen and sat back. "Sure, but I have one more question first."

"Man, I really gotta go." He sucked in a breath.

"So let's make this fast. You said earlier that you had nothing to do with what Forrest had going on. What did Forrest have going on?"

Rory unfolded his arms and sat up, joining Jefferson with his elbows on the table. This had the desired effect on Leon, who stared open-mouthed at the two of them.

"I didn't mean nothing by that. When you cops came around, I just figured you all know something I don't."

Sitting back again, Rory ran a hand over his beard. "I don't think that's good enough."

"Come on, dude. I have to pee," Leon whined.

Valencia shifted in his seat, as if he too needed the restroom. Jefferson guessed instead that the man objected to them not letting Leon relieve himself.

The detectives stared back, waiting.

"Mm," Leon growled. "Isn't this torture or something?"

"Forrest?" Rory reminded him.

The man slapped his palms on his thighs. "Come on. Can't you guess? Drugs, man. He sells stuff. All kinds of stuff. Can I go now?"

"Anything else?" Jefferson asked, tapping his pen on the table.

"Like what?"

"You tell us."

Shifting in his chair, his eyes flew spasmodically around the room. "I don't know. He's on his computer a lot, but I swear. That's all I know." He sucked in another breath. "Can I go now?"

Jefferson stood. "I think we're done. For now."

He opened the door and motioned for the officer to take Leon, who burst from the room like a horse on fire.

Chapter Seventeen

When MJ opened the door of her house, Edgar was ecstatic, his toenails clicking on the floor as his black and white body wriggled like a leaping tap dancer.

"Hey, buddy," she said, hanging up her bag.

The exhaustion of the day hit her on the drive home. Physically, she needed more sleep. Mentally, her heart still hurt from the meeting with their club kids this afternoon.

Luis took it the worst. He'd worked the closest with Mr. Newman, so it was more like losing a friend for him.

MJ was glad his parents picked him up. The boy needed their hugs tonight.

When the clock hit 2:40 p.m., her contractual time to leave for the day, MJ didn't stay to do any of her usual tidying up, copies, or planning. She needed time to relax. Maybe she'd even go to bed early.

She poured a cup of food into Edgar's bowl, his big brown eyes watching her greedily.

And then there was Shannon's message from Jefferson.

As much as MJ pushed this man out of her mind, something still clanged against her heart every time she remembered Shannon's excitement.

Was she just being selfish? Thinking that Jefferson was hers even though she'd never pursued him, expressed no feelings about him? Was she just being territorial?

She put on her navy Mariner Middle School beanie and grabbed her gloves. "Come on, boy," she said to Edgar. "Let's get outside."

The cold assaulted her as soon as they stepped out the door. Wind whipped against her face as if it coveted her beanie. She knew from experience, however, that once they descended the stairs to the wet sand below, away from the high bank, the inlet would shield them from some of the wind's ferocity.

Weather like this usually guaranteed the beach would be empty. MJ unclipped Edgar's leash and stuck it in her pocket. Descending the stairs would be less hazardous if she wasn't trying to hold back a dog excited to catch his ball, no matter the weather.

She was right. The beach, while still pummeling them with cold, protected them from the thrashing wind.

Edgar bounded after his ball as MJ walked the beach, taking in the relative silence. Passing the sea scoured driftwood log, MJ remembered sitting there, putting her shoes on, talking with Jefferson.

His expensive loafers were sandy again.

A smile flirted around her mouth, and she closed it off, scolding herself. Think of something else, MJ.

When her phone buzzed in her pocket, she sighed with gratitude.

Flicking the screen, she saw that it was Meredith Hamblin, Diana's mom.

"Hi Meredith," she said, putting the phone to her ear with one hand while throwing the ball for Edgar with the other.

"Hi, MJ. Sorry to bother you at home."

"Oh, that's fine. You know I'm always happy to talk to a Hamblin. What's up?"

A sigh came over the line. "Of course, we all know about Mr. Newman, the man from the senior center. And you know Diana. Her brain never takes a break. She just really wants to talk to you about it. I told her I'd call and ask you first."

"It's been tough for all the kids. I would love to talk to her. I can come over if that's better."

"That would be wonderful," she said, relief in her voice. "She's got a bee in her bonnet, but she won't tell me anything about it."

MJ smiled to herself. Diana sure had her own mind.

"I'll see you in about an hour?"

"Great. I'll have some tulsi mint tea ready for you."

Chapter Eighteen

The Hamblin farm sat at the end of a bumpy gravel drive, made worse by all the recent rain. The potholes were now water-filled craters that could support a lake ecosystem.

MJ's Bronco handled them just fine, but it wasn't a smooth ride. Of course, if she wanted a smooth ride, she'd buy one of the many soulless SUVs offered on the market.

Edgar sat in the passenger seat, his pink tongue lolling as he panted, fogging up the window. Diana loved Edgar, and MJ hated to leave him alone again. Claire usually took him out in the afternoon, except on really rainy days like they'd experienced this week. The dog got along well with Zeus and Athena, the two golden retrievers at the farm. It made sense to bring him along.

The heater blasted MJ's face with warm air, but the chill refused to leave her bones. A light curtain of mist still shrouded the day, revealing hints of a showy blue sky waiting just on the other side.

Though it was indeed cold, MJ doubted the reports of an oncoming snowstorm, at least in the lowlands.

Northwest winters rarely saw the convergence of freezing air and moisture needed to bring on the white stuff. Usually, the water-heavy clouds warmed the air just enough to ensure a rainy Christmas. If the temperatures fell to freezing or below, they could almost count on a clear sky of the sharpest blue.

But sometimes . . .

She hoped it wasn't this time. No flight delays, please, she thought as she came to a stop next to the farmhouse.

Edgar began wriggling and whining at the sight of the house, pressing his nose to the car window and then looking back at MJ, who was not moving fast enough for him. Though it pained him, Edgar waited in his seat until she was out of the car. Then she gave him a quiet, "Okay," which meant he could exit as well.

Diana came out to meet them, Zeus and Athena squeezing through the screen door behind her.

MJ waved hello as Edgar scurried past her legs.

Immediately, the three dogs began chasing each other in circles, through the front yard, down to the pasture fence, and back again.

"Edgar!" Diana called when dogs zoomed toward her.

He stopped in his tracks and trotted over to her, luxuriating in the petting and words of affection she offered. Then Zeus landed in front of him, doing a jumping downward dog that dared Edgar to chase him again. That was all it took.

MJ waved a hand at the dogs. "Let them run each other ragged," she said to Diana, pointing to the back door. "But I'm as cold as a polar bear's nose."

"Is that cold?"

MJ chuckled. "No idea."

"Well, I'm as cold as my mom's stare after my dad buys her a cookbook for Christmas," said the girl, rubbing her hands over her arms. She'd come out in just an Orca High School volleyball T-shirt and sweatpants.

"No!" said MJ.

The girl gave a grim smile. "At least that's what he told us. But that could just be him trying to keep his actual gift a secret. But brrr. Let's go."

Diana ran up the steps and opened the door, holding it for MJ.

A wall of heat greeted them as they stepped into the kitchen. Though MJ couldn't see it yet, she knew a wood-burning stove blazed in the living room. The heat it produced was strong and earthy—a wildfire in a metal prison giving off an angry heat. MJ could feel the chill leaving her as the warmth overtook it.

Meredith stood at the counter, pulling down mugs and plating some cookies in her methodical, calm way. The woman never seemed flustered, even by the demands of her five children. She wore a ready smile that made everyone feel as though their comfort was her chief concern.

This calm extended to the kitchen. It wasn't a cheery yellow, but more of a creamy contented lemon; happiness that didn't need to shout because it was a constant state of being. The kitchen was awash in it: the walls, the cabinets, and the rugs covering the white oak flooring.

"Hello, MJ," she said, turning to place the mugs on the round kitchen table. "Thank you for making the trip out here. As promised, here is your tulsi mint. I'm having the same, and Diana has some hot cocoa."

"Perfect." MJ took her coat off and hung it on the chair where Meredith placed her tea.

They all sat down, and Diana immediately grabbed a cookie. "You should try these," she said to MJ after a bite. "They're Becca's famous oatmeal chocolate chip."

"Oh, is Becca home?" she asked, reaching for a cookie.

Meredith sighed happily. "Yes. Both she and Abe are home for Christmas break. I love having all my babies back under one roof."

Becca and Abe were twins and the oldest children in the Hamblin household. MJ couldn't remember which college they went to last fall, but it was somewhere in Idaho.

MJ gazed around the room. "But it's so quiet? No Abe and Becca harmonies?"

All the Hamblin children had some musical talent, but Becca and Abe stood out as they were always singing.

Meredith shook her head. "Sadly, no. Dominick took the other kids to do some Christmas shopping, though I'm not sure I was supposed to know that," Meredith said, taking a sip of her tea.

This prompted a wide-eyed, open-mouthed look from Diana. "No, you were not supposed to know that."

Meredith shrugged. "Your dad isn't great at keeping secrets." She winked at her daughter. "But you should share your thoughts with Ms. Brooks so she can get on with her day."

Diana finished her cookie. Then she folded her hands in front of her with the serious expression of a judge.

"Do you know if Mrs. Van Buren knows that Mr. Newman died?" the girl asked, her blue eyes steady but soft.

MJ considered the question. It was possible the woman knew. It was also quite possible she didn't. "I'm not sure," MJ said, finally. "That's a good question."

"It's just, I was thinking about it, and you remember how they had that . . . argument?" She wrinkled her nose. "I'm not sure that's what you'd call it."

MJ nodded. "I remember."

"What if Mrs. Van Buren finds out he died, and she's all alone, and she thinks it's her fault? Like people can have heart attacks because of stress or something, right?"

Before MJ could respond, Diana continued in a flurry of words.

"Mrs. Van Buren told me that her kids live far away. So do her grandkids, and they don't come to see her except like once a year or something. And I think she's kind of lonely. So . . ." Her eyes flitted between MJ and her mom. "I'm worried about her finding out when no one is around."

A mist found its way into MJ's eyes. This young girl was giving a clinic in compassion right now. MJ took a sip of tea and swallowed her emotions down with it.

"I see what you mean," she said when she could trust her voice. "And I'm sure Mrs. Van Buren would appreciate your concern. So, what do you think we should do?"

Diana bit her bottom lip. "I thought about going over there," she said, eyeing her mother. "But I'm just a kid, and my mom doesn't know her at all. So I was thinking . . ."

She stopped, and MJ knew what the rest of the sentence would be.

"You were thinking I could go," she finished for her.

Diana nodded like MJ had just offered her an ice cream sundae.

"I could do that," she agreed.

"Now, now," said Meredith, setting her mug down on the table. "Don't feel pressured by my Ms. Diana here. I wasn't exactly sure what she was going to ask of you. If this isn't something you feel comfortable doing, we understand that. Don't we Diana."

Diana completely missed Meredith's stern eyes. The girl had already launched into her next argument.

"Yes," Diana agreed. "But Ms. Brooks does all kinds of stuff like this, even police work. She brought Jada back home and everything."

"A lot of very brave people helped bring Jada home," MJ said. A picture of Jefferson driving the police cruiser pushed into her mind. She squeezed her eyes briefly to scatter the memory. "But really, I don't mind checking in with Millie."

With a grinning side-eye, she said to Diana, "Since you seem to have thought this out, do you have any brainy ideas on how I can get her address? The senior center is not likely to give that information out."

Suddenly sitting straight in her seat with a pointer finger in the air, Diana nodded once before jumping from her chair. Then she dashed into the living room, returning with an envelope in her hand.

"Mrs. Van Buren gave me this before she left yesterday." She handed it to MJ.

It was a Christmas card, and in the upper left-hand corner of the envelope sat a neat rectangular sticker. It had a Christmas tree on the left side and the words "Mr. and Mrs. Van Buren" with a street address on the other.

MJ imagined Millie pasting this sticker on all her Christmas card envelopes, reminded with each one that the husband she loved was gone. She had to wonder if using these old labels was less painful than getting new ones. New address labels that would say only Mrs. Van Buren. MJ's thoughts drifted to a place she'd rather not go, the march of time and the fact that no one could avoid the part of life that included death; our own and worse, the deaths of those we love.

Taking out her phone, MJ took a picture of the sticker. Then she shook the melancholy away for the second time that day and grinned at Diana, who was visibly relieved.

"Problem solved," she said, unsure how she would approach this task she'd just agreed to.

Chapter Nineteen

After dropping Edgar at home, MJ drove to Millie Van Buren's house.

Like a rain cloud pushed along by the wind, she dreaded the task ahead. In truth, she did not know Millie well enough to be the bearer of such bad news. She kept playing scenarios in her head, trying to find one in which the coming interaction wouldn't feel awkward. It didn't work.

But another scenario also played out in her mind; one more awful to contemplate. Millie sits alone as someone calls with the news, or she reads it in the newspaper.

That scenario, MJ couldn't stomach. And so, she pressed on.

The address on Diana's envelope led to a historic neighborhood of craftsman homes near downtown West Sound.

The sun, ready to disappear so early this time of year, was well on its way toward sunset. Despite the fading light, MJ marveled at the restored homes up and down the streets.

A few homes still needed love, but most appeared as if built yesterday.

Millie's house was in the latter category. The immaculate yard showcased a massive porch of river rock connected with dark timber posts in a color she couldn't quite make out. Maybe a kind of espresso, she thought. A deep evergreen traced the roofline, which included two gables of lace-curtained windows.

The sight of the stunning home left MJ in awe as she made her way up the stairs to the rust-colored front door. A motion-sensor light flashed as soon as she began her ascent, making her feel awkward in the spotlight.

Someone had to be helping Millie with her yard and the upkeep of her home. Maybe she had more contacts and people in her life than Diana feared. Maybe this was a mistake, and MJ would feel foolish for interfering.

She didn't think so, though. Millie told her at the senior center that she and Mr. Newman were old friends. Millie's husband was dead, and now one of her closest friends as well. MJ had to imagine this news would hit her hard. Checking on her couldn't hurt, but not checking on her could have the opposite effect.

Taking a deep breath, she raised her hand and knocked on the door.

To her surprise, the door opened immediately.

"Oh," she said, stepping back. "Hi Mrs. Van Buren. I hope you remember me."

The older woman looked her up and down with shrewd eyes. "Of course I do. You're the teacher from the computer club." She pulled her pink cardigan closer around her.

MJ could hear a TV blaring from inside the house. She stuffed her hands inside her pockets. What the heck was she doing here? The expression on Millie's face asked the same question, the guarded eyes of a woman not used to random visitors. Shannon was right. None of this was her problem. She should just scurry away and let someone else deal with it.

But as MJ gazed at the woman, seeing no awareness of the awful news about Ira, she knew for certain that no one had thought to tell

Millie. The address label flashed into her mind. Mr. and Mrs. Van Buren. Millie was losing her past one life at a time.

MJ closed her eyes briefly, hating this task for the pain it would bring, but knowing she couldn't turn back now.

"Can I come in for a few minutes? I have something I want to talk to you about." Little puffs of cloud appeared as her words fell into the cold air.

Millie stared at her, and MJ felt sure the woman would refuse.

"For a minute," Millie said as she turned, shuffling away from the door in her slippered feet. "Take your shoes off," she said, still walking away.

MJ closed the door and slipped off her boots. Then she followed Millie's retreating figure down a dark paneled hallway. Family photos lined the wall, some from decades ago, and some with small children that looked much more recent.

Among the array of pictures, a gold-framed photo from the fifties or sixties caught MJ's attention. It had to be a wedding portrait of Millie and her husband. They looked so young, like kids, really. They were a handsome couple.

Millie looked back just in time to see MJ turn away from the portrait. She didn't smile, but she didn't look angry either. It almost seemed as if she wore a purposefully neutral face, like admitting any emotion would open too many heartaches.

She took a right turn into the room at the back of the house. MJ followed.

Here sat the TV. On the screen, Kelly Clarkson smiled and chatted with another Hollywood somebody. This pricked something in MJ's memory about the singer having a talk show.

Two pale green recliners faced the TV with a small side table between them. Millie sat in the one closest and motioned for MJ to sit in the other. With her more nimble hand, the older woman picked up a remote and turned down the TV.

"Now, what can I help you with?" Millie's eyes were not unfriendly, but they narrowed slightly, as if prepared to tell MJ to get lost.

That was fair, MJ thought. This was an out-of-the-blue visit.

"First, I love your home. It's beautiful."

Millie gave a curt nod. "Thank you."

Realizing the woman did not want to engage in small talk, MJ dove in.

"Have you heard anything from the senior center, or perhaps from a friend about Mr. Newman?"

Millie's eyes were slits of suspicion now as her wrinkled brow descended in confusion. "What a strange question. Why would I hear anything about Ira?"

MJ noticed the use of Newman's first name. She hated having to be here, not wanting to say the words that might break this woman's heart.

"I'm here because we had some bad news, and I know you were friends with Mr. Newman." She drew in a breath before continuing. "Mr. Newman passed away last night."

The woman stared. She didn't say a word, but her face drained of color so quickly that MJ feared she might faint.

She rushed out of her seat and kneeled beside her.

"Millie? Are you okay?"

No verbal response came. She just continued with that vacant stare. MJ touched her hand.

"Millie, I need you to speak to me. Let me know you are okay, or I'm going to have to call 911."

Finally, the woman faced MJ with a slow turn of the head. "How?" she whispered.

"I don't think they know," she responded gently. "He seems to have passed in his sleep."

Tears formed in her eyes. "Oh, Ira. My dear Ira."

"Is there anyone I can call? Family, friend, maybe a pastor or something?"

Millie sobbed now. "I can't believe the things I said to him. And now he's gone."

MJ spotted a tissue box on the coffee table. She handed it to Millie. "Here, sit back and take some deep breaths. I'm going to make you a hot drink. Tea or coffee?"

The only response was a low moan as Millie continued to cry.

Patting the woman's shoulder, MJ decided to make whatever was in the kitchen. "I'll be right back."

Diana had made the right call. Millie showed clear distress at the news about Mr. Newman. MJ appreciated the girl's thoughtfulness even more. But Millie needed more than a stranger to comfort her, and MJ had no idea who to call.

Thankfully, Millie had a makeshift beverage center on her counter. A kettle and several types of tea stood stationed there. In the cupboard right above, MJ found mugs.

While filling the kettle from the kitchen island's sink, MJ noticed magnets clinging to the refrigerator door. She set the kettle to boil and then walked over to investigate them.

A bone-shaped magnet said West Sound Veterinary Clinic, which MJ found odd as she had noticed no pets in the house. Cats, she knew, could make themselves scarce, unlike dogs who never want to be left out of the action.

There was a bright green one with a barbell that MJ guessed was a gym of some kind. The name Senior Strength shouted in a bold black font.

Next to that hung a yellow square with a cross at the top and the words Cecil Bay United Methodist, Reverend Amelia Ackerman, Lead Pastor. It also listed a phone number.

Bingo.

MJ pulled out her phone and dialed the number. It rang without an answer, and just when she thought the call would go to voicemail, a cheery female voice said, "Cecil Bay United Methodists. I hope you're having a blessed day. This is Virgina. How can I help you?"

That was quite an impressive greeting, MJ thought. "Hello. My name is MJ. I'm here at the home of someone who, I think, goes to your church. Her name is Millie Van Buren?"

"Oh, yes. I know Millie very well." The woman sucked in a breath. "Oh dear. Has Millie heard about Ira? We just got the news from his son this morning. How is she doing?"

This statement relieved some of MJ's concern. Millie had people that knew both her and Ira.

"That's why I'm calling. She knows about Mr. Newman, and she's very upset. I don't think she should be alone. Is there someone from your church that could come check in with her?"

"Are you a relative or a friend?"

MJ gazed at the ceiling. How to explain?

"It's kind of a long story. The short version is that I'm a teacher, and we have a student-run computer class at the senior center. Both Millie and Ira attended. One of our high school students suggested I check on Millie once we heard the news about Mr. Newman."

The kettle clicked off and MJ put the phone on speaker so she could make the tea while talking.

"Sorry," she said. "I guess that was still the long version."

"Don't apologize, MJ. It sounds like you have some wonderful students and bless you for checking on Millie."

"Thank you. It was no problem. I just think she would benefit from a familiar face."

"Of course," agreed Virginia. "And I know just the ladies for the job. Don't you worry. I will call them right now. Can I call you back at this number?"

"Yes. That's fine."

"I will let you know when they will be there. Can you wait until then?"

"Of course. Thank you."

She carried the tea into the family room. Kelly Clarkson was singing on the TV, just barely loud enough to hear. Millie had the leg rest up on her recliner. Her eyes were closed, sending a jolt of panic through MJ.

Setting the tea on the side table, MJ spoke quietly. "Millie?"

She answered with a ragged intake of breath, her eyes still closed. "I never thought Ira would die before me." She clutched a well-used tissue in her hand.

"I'm so sorry, Millie. It sounds like you were close to Ira."

Her bottom lip quivered as she opened her eyes. "We used to be closer. Ira always thought he had to take care of me."

"Here, have some tea. I brought some of the sweeteners you had in the kitchen. Do you want any milk or creamer?"

She shook her head. "No, just sweetener is fine."

MJ dumped in a packet and stirred, handing Millie the mug.

She took a small sip and then set it back on the table. "I can't fathom that he's gone. Ira didn't even take any medication. How could he just die?" A desperation seized control of her features, her eyes wide and red with crying. "You're sure it was a natural cause?"

"I don't know, Millie. I'm sorry. We heard from the senior center, and I'm not sure they know many details, just that he seems to have passed in his sleep."

This appeared to ease her mind. "At least there is that. I hate to think of him suffering."

"How long have you known Mr. Newman?" MJ ventured, hoping talking about Ira might provide some comfort.

Millie offered her a weak smile. "Oh, about thirty years. Ira and my husband were best friends, hunting and poker buddies. Ira's wife and I were not as great of friends," she chuckled. "We got along well enough. The four of us spent a lot of time together."

She picked up the tea, balancing the mug bottom with her stiff hand, and took a sip before setting it back down. "When our spouses died, Ira and I took solace in spending time together." A tear escaped. MJ handed her another tissue. "He was a good man, but he wanted to marry me. I didn't feel that way about him."

A fresh wave a grief contorted her face. "Darn you, Ira!" she bellowed, wiping away a new crop of tears.

MJ handed her more tissues, not knowing what else to do. As much as she wanted to help Millie, she felt inadequate for the task.

"You're probably wondering why we argued the other night," Millie said suddenly.

Shrugging, MJ said, "It's not my business, but I'll admit to being curious."

"A few weeks ago, I made the mistake of telling Ira that I met someone else." She glanced up at MJ, an upturn to her lips that was both shy and sad.

"Oh," said MJ, surprised by this revelation.

"I know," said Millie. "I'm old, but even old people want to be in love." She shook her head. "Ira thought it was enough to not be alone.

He said I should marry him, even if I didn't love him romantically; that at our age, it didn't matter as much."

She drank another sip of tea. "Anyway, he kept trying to butt in on my relationship, like I couldn't take care of myself. I finally had to tell him to leave me . . . alone." The last word came out in a sob. "I'm sorry."

MJ reached across the table and squeezed Millie's hand. Of all the reasons MJ might have imagined for Ira's outburst, this wasn't it. But why shouldn't it be? She scolded herself for being narrow-minded. Perhaps this new love interest is who Millie needed right now.

"Do you want me to call your—"

"No!" she almost shouted. "Sorry, no dear. I will tell him later. He's busy this time of day."

"Okay. Just let me know if you change your mind."

When MJ's phone buzzed in her pocket, she patted Millie's hand. "I'll be right back. Do you want anything from the kitchen?"

Millie shook her head while continuing to dry her eyes.

It was Virginia, telling her that two ladies from the church would be at Millie's house in fifteen minutes.

MJ decided not to tell Millie. That could blow up in her face, but there was also a good chance that Millie would have refused visitors if asked.

Maybe Millie's mystery man would show up later? After the woman's frantic reaction to calling him, MJ found the story of this new romance to be strange. She wondered if Ira thought the same thing.

Chapter Twenty

C uriosity got the better of MJ.

And it wasn't just because Millie had a more active love life than she did.

Ira Newman's apparent suspicion of the woman's new love had MJ's mystery antennae fully activated. Was it just jealousy, or did Ira know something about this person, something that suggested Millie was in danger?

Asking the woman herself was out of the question. When the church ladies showed up, Millie gave MJ the coldest stare of her life. They would not be exchanging Christmas cards anytime soon.

No, she was definitely on Millie's naughty list. She also wasn't on her KIT friend list, which might make her search on the social media site useless.

Nevertheless, MJ made herself a cup of tea and sat down with her laptop open to the site. MJ had a profile, but she rarely checked it, using it just to keep in touch with aunts, uncles, cousins, and a few friends from high school. Social media could be a minefield for teachers, so she limited her presence there.

Typing Millie's name in the search bar, MJ hoped the uniqueness of it would make the woman easy to find.

"Voila! There you are," she whispered to herself.

The top two search results were both for Millie Van Burens, but the second one had a profile picture of a much younger woman. The profile picture for the first result was a gray cat. That had to be her Millie.

MJ clicked on the profile, quickly realizing it was set to "private." Undeterred, she scrolled through the list of past profile pictures. There were only two, and MJ remembered it was only a couple of months ago that the club kids had helped Millie set up her KIT account. The other two profile pictures were flowers.

There was only one public post. MJ clicked on it and a picture of the same cat as the profile picture filled her screen. Its strange gold eyes stared back at her from a coat of blue-gray fur, like a little storm cloud.

Below the picture, Millie had written, "I'll miss you, my little Queenie. Keep Walter company in heaven."

MJ felt another wave of sadness for Millie. Queenie was likely not just a pet, but a companion for the woman. MJ knew how that felt. Losing Edgar would be devastating.

She glanced down at the dog, resting contentedly at her feet. She'd miss him while in Las Vegas. But he would have adventures with Justin, who planned to take him to a cabin near White Pass. Edgar would likely get to play in the snow, which he loved.

She reached down to pet him and then went back to her search on Millie's profile.

Luckily, the profile friends list was not private. As she scrolled over it, MJ sat back in surprise. She and Millie had a mutual friend.

Claire knew Millie.

Claire knew Millie. Jefferson and Shannon. These intersecting friend circles were going to make her dizzy.

She chalked it up to an interesting coincidence, but not much more than that. Maybe Claire knew Ira, too. If they were all friends, Claire might be another good person to call Millie and check on her. MJ would suggest it later.

The rest of Millie Van Buren's friend list was blessedly short. There were a few people that MJ pegged as Millie's children or grandchildren, judging by the shared last name.

She clicked on a few others, mostly senior women. Then she found Oloff Svensson. The name stuck out not only because of its Swedish origin but also because Oloff was the only man on Millie's friend list that wasn't a relative.

His profile picture showed a smiling man with a mane of silver hair and piercing blue eyes. In the photo, he held a glass of wine and appeared to be in a plush restaurant.

"Handsome man," MJ said out loud. Edgar glanced up at her. "I mean, for an older guy," she assured the dog.

His head fell back to his paws as if understanding the conversation would not lead to a treat or a trip outside and was therefore boring.

Oloff's profile was public. However, he'd only posted ten times. Each post contained a picture of him in a different setting: at the beach, at a desk wearing a white lab coat and stethoscope, walking a dog in the woods, and the strangest of all, sitting in a leather chair reading the Bible.

Reading the Bible wasn't strange, but who takes a picture of themselves doing it?

The other curious thing was that the posts, save a couple of exceptions, were all made on the same day, September tenth, just a few months ago.

The feeling that this was a scam profile grew when MJ checked Oloff's friend list. There she saw Millie, along with a few other women. There were a couple of other men, so MJ clicked on their profiles.

What she found there followed the same pattern.

New profile. Few friends. Few posts, all of which were created on the same day.

The profiles all fed off of each other, creating the appearance of friends when they could all potentially be the same person.

If this Oloff was Millie's new love, Diana had been right.

Millie was being scammed, and MJ would put money on the idea that Ira knew it.

Chapter Twenty-One

As Jefferson and Rory were heading to an afternoon briefing, Valencia caught up with them from behind.

"Detectives, I have a report for you."

Jefferson desperately wanted to continue walking, but he stopped and turned to face him. "A report?"

"Yes, I typed up my notes from your interview with Leon. I added some comments, areas for improvement, what I think you did well." He nodded toward Jefferson when he said the last part, which far from being a compliment, would instead earn him sarcastic scorn from his partner.

Valencia handed them each a packet of printed paper. "Here's a copy for each of you. We can sit down and go over it when you have some time."

"Sure thing," said Rory.

Jefferson took the report with a quick nod. "Thanks. We have to go—"

"To the briefing," Valencia interrupted. "Yes, I know. I won't keep you. Just wanted to share it with you before you head out somewhere."

"Hughes! Jackson!" bellowed the chief from the briefing room door. "Get in here."

They did as instructed, joining Mendez and Larson already seated around the table. Other than the chief, they were the extent of the briefing attendees.

"Hughes and Jackson, I want to hear what you've found so far regarding Ira Newman's death. If we need to include a few officers, we'll do that later."

"Understood," said Jefferson. "So far, we have nothing solid to suggest Ira's death was suspicious. Without the autopsy, we're just tracing his movements, looking for anomalies. There could be something off with his fitness trainer, but like I said, not concrete. Rob Newman brought up the name Warren Harris, one of the guys Ira put away. I think his arrest was before my time here."

"I remember," nodded the chief. "Real nasty character."

"Well, he was paroled last week."

The chief gave one heavy nod. "Get an officer on that. Find out who his parole officer is, where he lives, works, etc."

"Got it."

"And the trainer is the reason for the earlier interview?" asked the chief.

"Not an interrogation, mind you," added Rory.

"Stuff it, Jackson," said the chief, his hard eyes signaling annoyance. "So, what is this suspicious activity?"

Stuff it? Jefferson stifled a smile before continuing. "Newman worked out at a gym called Senior Strength. Their clients are all senior citizens." He explained why they believed Newman's trainer, Forrest Bernard, may be missing.

"Ira still got his workout in, though," Rory said, glancing mischievously at his partner.

"That's not pertinent." Jefferson glared.

Until now, Larson had been scrolling on his phone. He dropped it on the table and sat back with amused attention. "I know when Hughes gets crabby, Jackson is dishing something good."

"Be careful, Jackson. If it is indeed not pertinent, Hughes won't be the only one crabby with you," warned Chief Carlson.

Rory stroked his beard. "Well, we did interview, not interrogate, the fill-in trainer, who is none other than Mr. Justin Brooks."

"Brooks? Of course," smirked Larson. "That guy loves his muscles. What better way to showcase your fitness than to work out with a bunch of geezers."

"Says the original geezer himself," joked Mendez.

"Ain't that the truth," mumbled Larson, rubbing the back of his neck.

The chief put a hand up. "We are wasting time. How is Brooks pertinent?"

"He told us that Ira was not himself that morning. That he seemed preoccupied," answered Rory, his arms folded across his chest.

The chief nodded. "That's something. Try not leaving anything else out, Detective Hughes."

"I won't, sir. And if I do, Jackson here always has my back."

Rory agreed with a single nod of his head. "Always."

The banter aside, Jefferson wasn't sure why he hadn't mentioned the interview with Justin. He told himself it was to save time. It did exactly the opposite.

The chief waved aside their snipes. "What information did you get from your recent arrest? He was staying at the trainer's apartment?"

Jefferson tapped his notepad with his pen. "Yep. His first instinct was to run, so we knew there was something he didn't want to talk about. He had some dope on him. Later, he told us Forrest has a little side business selling the stuff. Said he hasn't seen Forrest in three days."

"Our guy, Leon, also mentioned something about computers. We need a warrant to check into that. Could be porn, identity theft, or nothing." Rory shrugged.

"And the odds of it being related to Ira's death are not great," added Jefferson. "Then we checked at the senior center where Ira attended a computer class run by students in the evening. The desk attendant said Ira stormed out of the building, upset about something. He didn't know what."

"And," Rory jumped in, "you'll never guess—"

"I'm getting there," Jefferson said through clenched teeth. Sometimes, Rory needed a good throw through a window.

"Oh, sorry," he said with a wink at Larson and Mendez. "You guys will enjoy this part."

"No!" said Mendez, appearing to guess what Jefferson would say. "You said student-run club." He put a fist to his mouth to hide his chuckle.

Then Larson caught on. "So, the other Brooks runs the club?"

Rory nodded, patting Jefferson on the shoulder. "It's true. But I won't even go into the rest. I don't think Jefferson here can handle it, and the chief might blow a gasket."

The chief indeed looked ready to throttle someone. "I am failing to find the humor in this situation. Let me remind you that Ira Newman deserves your respect and attention. Save the badgering for another time."

"Or we could just not have the badgering," suggested Jefferson, knowing full well that if the shoe was on the other foot, he'd be all in.

"Sorry, son. I don't think that's possible." Despite his strong words, even the chief had a glimmer in his eye. "Now, how is MJ, and what, if anything, did she tell you?"

Jefferson cleared his throat. "We haven't spoken to her yet. School has only been out for a bit. We'll call her as soon as the briefing is over." He responded directly to the chief without looking at any of his detective colleagues. "The senior center desk attendant seems to think she and the other teacher in the room saw whatever upset Ira."

The chief nodded. "Sounds good for now. Any time frame on the autopsy?"

"Not yet," said Jefferson. "Underhill has to finish up with their guy." He motioned with his head toward Larson and Mendez.

Larson was back to scrolling on his phone. "Yep," he said, his eyes still on the screen. "She said later today we can head over. Any minute now."

Larson showed his screen to Mendez, who squinted for a couple of seconds before nodding.

"I think so," he said.

This caught the chief's attention. He cocked his head in their direction. "Something interesting on your phone, detective?"

Larson sat up and passed the phone to Jefferson. "This is your trainer, right?"

Jefferson and Rory both glanced at the picture. It was the staff page from the Senior Strength website. Larson had zoomed into a picture of a smiling young man with dark, curly hair.

"Yeah, that's him." Jefferson confirmed.

Larson then passed his phone to the chief. "We can't be sure," he told them, "but it's possible your missing guy is our guy. In fact, I'd even venture to say it's probable."

This revelation quieted the conversation like a collective pause.

That same current of energy as earlier lit up Jefferson's mind, and he knew Larson was right. Forrest was dead. Unfortunately, it made too much sense.

And if the dead body discovered at Shopside was indeed Forrest Bernard, then they couldn't ignore the trainer's potential connection to Ira's death

The chief's jaw tightened, his eyes like ice. The same pieces seemed to fall into place for him. "Find out. I want to know before today is over. If that means a warrant to get into the trainer's apartment, I will make it happen. This is priority one."

He inhaled deeply, his nostrils flaring with angry determination. He threw his shoulders back and started barking commands.

"Larson. You and Mendez get over to that apartment and wait. I'll have a warrant within the hour. Collect DNA samples, but also look for pictures that show tattoos or other identifiers, because we all know the snail's pace of DNA results. Look for contact info for family or friends." He waved a hand. "I know you know what to do."

The chief paused just long enough to take a breath. Jefferson jumped in, bracing for the angry glare that was sure to come his way.

"Sir. We will check with Leon Albright as well, about identifying marks. But he also told us that Forrest has an ex-girlfriend in the area. She might have more, uh, knowledge of bodily marks. We have her name."

"Fine," he said sharply. "Make use of it. The more corroboration we have that the dead man is the trainer, the better. If we can't find family members, then his friends will be the next best people for identification. Also, get a hold of MJ. Find out if there is anything to this supposed altercation."

"Sir," Jefferson protested. "You know if we call her, she's just going to want to solve the case."

The chief stood, his signal that all this talking must now turn to action. He paused, his eyes of steel unwavering but thoughtful as he considered the detective. "Has that ever been a bad thing, Hughes?"

That gaze bored into him, and Jefferson couldn't withstand it. He looked down, picking up his notepad. "No, sir."

"Then let's get going, son." He was quiet for one more heartbeat, then he bellowed at Larson. "Find some officers to print pictures and labels and start this investigation board."

"Oh, and Hughes," the chief said, holding his pen out like a sword. "Call Underhill and ask her to push Ira's autopsy to the top after the Shopside Docks man." He dropped the pen to his side as he seemed to rethink that demand. "Never mind. I'll call her. Maybe as a personal favor, I can persuade her to present the findings to the team here at the station." He nodded, as if confirming this change in direction with himself. "Good. That's all."

Chapter Twenty-Two

Leon Albright provided no help when asked about identifying marks for Forrest.

He'd scrunched up his face and said, "We ain't sitting around looking at each other naked, dude."

Jefferson had to admit he'd probably answer in much the same way if asked.

He and Rory were back in the hub, getting ready to contact the ex-girlfriend, Emily Simons, as well as MJ and Shannon.

"I'll get a number for Emily," offered Rory. "You set up an interview with MJ and her friend."

Rolling his phone in his hand, Jefferson considered this arrangement. Which woman should he call first? Would Shannon get angry if he called MJ before he called her? But calling Shannon before MJ, and about a case, just felt weird. He knew MJ so much better.

"No, I think we should do it the other way around. I'll call Emily Simons."

Rory rocked back in his desk chair. "Oh, no you don't. You got yourself into this mess, and I refuse to let you rob me of the entertainment it will provide."

His chair tipped forward, legs making contact with the ground. "Besides. I already have her contact info. Sort of."

"What? How?"

"Easy peasy. I found her KIT profile."

"How do you know it's the right Emily Simons?"

Rory turned his computer so Jefferson could see the profile's cover photo. Two German shepherds flanked a smiling Black woman. She sported a Seahawks beanie, out of which hung two dark braids. Her eyes, however, were the most striking part of the photo. They glowed a light amber. The effect was so stunning that Jefferson wondered if it was real.

"Wow. Beautiful girl."

"Don't even think about it, Jeffy. You've got enough women on your dance card."

"Noticing is not the same as thinking about it. As a married man, I'm sure you understand that even better than me."

Rory scoffed. "I didn't even notice she was attractive until you said something."

"Whatever. So, what did you find?"

Returning his screen to face himself, Rory added, "Her profile is private, but there is one picture here with Alejandro Delgado, who I just happen to know is the owner of Agua Azul. I'm not a betting man, but I bet Agua Azul is where Ms. Simons works." He froze and stared into the distance. "That sounds so good right now. After this, let's go get a burrito. In fact, let me call. If she's there, we can grab lunch and talk to her. It's a twofer."

"And MJ?"

Rory let out a heavy sigh. "Alright. You agree to the burrito thing, and I'll call your ladies."

This characterization of MJ and Shannon deserved a protest, but Jefferson didn't want to risk Rory changing his mind.

"Deal."

Chapter
Twenty-Three

R ory's hunch turned out to be correct.

He pointed out to Jefferson that being a frequent burrito buyer comes with some perks, like having the owner's phone number. Telling the man they needed information for a case probably didn't hurt, either.

Alejandro confirmed Emily was an employee, and while not currently there, she was due to start a shift in thirty minutes.

Just enough time to eat a burrito.

"All that's left to do before getting some Agua Azul goodness is sort out your love life. I mean, call the ladies." Rory winked. "Give me MJ's number." He held his phone, ready to dial.

"This is not to be used for anything other than the intended purpose. I don't know what trick you could pull, but I don't trust you, Jackson."

"Come on, you big baby. Just give me the number."

Jefferson read out the numbers as Rory typed on his phone. As soon as he hit the last number, Rory jumped out of his seat and ran to the empty briefing room.

After some confusion, Jefferson dashed after him. "Jackson!"

He was too late. Rory had locked the door.

"Jackson!" he bellowed through the door.

A female officer working at a desk nearby glanced up, caught sight of Jefferson, and then shook her head as if to say, "Boys." Then she turned her attention back to her computer.

"Jackson," he said with less volume.

Nothing. He could hear Rory's voice on the other side, but the briefing room had thick walls and a solid door for a reason.

He ran a hand through his hair, holding the longish locks at the top, pacing outside the door. What was that fiend up to? He should've just called MJ himself. Trusting Rory was a mistake.

The door flew open just as he stopped in front of it. With a scrunched brow and up-and-down look from the corner of his eye, Rory said, "What's eating you?"

"What's eating me? What did you say to her?"

"You need to relax," Rory said, heading back to his desk. "We have a meeting at MJ's house at seven. She's going to call Shannon, and they'll both be there."

Jefferson slapped his forehead. "Are you kidding me? Together?"

The white line of a toothy grin popped through Rory's ginger beard. "Together."

"You did that on purpose."

"Of course. Best use of resources." Though a grin attached itself to his beard, Rory's eyes were still, and alarmingly serious.

"Besides, partner. I think you'll thank me in the long run."

"I can't, for the life of me, fathom how."

He rested his hand on his chest. "Just trust this man with more experience in the romantic arts. Now, let's go get that burrito."

Chapter
Twenty-Four

In less than fifteen minutes, Rory and Jefferson sat in a booth at Agua Azul, digging into their burritos. Fifteen minutes later, Alejandro came over to their table with a young woman Jefferson recognized from her KIT profile.

"Gentlemen," said Alejandro in his thick Mexican accent. "It's okay for you to speak with Emily. I cover," he said, grinning and pointing to himself and then at the podium where the hostess usually stood.

The girl, standing a head taller than Alejandro, looked less enthused than her boss about this prospect. Her eyes were even more stunning in person. Even as they fell on the detectives with narrowed suspicion, Jefferson found it hard to look away.

Rory stood up and moved to Jefferson's side of the booth, dragging his burrito and Coke with him.

"Please, have a seat," he said.

Emily, still wearing a maroon peacoat, slid into the booth.

"Take the time you need," Alejandro said before leaving to greet a couple at the podium.

The young woman sat straight against the back of the booth, her posture stiff and wary. A massive bun of dark hair sat atop her head, skirted by a wide black headband. She kept her hands in her coat pockets, those amber eyes shifting between the detectives.

A trumpet-heavy mariachi version of "Eye of the Tiger" wafted through the air of the restaurant, and colorful hand-painted ocean murals covered the walls, complete with larger-than-life sea turtles and a variety of other salt-water creatures.

Jefferson had only been in the restaurant a handful of times. Most of the West Sound police ate from the Agua Azul food truck that parked near the station two days a week.

"Thank you for speaking with us, Emily."

"I don't think I really had a choice," she said, annoyed. "Alejandro just herded me over here."

"Yeah, sorry about that. But I'm Detective Hughes, and this is Detective Jackson. You're not in any trouble or anything. We just have a few questions about a friend of yours." He paused. "Or more like a former friend."

She rolled her eyes up to the ceiling with a heavy sigh. "Let me guess. Forrest."

"Why would you guess Forrest?" asked Rory.

She pulled her hands free and sat forward. "Look, can we just cut to the chase? I have not seen Forrest in more than a year. I don't date him anymore, and I seriously regret that I ever did. The guy is a narcissistic idiot who doesn't care who he hurts as long as he can make money."

Jefferson cocked his head. "For example?"

Sitting back again, she folded her arms. "Can you tell me what he did? Like, why are you here?"

The detectives exchanged a glance.

Her crossed arms relaxed, and her voice lost its edge. "Is he dead?"

Jefferson met her gaze. "No one has seen him for a few days. He may be missing."

She planted her elbows on the table, her forehead on her palm. "I told him this would happen. I told him." Her eyes flashed up to Jefferson's. "So, you're looking for him? That's why you're here?"

"You could say that," Jefferson said. "But I'll be honest with you. A body was found this morning—"

"Oh no," she whispered, wrapping an arm around her stomach.

"We don't know that it's Forrest," he cautioned. "But we think it's possible."

The way she touched her fingers to her lips, Jefferson worried she might be sick. Then she spoke again.

"Look, we didn't part on good terms, but," she shook her head as tears invaded her amber eyes. "I'd never want anything bad to happen to him."

Rory reassured her. "We're not thinking that at all, that you would have anything to do with it. What we need is for you to help us determine if the man found this morning is Forrest."

"You mean like ID him?" Her eyes were wide in disbelief. "No way. I can't do that." She put her palms up, and Jefferson noticed a slight tremor in her hands.

"We wouldn't ask that unless there aren't any other options, and of course you can always say no," Jefferson explained. "Instead, we'd like you to think carefully about any identifying features you remember about Forrest. Tattoos, birthmarks, scars . . . anything like that."

She licked her lips and nodded. "I can do that."

They both watched her expectantly as she worked to compose herself.

"Um, he didn't really like tattoos because he said they were unhealthy, could lead to disease and stuff, but he had a scar. He told me it was from getting his appendix out, but who knows if that was even true." She closed her eyes as if trying to see it in her mind. "It was right here," she pointed to her own stomach. Realizing they couldn't see, she stood and made a small slit-like motion on the right side, the lowest part of her abdomen.

"That looks like appendix," said Rory.

Emily sat back down. "I learned not to trust much of what he said, so . . ."

Forrest Bernard was turning out to be quite an interesting character. He obviously lived off his charm and seemed to use it for nefarious purposes if Emily was to be believed, and Jefferson didn't think she had any reason to lie.

"You said he hurt people. What did you mean?"

She grabbed a napkin from the dispenser on the table and wiped her nose, the slight tremor in her hand still visible. "I don't mean literally hurt people like some kind of goon. It's more like he did things that eventually hurt people."

Her eyes flitted between them. There was a question in them, one she hesitated to ask. Jefferson sensed she wouldn't say more unless she knew the answer.

"We know he was selling drugs," he said.

She nodded quietly, glancing down at the napkin in her hand. "So that's one way he hurts people. Some of them are people I know."

"Is there another way he hurt people?" asked Rory.

She nodded again. "Some of it was just stupid stuff, you know, but that gym he works at . . . " she sucked in a breath and blew it out, her eyes suddenly hard and fiery. "That place made me so mad. I quit, but Forrest, he didn't care. He said most of those people had plenty of money and nowhere to spend it."

Jefferson put a hand up. "Wait, back up. So, what were they doing that made you mad?"

"Oh, just selling them old folks all kinds of stuff they don't need. Their stupid useless supplements, shakes, clothes, workout gear . . . you name it. They're just hustling those people. Promising them longer life if they buy their junk. Disgusting." She let out a derisive laugh. "Forrest is good at it. I fell for his stupid charm, so I can't blame anyone else for doing the same."

"So unethical, but not anything illegal?" clarified Rory.

She shrugged, pulling at the napkin and crinkling it again. "Not that I know of, but I wouldn't put it past them."

The rate of new customers at the podium had been steadily increasing over the course of their interview. Alejandro had thrown a few furtive glances their way.

Jefferson gave her an appreciative half smile. "We should let you get to work. Just one last question and then we'll be on our way."

"Sure."

"Do you know of any family Forrest has in the area, or somewhere he might stay or hide out?"

"No. He never talked about his family. I think they are in California or something. He only really hung out with my friends, but none of them talk to him anymore. Except Leon, but Leon is a serious loser." With pressed lips, she sent an angry puff of air through her nose. "Because of Forrest and his drugs."

Forrest sounded like a real winner. Preying on the elderly and addicting his friends to drugs. It would not surprise Jefferson to learn that the man had come to a tragic end in the Puget Sound, either by his own hand or that of a murderer.

***

"We're still sitting outside the apartment, running the heater. It's cold as blazes out here," Larson grumbled on the other end of the phone.

"That makes no sense," countered Jefferson.

"Sure it does. How'd we end up with this gig, anyway? You two are out eating burritos while we freeze to death in the parking lot of a rot-invested apartment complex."

"You could have pulled rank."

"I'll remember that next time. What'd the ex tell you?"

Jefferson turned his eyes out the window as he and Rory made the familiar drive toward MJ's house on Stanton Inlet. The sunsets came early this time of year. Today's had come and gone. Where the Sound should be, he only saw a mass of nothing, like a gaping hole between the lights twinkling on each side of the inlet.

"Appendix scar, lower right abdomen."

Larson grunted. "I'm not sure that's much help. It's too common." He could hear him bang on the steering wheel. "Dang it!"

"Chief having warrant trouble?"

"Yep. I think we might call it a night. Not much is going to happen this late. I'll make sure Underhill knows about the scar."

Jefferson desperately wanted to keep Larson on the phone. Otherwise, his mind would default to imagining the torture he was about to endure at MJ's house.

Unfortunately, he couldn't think of a way to drag it out, and Larson was not the man to chit chat. Jefferson wasn't either, but this situation was messing with his head.

Why in the world did Rory think Jefferson would thank him for creating the most awkward situation imaginable? No, this would require significant payback.

Chapter Twenty-Five

"**I**'m finally alone again."

"I've been waiting," replied Oloff.

Millie cringed. She hated to upset Oloff. He was too busy to wait around for her. Anger flared at that teacher. How dare she call people from church to come over without asking?

"Sorry, I had to get rid of some ladies from church."

"Visitors?"

Millie took a deep breath. As she thought about Ira and the reason for the ladies' visit, she felt a fresh stab of grief.

"Ira, the man I told you about, he died."

The screen stared back, unchanged, for several seconds. Millie adjusted the seat pad under her bottom. Sometimes her hips ached terribly after sitting in this office chair and chatting for so long.

Finally, after what felt like an eternity, Oloff responded.

"He won't be bothering you anymore."

Millie's fingers froze on the keyboard. A chill gripped her, like someone pouring ice water down her back.

An unexpected pang of hurt slashed at her heart. Such a callous thing to say. Was Oloff trying to be funny?

How was she to respond? Thankfully, he put her out of her misery.

"Sorry. Insensitive."

"Yes, a little. He was a dear friend."

"Just a friend?"

Millie rolled her eyes with a satisfied smile. Oloff sounded jealous. "Yes. Just a friend."

"How?"

"How what?"

"How did your 'just friend' die?"

Millie realized she still didn't know what happened. Ira took such good care of himself, she found it hard to believe he had a sudden heart attack or anything.

"I don't know. The woman who told me didn't have details."

"And who was that?"

"The woman?"

"Yes."

"A teacher from the middle school. She's quite a nosy girl."

"Nosy?"

"She runs the computer club at the senior center. Last time, she told me I was being scammed because I wanted to use GreenShare. Like I'm some helpless fool." Sure, she'd lied about her reason for wanting to use the program, but that didn't mean she couldn't think for herself.

"That's rude."

"Exactly," wrote Millie, the offense growing bigger in her mind by the second. "She told me about Ira, which I appreciate, but then she called the church people. All I wanted to do was to talk to you, but I had to spend an hour convincing them I was fine being alone."

"She should mind her own business. What's her name?"

Why did he care about the teacher's name? "It doesn't matter."

"Just curious. I like to know what it's like to be in your world."

Millie chuckled. Could he really care about such silly details. "Her name is MJ Brooks. I'm sure she's a great teacher, but she's too nosy for my liking."

"She's treating you like a student."

Staring at the screen, Millie felt a thump in her chest. She hated Oloff to see her as weak. Old and weak. In truth, she'd been slightly annoyed by the teacher, but Millie had at least considered her respectful. But when Oloff put it that way, she could see his point.

"You're right. She even had my old friend Claire call me. I haven't talked to her in at least five years, but the teacher lives at Claire's house. She must have been blabbing to her about me."

"Claire?"

"Claire O'Neil. She has a beautiful house up Stanton Inlet, right on the water."

"Sounds interesting."

A fierce wind batted at the window, causing Millie to look away from the screen. One small table lamp lit a corner of the room. That and the computer were the only things keeping the night at bay. Though it wasn't late, the darkness seemed deeper and more sinister than usual. What if the power went out?

Maybe she ought to go grab her flashlight. With her stiff legs and hips, stumbling around in the dark could be dangerous. She could easily fall. This thought suddenly made her feel very alone. Would Ira still be alive if he hadn't lived by himself?

"It's windy here," she typed. "I'm going to find a flashlight just in case. I'll be right back, love."

"Be safe," Oloff typed with a string of red hearts.

Turning on lights as she went, Millie shuffled through the kitchen to the laundry room, where her husband had always kept the flashlights. Realizing she'd never checked them, she couldn't be sure they worked, or that she had the right batteries.

Opening the cupboard over the laundry room sink, she found two flashlights. She picked the biggest one and turned it on. It worked, but gave off a deep yellow light, barely enough to see.

Holding the flashlight handle against her chest with her stiff left hand, she unscrewed the top. Size D batteries. Millie blew out a relieved breath when she saw a plethora of batteries in one of the drawers. Finding the correct ones, she emptied the batteries out of the flashlight and put in a new set.

When she next pushed the button, a bright stream of light shone into the room.

Just then, a loud bang sounded from the backyard.

Millie's heart jumped into her throat.

It had to be the wind, she told herself. No one would be out in this weather, and certainly not in her backyard.

Gingerly, she carried the flashlight with her into the family room. A light blazed through the family room windows. Something had triggered the motion sensor.

Before moving any farther, Millie stopped to take several slow, deep breaths. It worried her when her heart beat so quickly. Besides the arthritis, the doctor said her heart had a leaky valve, not a serious concern right now, but he told her to reduce the stress in her life.

This was not helping.

After a few seconds, the flutter in her chest eased, and she felt brave enough to look outside.

Peering through a slit in the blinds, she could clearly see one of her deck chairs had careened into the deck railing.

Millie laughed and chided herself for being so scared as she checked the door to the deck, ensuring it was locked. Afterward, she took her flashlight and made the return trip to the office, where she could continue her conversation with Oloff.

***

As she settled back into the chair, Millie realized she felt quite tired. This might be a good time to say goodnight to Oloff and head upstairs to bed. She'd rather sleep through this windstorm. Then, if the power went out, she wouldn't even know until the morning.

"I'm back," she typed.

Oloff obviously had gone nowhere. He responded right away.

"That took a while."

"I had to find batteries. Then there was a noise outside. Just a deck chair. But silly me, it got my heart going."

"I don't like you being alone."

"That's why you should come here."

His response was longer in coming this time. Millie wondered if she should remind him of her offer to pay for the ticket to Seattle.

"I have a different idea." Finally appeared on the screen. He followed his words with a pair of googly eyes.

She twisted her lips and gazed at the screen with curious, narrowed eyes. What did he have up his sleeve?

"I'm listening."

"You should come here."

Her eyes widened in shock. What was he thinking? He was having a hard time making ends meet with just himself to worry about. How could they both live there? "But isn't it hard enough for you to make it alone?"

"Found a new investor. He's putting me up in a new apartment. Here's a picture."

As the picture loaded, Millie twisted her hands together. She loved Oloff, but living in something like that building they were renovating would not work for her.

When the picture appeared, Millie sucked in a breath. It was beautiful. The living room had a glass wall that showed a stunning vista of the ocean. The rest of the room held sleek white furniture in a modern design.

"What do you think?"

"You get to live in that apartment?"

"Yes. And I want you with me."

Staring at the picture, Millie could almost see herself standing in front of those windows. Of course, she'd be wearing an elegant linen pantsuit, and she'd have a drink in her hand, something fruity and fun. Oloff would slide next to her, his arm around her waist, a drink in his other hand.

"It's a little scary. I've never been to Africa."

"It's beautiful and warm. You'll love it here. So many amazing things."

Thoughts of going to bed had vanished. Energy coursed through her now.

Why not? Her kids rarely came to visit. And maybe they would enjoy coming to see her in Africa. With Ira gone, she didn't have any friends left in the area. She didn't consider those church ladies to be her friends. They were so much younger than her.

Millie sat back and stared at the computer screen. She was *actually* thinking about it. Wouldn't it be so unexpected? How many years did she have left in her life? Why not spend them doing what she wanted, with whom she wanted?

The dream faded from her vision when she realized Oloff was typing again.

"We could get married."

Even though the idea seemed shocking and ridiculous, Millie smiled from ear to ear. He wanted to marry her.

"My new investor has millions. He's a philanthropist. Wants me to open clinics all over Africa. I want you by my side."

Worry tempered Millie's enthusiasm. All that travel. What if she slowed him down?

"I hope I can keep up with you."

He sent a smiley emoji. "I'm a doctor. You'll be my favorite patient."

Love overflowed her heart. He understood her health fears, even with her vague response. Oloff really knew her. He would take care of her. He would make her last years on this earth happier than she could have ever imagined they would be.

"So, is that a proposal?" she typed, her lips curling into a wicked grin.

"That's exactly what it is."

Millie bit her fingernail, hardly believing what she was about to do.

"Yes! I will marry you. And yes, I want to move to Zimbabwe to be with you."

Oloff sent a string of hearts, blushing faces, and clapping hands.

"I can set up an international account for you. Will you sell the house?"

The reality of the change ahead suddenly felt heavy, almost too heavy. This house had meant so much to her and Walter. They'd raised all their kids here. Selling it would break her heart, but she knew it would be for the best.

"Yes. But it will be hard."

"Hard to sell?"

"No. My heart."

"Just look at that picture again, my love. Adventure awaits."

"My kids won't understand."

He seemed to consider his answer, as it didn't come right away.

"You should wait to tell them."

"Why?"

"They will try to talk you out of it. Kids don't like their parents being so independent."

Millie nodded to herself. Why did young people always think they knew best?

"You're right. I'll wait until I'm just about to leave."

"Good. I'll send you bank info tomorrow. Looking for a wedding venue. What do you think of this?"

Another picture filled the screen. This time it was an African prairie. A boisterous number of white lilies adorned an arch set in a field. A lovely bride and groomed kissed beneath it. Giraffes and zebras grazed in the background as the setting sun plated the entire scene in gold.

A warmth seemed to flow out of the picture and wrap around Millie's heart. How could this be happening?

No more questions, she told herself. No more fear. Instead, she would dream about this new life, make plans, and ensure nothing stopped her from being able to walk off the plane and wrap her arms around this wonderful man.

Chapter Twenty-Six

C ould this get any worse?

MJ stared at her phone. It was weird enough that Rory Jackson called her instead of Jefferson. Now she had to ask Shannon to come over so the four of them could sit in the same room and go over some "questions" from the detectives.

Questions about what? Rory had been purposefully vague, she thought. Something about the senior center, he said.

The questions had to be connected to Ira Newman. His death felt unnatural, too unexpected. The police must have a reason to suspect foul play.

Just the thought of that gave her goosebumps, and not the good kind. The kind that felt too much like a warning.

Why would anyone want to hurt Ira Newman?

Her mind wandered down several rabbit holes before being abruptly halted by the reminder that she needed to call Shannon. That sent her mind whirling in another direction.

Watching Shannon and Jefferson flirt their way through an interview might drive her to the edge of insanity.

First, Jefferson wasn't super flirty. He had his charming ways—that annoying crooked smile, for one, and his blue eyes that could mirror the sky one minute and the ocean the next. They changed with his mood, and she'd seen most of his colors.

What she didn't want to see was the flirty, distracted Detective Hughes. The one less focused on his work than on a pretty face. That Jefferson would be just like every other man. The Jefferson she . . . respected, that was the word, would put his desire to catch a killer above every other feeling.

But was that a good thing? Didn't he deserve to have a relationship that made him happy? Could he possibly pick anyone in the world better than Shannon Davis?

Holding her phone so that her reflection stared back at her from its lifeless black screen, MJ knew she couldn't deny the answer.

Time to quit twisting herself into knots and make the call.

***

Only Edgar and Shannon seemed blissfully unaware of the tension in the room.

MJ had started by getting everyone drinks. Black coffee for Rory, sparkling lemon water for Jefferson, coffee with cream for Shannon, and tulsi mint tea for herself.

Now, MJ and Shannon sat on the couch. Jefferson sat in the armchair. Rory sat in a kitchen chair he pulled over for himself. And Edgar lay on his dog bed, his copper eyes shifting between all of them.

The stage was set, but no one seemed ready to start the show.

"Sure is windy out there," remarked Shannon, her eyes darting to Jefferson and away again.

He smiled, but it wasn't his confident crooked smile. Instead, it skittered on and off his face like a squirrel that darts into the road only to dash back to safety at the sight of a car.

Earlier, when MJ had opened the door to the two detectives on her porch, she couldn't deny the hitch in her heart as her eyes briefly found Jefferson's.

That day on the beach was the last time they'd seen each other, and the way it ended still haunted her. She wondered if he even thought about it.

Shannon had arrived a few minutes after them. When she saw Jefferson, a gentle pink had risen to her cheeks. MJ still cringed as she thought about how the two greeted each other. They reminded her of middle schoolers who'd just decided to start "talking" to each other, the new middle school vernacular for "going with."

But this moment, right now, was the most awkward. The two detectives seemed to be off their game.

She glanced at Rory in the stiff kitchen chair, one foot resting on the opposite knee. He wasn't smiling, but he wasn't "not" smiling. He seemed to take in every movement of the other three like they were a flock of unusual birds.

She bristled at this observation. He must know about Jefferson and Shannon. The two of them probably had "guy" talk about it. Jefferson probably told his partner how beautiful Shannon was, and all the places he planned to take her. Imagining this idle chitchat about dating did nothing for her mood.

Time to get this over with.

"So, Detectives," she said, knowing how much she sounded like a teacher. "What can we help you with?" Her eyes were on Rory as she spoke, but she forced herself to cast a quick glance at Jefferson.

His eyes met hers, their shade a kind of blue she'd never seen before. Gray, she thought, like they were stuck between something lighter and something darker.

Then he dropped his gaze to pull a notebook out of his pocket.

"Thank you for meeting with us," Rory said. "We know it's late." That seemed to be all he would say as he gave Jefferson an expectant look.

MJ sensed the detectives were not on the same page in this interview. They normally played off of each other like they were reading each other's minds.

Jefferson's hard look at Rory confirmed her suspicions.

Regardless, he sat forward, pen in hand and notepad on his knee. "We were at the West Sound Senior Center earlier today, and the attendant informed us you two, MJ and Shannon," an awkward grin came and went as he hurried on, "ran a computer club for some patrons there."

MJ nodded.

"That's true," said Shannon.

"And did you interact with a man named Ira Newman?"

Shannon and MJ exchanged a look.

"Yes, we knew Ira." MJ sighed. "We had to break the news of his death to our students this afternoon."

"I'm sorry," said Jefferson said, grimacing. "I guess you would have to. That must have been hard." His eyes seesawed between them as if unsure of where to land.

Shannon nodded with melancholy in her earth brown eyes. "A few took it really hard."

Jefferson cleared his throat. "The attendant also suggested Mr. Newman may have been involved in an altercation during his time with you. Do you recall anything like that?"

Shannon shrugged with the slightest upturn to her lips. "Well—"

"Wait," MJ broke in. "Sorry Shannon, but Detective Hughes, are you suggesting that there is something suspicious about Mr. Newman's death?"

He sat back, his eyes now fixed on hers. "Did I say that?"

"You sort of did," she replied. "I mean, how many innocent deaths by natural causes have you investigated this year?"

"Ms. Brooks," he said, matching her formality. "I can't tell you what may or may not be true about this case—"

"So it is a case."

"For lack of a better word."

"I can give you some better words if you need them. Inquiry, probe, query, exploration—"

"MJ."

"Jefferson."

Suddenly, his crooked smile crept up and wrinkled his eyes. "You can't ever do a normal interview, can you?"

Despite herself, she smiled back and lifted her shoulders. "Sorry, not sorry?"

He sighed and ran a hand through his hair. "Look, there is a lot we don't know. We do not know that Ira Newman's death was anything other than what it appears. A natural death. We're checking into it as a favor to his son, who suspects there may be more to this than meets the eye. Ira is one of us, a retired detective, so it's possible—though unlikely—that someone with a grudge had it out for him."

"Wow," said Shannon. "I can't imagine that. He seemed like such a nice man."

Jefferson nodded with a quick flick of his eyes toward her. She smiled at him, but his eyes had already moved back to MJ.

With a sense of panic for her friend's feelings, MJ checked to see if Shannon had felt this slight, as unintended as it was.

If she did, Shannon put on a brave face. She took a sip of her coffee, putting it down with a pleasant smile.

Rory chose this moment to put in his two cents. "I don't think the guys he put away would see it like that," he said with a stroke of his ginger beard.

Shannon gave a light laugh. "No, I would guess not."

"So, what can you tell us about the computer club?" Jefferson tried again.

And again, he directed his question to MJ.

"We both saw it, so maybe Shannon wants to say?"

"Oh no," responded her friend. "You go ahead, MJ."

Was there ice in her tone?

MJ shot Rory a plea for help. He definitely had a grin buried in that beard of his.

"You know what?" she said, standing. "I have some cookies in the kitchen. I'll go get them. Shannon, you explain what happened."

As soon as she stood, Edgar was on his feet, ready to follow her.

In the kitchen, she hid herself behind the wall to avoid being seen. Kneeling down, she grabbed Edgar's head and buried herself in his silky fur. What was going on out there? Maybe she would prefer a flirty Jefferson to this. It was excruciating.

What if Shannon thought MJ was stealing Jefferson's attention on purpose? Would her friend see that he only found MJ easier to talk to because they knew each other?

That's all it is, she told herself. She just had to help him get to know Shannon.

"That's what I'll do," she whispered to Edgar.

Chapter
Twenty-Seven

"So, he had an argument with an elderly woman? That's the altercation?" asked Jefferson.

MJ set the cookies down on the coffee table.

That was all the motivation Rory needed. He pulled his chair closer to the group and availed himself of an iced snowman.

"Yeah, that's pretty much it," Shannon said, taking a sip of her coffee, her eyes blinking over the top at Jefferson.

MJ squirmed. That wasn't all there was to it. She balled her hands into fists, clenching and unclenching them on her lap.

Don't do it, she told herself. Didn't you just resolve to help Jefferson get to know Shannon? If you take over the conversation now, Shannon will definitely think you are sabotaging her chances with Jefferson.

But what was she to do? The police needed to know that there was more to the argument between Millie and Mr. Newman.

"MJ?" said Jefferson, drawing his brows together. "You look like you have something to say."

Was she really so obvious?

She bit her bottom lip and moved her head slowly from side to side. "No. I'm fine."

He wasn't buying it. His questioning blue eyes stared directly into hers. In her mind, she begged him to stop because she couldn't look away. And the longer their eyes remained locked, the deeper the question became, until it seemed to burn in his eyes. And then she knew the question had changed. It sat there in the steadiness of his stare, wondering but also hurting.

He wanted to know why she dropped his hand at the beach.

Her breath caught in her throat, and she dropped her eyes.

Trying to still her heart, MJ grabbed a cookie and took a huge bite, chewing and breathing raggedly through her nose.

"What is it MJ," asked Shannon, worried.

After swallowing the far too big of a bite, MJ ate the last bit, waving away any concern and ignoring her still stuttering heart. "I'm fine. But Jefferson, as much as it pains me to say it, you're right." She blew a stray curl from her forehead. When it didn't move, she tucked it behind her ear.

"It's not my story to share, so I wasn't sure I should say anything," she lied. The only reason she'd held back was to keep Shannon from feeling sidelined. Despite her best efforts, MJ had done all the talking. She fought the rising sense of guilt as Jefferson spent most of his focus on her. Though, to her shame, a part of her also enjoyed it.

Why were they doing this interview together, anyway? Whose bright idea was this? It couldn't be Jefferson. He looked as comfortable as a snowman in Miami.

All she could do was hope that Shannon chalked it up to familiarity. The detective and MJ knew each other well so their comfort with each other should be expected. Right?

"I found out what caused that argument between Millie and Mr. Newman," she added, glancing apologetically at Shannon. "I haven't had the chance to tell you."

Shannon rolled her eyes. "Of course you found out." She turned to Jefferson, jabbing a thumb toward MJ. "This girl can't leave it alone."

"Oh, I know that all too well," he said, shaking his head at MJ. There was that crooked smile again.

MJ glimpsed Rory, who had been unusually quiet. He sat forward with his elbows on his knees, his fingers steepled under his chin like a professor observing a student presentation.

"So, spill it," Jefferson said.

She licked her lips. "I went over to Millie's house earlier today."

"What?" Shannon gasped. "When? Why?"

"Diana was worried about Millie being alone when she learned about Ira's death. I agreed to check in on her."

"Wait, who is Diana?" asked Jefferson, pen ready.

"Just—"

"She's a student at the high school," said Shannon, jumping in. "She helps with the computer club."

"Anyway," said MJ, "she was right. Millie was upset once I told her about Ira. So, I stayed for a while. We were talking about Ira when Millie just came out with it. I didn't even ask. And the reason for their fight might surprise you."

"If you are trying to build suspense, MJ . . ." Jefferson nudged.

She shot him a half-hearted glare. "I'm getting there." She turned to Shannon and then Rory. "As I was saying, Millie claims Ira was essentially jealous because she has a new love interest."

Shannon's mouth fell open. "Were Millie and Mr. Newman a thing?"

"Hmm, not really. Millie only considered him a friend, but Ira wanted to marry her. According to him, being with someone was better than being alone."

Rory had been so quiet that MJ jumped when he leaned forward and spoke.

"Let me get this straight. Millie wants to be with the person she loves; the person who makes her feel alive. And she's willing to fight for that kind of love, even if it would hurt Ira's feelings?" His steady eyes held just a hint of amusement, as if this might be a joke, but might also be serious.

The other three stared at him. No one seemed to know how to respond to Rory's unusual rephrasing of MJ's words. No one moved as the silence stretched out uncomfortably.

MJ chanced a look at Jefferson. He hid his eyes by staring down at his notepad, tapping it aggressively with his pen.

Then she turned to consider Rory with questioning eyes. "That's putting it more poetically than she did," ventured MJ. "But I guess she meant something along those lines?"

Rory sat back. "I just wondered." He folded his arms and grinned.

MJ eyed him. What was he playing at? As much as Rory loved joking and making his partner uncomfortable, this was different. He wanted to make a point.

When Jefferson finally looked up, the hard set of his jaw suggested he understood Rory's cryptic comment, even if she didn't.

"You'll have to forgive my partner," he said. "It's been a long day. He gets weird when he needs sleep."

Rory nodded. "It's true."

Jefferson fixed him with a deadly stare. "In fact, I should have left you back at the station for all the help you've been."

The other man yawned. "Like you said, it's been a long day. So, MJ," he asked, moving his attention to her. "Do you know who Millie's other man is? Could there have been some animosity between Ira and him? Maybe someone else at the senior center?"

"Well, I offered to contact him since Millie was so upset. Her response was a frantic and aggressive no." She sat forward, using her hand to punctuate her ideas. Her mind had shifted completely to the case now. "It was so weird that it made me wonder if there was something off about him." She looked between the two detectives, flooded with a familiar energetic curiosity that drove her to search for answers. "And maybe Ira knew something."

"That's a leap," Jefferson said, his features slightly more relaxed.

"It seems a little far-fetched," chimed in Shannon, grinning at Jefferson. "But MJ's been right before."

"Thanks for the support," she said, giving Shannon a friendly elbow to the ribs.

"It's too bad you didn't ask for his name," added Jefferson.

MJ forced back a grin. He wouldn't like this next part, but he wouldn't hate it.

"You're right. I didn't ask Millie, but—"

"Oh, I can't wait to hear this," grinned Rory.

That smile she'd forced down crept out anyway. "I searched her social media profile, and I think I found the guy."

"MJ, you've been busy," said Shannon.

Jefferson stared, but his lips quirked with humor. "As expected. Who is he?"

"I can't be completely sure this is *the* guy, but if it is, Millie is in over her head."

She explained what she'd uncovered about Oloff, even opening her laptop to show them the profile.

"If this is what Millie and Ira were arguing about, then I think Ira knew she was being scammed."

Jefferson looked skeptical. "Do you really think she'd fall for that?"

MJ settled serious eyes on him. "I think you underestimate the power of loneliness."

"I'm not sure I do," He said it quickly, seemingly without thinking.

Casting her eyes down to the laptop, MJ nodded, not sure what to say to that. Before she could analyze his comment, the detective moved on, as if realizing he'd showed a card he preferred to keep hidden.

"Anyway," he sighed. "Any theories are moot until we know the cause of death, so don't go getting yourself caught up in this, MJ," he warned.

"I won't think about it ever again," she promised, fingers crossed behind her back.

"Yeah, right," he smirked.

Rory grabbed another cookie. "By the way," he said. "We had a pleasant conversation with Justin today."

Jefferson sat back, his pen falling to the floor. "For heaven's sake, Jackson. Do you want to give her the entire case file?"

For how crazy this interview had been, she did not expect to hear her ex-husband's name. "Justin?" MJ asked, ignoring Jefferson's outburst.

"Yep," Rory responded, also not looking at his partner. "He works, or I guess it's more accurate to say volunteers, at the gym Ira attended. Senior Strength?"

"Justin knew Ira?" She didn't look anywhere but at Rory, determined to find out as quickly as possible how Justin fit into this situation, something Jefferson clearly did not plan to tell her.

"He filled in for Ira's regular trainer a few times, a guy named Forrest. Ring any bells?"

MJ pressed her lips together. Even though she and Justin had divorced, she had to spend far too much breath explaining to people that they were not together, not involved. Justin's good looks were the prime culprit. People couldn't believe she would let a man like that go. Even Justin didn't believe it. It was exhausting. She wanted to stay on friendly terms with him, but sometimes he made it difficult.

"Other than Justin coming here to pick up or drop of Edgar, we don't spend time together," she managed.

At the mention of his name, the dog pushed himself out of his bed and trotted to the side of the couch. MJ reached down to pet his head. "I didn't know he was helping at the gym, and I certainly don't know anyone named Forrest."

Rory gave a quick grunt. "Interesting."

"How is that interesting?"

She glanced at Jefferson to see if he would add anything. He watched her with a furrowed brow, as if she were the day's Wordle and he was on try number five, but he said nothing.

"Do you think Justin is involved somehow? I don't believe that for a second. You guys know him. He doesn't have an evil bone in his body. An overprotective hero complex maybe, but not evil."

"But he has a lot of muscle," said Rory.

"A lot of muscle," agreed Shannon. "But there's also a big heart under there. He's always helping someone."

Jefferson shot her a look of surprise.

A flattering blush landed on her cheeks at his attention. "I mean from what MJ tells me."

This answer annoyed MJ. It wasn't like the two of them chatted about Justin's life on the regular. She made it sound as if MJ followed her ex-husband's life like a documentarian.

"It's not like I know his every move," she corrected. "But his heart is in the right place with all of his volunteering. I can't deny that," said MJ.

"I take it he hasn't mentioned training people at the gym or Ira in particular?" asked Jefferson. Gone were the smiles, replaced by a combative stillness in his long body as he waited for her answer.

MJ stared as if he had asked for instructions on an assignment after she spent ten minutes explaining it. Did he think she was lying about her relationship with Justin?

With a superhuman effort at calm, she answered in a low, measured tone, her eyes never leaving him. "The last time I spoke to Justin was a week ago. He is watching Edgar while I am in Las Vegas. That is all we talked about."

"That's all?"

"That's all."

The air prickled between them as they continued in a staring stand-off. MJ's heartbeat quickened, but she didn't know which emotion roiling inside of her was responsible.

With a loud clap of his hands, Rory said, "Glad that's straightened out. It's not like Justin is a suspect or anything. I only mentioned it because it's such a strange coincidence that you both knew Ira."

This ended the standoff, and each side retreated, both staring at Rory, who looked very pleased with himself, having accomplished whatever goal he'd set for this interview.

"That is a strange coincidence," agreed Shannon. "But then again, this isn't a big city."

Trying to regain some measure of focus, MJ asked, "What did Justin tell you about Ira?"

Rory sat back, folding his arms. "Not much, really. Just that Ira wasn't being his usual self yesterday morning, seemed distracted."

"Wait." MJ pushed herself to the edge of the couch and stared at Rory. "Did you say Senior Strength?"

"That's the name of the gym," Rory confirmed.

A spark of recognition ignited in MJ's brain. She'd seen that name.

"I saw a magnet with that name on Millie's fridge. Maybe she knew that trainer, too."

"Or maybe she met herself a hot, strong senior," Rory said, wiggling his eyebrows up and down.

"It's another connection, though," MJ said.

"Maybe," said Jefferson. "But the gym caters to seniors, so it's not that surprising."

Before MJ could ask another question, Jefferson pulled out his phone, buzzing with a call. He hurried to his feet and rushed to answer it in the kitchen.

Shannon stood as well, stretching her arms overhead. "There doesn't seem to be much else to talk about, and I am beat. Is it okay if I take off?" she asked Rory.

Rory joined her in standing, adjusting his suit coat and smoothing his tie. After a second, MJ also stood.

"Sure," said Rory. "I think we've covered everything."

Shoving his phone back in his pocket, Jefferson's brisk step brought him back into the room. "Jackson. We have to go. Got a fingerprint hit on Shopside guy."

Chapter
Twenty-Eight

E ven the cold air descending on West Sound couldn't match the frosty atmosphere of the detectives' ride to the station.

At least for Jefferson. Rory whistled Christmas tunes all the way.

Obnoxious, yes. But it meant they didn't have to talk. While Jefferson wanted to rip into Rory for whatever that was at MJ's house, he knew now would not be a good time.

That interview felt like his brain had been on a medieval rack, one side trying to pay attention to Shannon; the other trying, and failing, to be aloof toward MJ.

He needed to cool off and get his head into Ira's case. And he predicted it would eventually transform into a case based on the growing murkiness of the man's last days. Right now, it was an "inquiry, probe, query, or exploration" as MJ had suggested with a truckload of sarcasm.

How did she break him down so fast? The detective facade he wore with other people, criminals and witnesses alike, kept him just distant enough to stay clinical in his observations.

But with MJ, she always found the loose thread that pulled his "cool" apart at the seams, until he was just him, more real than he liked to be.

At least that's what he used to think. If he was honest with himself, the way MJ peeled away his protective layers was freeing. She never accepted the walls he put up, whether about himself or a case. MJ would climb and climb until she peeked over the top to see the truth.

Maybe he should have ripped into Rory to avoid too much thinking about MJ.

When they finally made it to the station, they went straight to the briefing room.

Larson glared at them from his seat. He was wearing sweats and a sweatshirt. Mendez wore jeans and a button down green plaid jacket over a t-shirt.

Jefferson knew what the clothes and the glare meant. The other two detectives made it home just in time to change, and then got the call to return to work.

In an end-of-shift uniform that had lost its snap was Officer Meyers, who nodded a hello but otherwise stayed quiet.

Chief Carlson sat at the head of the table, his flinty eyes alert but accompanied by bruised circles beneath them. Next to him was the much fresher face of Stacey Underhill, the medical examiner.

"Thank you for coming gentlemen," said the chief. "We are lucky to have Dr. Underhill here. She kindly took some time before heading home to share her findings in person." He clasped his hands on the table. "I know it's late, so we'll just get on with it." He motioned toward Stacey. "Dr. Underhill."

"Thank you, Chief Carlson." She turned a bright, toothy grin on the detectives. "Aren't you fellas lucky? It's like a late night at Horror Fest with Dr. Underhill."

"It doesn't matter the time of day," drawled Larson. "Your reports are always full of horror."

"Well, thank you," Stacey said, flipping her long, blonde hair behind her shoulders. "That means a lot coming from a grump like you."

Larson snickered. "You know it."

She passed stapled reports around to the detectives. "This is the first report, and it's for the man found at Shopside Docks. First, fingerprints came up with two different hits when put in the local and national databases," she said with a glance at Jefferson and Rory, "Before you two arrived, we discussed that one of the names, Forrest Bernard, is likely a false identity."

With a slow breath through his nose, Jefferson rubbed a finger across his chin. "So it is him. That's too bad. I was pulling for the guy, hoping we'd discover he was hiding out, instead of floating in the sound."

"I'm sure he would have preferred that as well," replied Stacey. "Instead, he seems to have run into a blunt instrument. We found the wound on the back of his skull once we removed debris and plant life from the body. There's an image on page . . . " She shuffled through the report. "It's on page five."

This created an almost synchronized rustling of paper as they all turned to see the image.

"The tissue around the wound is too degraded to offer reliable data, but the shape of the damage to the skull suggests something like a hammer, but a wide one. Or something like that."

The image was jarring something in Jefferson's memory, but he couldn't put a finger on it. "So, no drowning?"

The ME smiled. "That's on page seven, but I'll give you the short answer. No. It appears someone struck the young man and then dumped him in the water. I'd say it's also possible that the two incidents were not simultaneous."

Rory looked up from the report. "Someone struck him in a different location and moved the body to the water?"

Stacey shrugged. "Could be the case. I can't say for certain so you'll have to figure that out."

Closing the report and sitting back, Rory said, "I guess we can get that warrant for Forrest's apartment now."

The chief nodded with a grim face. "And we'll be looking at Leon Albright as suspect number one. We need to interview him again with this new information."

"And the other name?" asked Jefferson.

"Meyers, share what you've been able to pull from out-of-state records," ordered the chief.

The young officer sat up straight. "Yes, sir." His eyes darted around the table as if he expected a firing squad.

He cleared his throat. "Yeah, so I ran his fingerprints again . . ." He trailed off, glancing at the chief.

"Go ahead," the chief said with a wave of his hand. "Nobody will bite you."

"Except maybe Larson," mumbled Mendez.

The young officer cleared his throat nervously but quickly continued.

"Locally, his prints identified him as Forrest Bernard. Got picked up for possession with an intent to sell in Seattle about a year ago." He attempted to pass a copy of the report to everyone, but his hands were shaking.

Stacey touched his arm with a sweet smile. "I can pass those for you."

This attention from the attractive doctor only increased his nerves. He swallowed and assented silently.

"Um, so . . . the second name came up in the FBI's national database as Advik Peterson. He has outstanding warrants in California for check fraud and financial elder abuse, both felonies. He was employed at the time by Hampton and Cole Care International."

"Not a good guy to work with West Sound seniors," said Mendez.

"Holy crap," said Larson. "Do you think he was stealing from Ira?"

The chief's face contorted into a scowl. "No. Ira was too suspicious, too savvy for that. But he might have caught on to this fella swindling other people."

Jefferson and Rory looked at each other.

"It's too big a coincidence," Rory said, speaking just to Jefferson. "MJ does it again."

"I know, unfortunately."

"You two care to enlighten the rest of us, or do you need to take your conversation outside?" The chief was clearly in no mood for messing around.

"We may have some related information," said Jefferson.

"Let's hear it."

"Ira had an argument the night he died with a woman, a friend of his named Millie." He hesitated before continuing. He hated to do it, but he had to explain how they got the information.

"According to MJ, who witnessed the argument—"

"Of course," chuckled Larson.

The chief turned a thunderous look on him and the senior detective went quiet.

"It seems Ira and Millie were arguing over a new romantic interest of hers, a boyfriend, I guess you'd say. Ira and she were close, but not like in love . . . at least she wasn't . . ." He stumbled over his words, realizing he was getting lost in the awkward romance weeds.

"And this is related, how?" coaxed the chief, his patience intact for now.

"Without recounting all the details, Millie may be the victim of an online scammer. I stress 'may' because we have not had time to confirm any of this. Ira may have figured it out."

The chief rubbed his chin, thinking it over. "Do you know if she is still in contact with the alleged scammer?"

"We just heard this tonight, so no."

He nodded. "Find out tomorrow. Forrest, Advik, whatever his name is, he's dead, so if she's still trading messages online, it might have nothing to do with Bernard or Ira," he said. "Tomorrow. Check into it."

Stacey Underhill cleared her throat. "Before you gentlemen get too carried away with your detective hypothesizing, I have more to share with you, and I have a hot bath calling my name at home."

Jefferson pressed his fingers into the bridge of his nose, his eyes fixed on the report in front of him. Knowing Stacey, there was no way she did not purposefully put the image of her in a bubble bath in every man's head.

Except maybe the chief, who gave the rest of them a scathing shot of his steely eyes. "Of course, Dr. Underhill. Please continue."

"Thank you. Since you mentioned Ira . . . on the chief's request, I pushed his autopsy to the front and finished it this evening. This was a hard one," she said, lowering her eyes. "It's never easy when it's one of our own. I didn't know Ira as well as you all, but I know he was one of the best."

Everyone silently agreed.

"So on to the clinical stuff because this is a shocker." Her eyes moved around the table to each of them. "Based on my examination, Ira Newman died of respiratory arrest."

With a slow nod and pursed lips, the chief released a breath from his nose. "A natural death, then."

"I didn't say that," Stacey cautioned. "There are some other troubling findings that need further testing."

The man closed his eyes briefly as if that act could make Stacey's next words disappear. Then he faced her with hard stare. "For instance?"

"I've given my thoughts in the summary of the report, for your reference," she said flipping the pages of her report. "It's on the last page. Anyone interested in the medical jargon version can read the whole thing. But I'll give you the summary of the summary."

She shook her head. "You are not going to like this." Taking a deep breath, she folded her hands together on the table. "I've read over Ira's medical history. I can find no reason this man should have stopped breathing in his sleep. No heart disease, no obesity, no asthma, no medications, no signs of choking—nothing. What I did find is extensive pulmonary edema. For you laymen, that's fluid in the lungs. Usually, I'd look for congestive heart failure, kidney disease, that type of thing. None of those fit Ira's case."

"What are you suggesting?" asked Larson. "Did he drown?"

She smiled. "No. It's not that kind of fluid. I'm suggesting that his death did not come about by a natural medical event." She held a finger up before anyone could respond. "That doesn't mean murder. There have been cases of people developing pulmonary edema after a head injury, but I didn't see any signs of trauma."

Jefferson watched Stacey curiously. It was not her style to mince words, but she seemed to be taking the long way around to her main point. And he had a good idea why.

"You think it's drugs. Opioids can cause fluid in the lungs," he said, watching as she cast a hurried glance at the chief.

Without a word, she nodded.

The chief's nostrils flared as he stared at Stacey. His breathing became slow and deep, his eyes like iron. "That's not possible." He turned away, his hard stare boring a hole into the table.

Stacey bowed her head at the chief's response. "I know it's not the news you wanted. Here is the report." She passed another stapled packet around. "As I said, the most important details are in the summary, but you have all of my notes and findings. Look," she said, turning to the chief, "I'm not certain it's drugs. I've ordered a full toxicology report, but you need to get into his house, check the scene for any evidence that drugs may be involved. It's possible he took something without knowing what it was or . . . well, I don't know what else, that's not my part of the job."

"We all understand our job here, thank you." The chief's words were unnecessarily harsh, and Jefferson knew the man would regret it later, if not immediately.

"It fits, in a way," said Rory. "We know his trainer was dealing drugs on the side. And, according to his girlfriend, Forrest could be very persuasive."

The chief continued to bore a hole into the table while the rest of them stared at each other, the somber news hanging on every face.

This explained why Ira's death had shocked everyone. He really was too healthy. It was a massive blow to think that he died in that way.

"But why?" asked Mendez. "If he was so healthy and keeping his body is good shape, why would such a man do drugs?"

"And how," muttered Larson. "Did you find needle tracks or anything?"

Stacey's eyebrows shot up. "No. I found none of the normal external signs of drug abuse. But we all know that if something is potent enough, people can overdose the first time they take an illicit drug."

"So he just wanted a high and ended up dead?" Rory said.

"I think there is a less likely possibility," Stacey said, her voice quiet, as if she knew the words would cut and she wanted to be careful. "We have to consider the possibility that he took the lethal dose . . . on purpose."

A vehement headshaking from the chief cut off any further conversation about this idea. "There is no way. Just no way."

"I had to say it," Stacey said.

"I understand that. And I'm sorry, I don't mean to kill the messenger, but I need to be very clear. I do not want anyone leaving this room to spread anything that would sully a good man's reputation without extensive, undeniable evidence. Do you understand?"

Everyone said that they did.

The chief stood. "Take the reports home. Read them. We will meet again tomorrow morning at seven and decide on our next steps. Go home and get some sleep." Then he turned and left, the door closing with a slam behind him.

Chapter Twenty-Nine

With a pounding heart, MJ shut the door.

The detectives were gone, and now she had to face Shannon.

Never, in all their years of friendship, had they let anything like this come between them, but tonight, MJ didn't know what to expect.

Plopping back onto the couch with a sigh, she glanced at Shannon. "Glad that's over."

"I'm not," said Shannon, sitting down beside her. "Jefferson hardly gave me the time of day," she pouted.

MJ sat sideways to face her. "I wouldn't worry about it. He's just so focused when he's working. It's almost like he's a different guy," she said, trying to console her. It wasn't a lie.

"He was definitely focused. Focused on you." Shannon gave her shoulder a playful slug, but MJ knew the words held more meaning than that.

To her dismay, her mind went blank as she searched for words to explain away what Shannon had insinuated. Nothing came, and MJ dropped her eyes to pull at a string hanging from the hem of her jeans.

"Shannon. I'm sorry," she said, raising her eyes. "I'm sure he didn't mean anything by it. Jefferson can be . . . insensitive isn't the word. It's more like the rules matter to him, so flirting during an interview—he likely went out of his way to avoid it. But I'm sorry if his attention to me made you feel bad."

Her friend's shoulders slumped. "Oh, MJ, I'm not mad at you. I'm not sure what I expected, anyway. Jefferson and I hardly know each other. And what you said makes sense. He really is a good guy."

"Yes, he is. And he only focused on me because we have history. Crime-solving history," she said, wriggling her eyebrows.

Shannon laughed. Then she held her arms out. "Here, give me a hug."

Squeezing her tight, MJ said, "He will get to know you and then he won't be able to think of anything else, poor guy."

Shannon pulled away with a shy smile. "I'm not sure about that."

"Well, I am. Now you better go home. We both have to work tomorrow, and being sleepy with a room full of middle schoolers is a recipe for disaster."

"True." Her face stilled and her tone became serious. "Do you really think someone murdered Mr. Newman?"

"I don't know, but if the police are this serious about investigating his death, I'd lean toward yes."

"I was afraid you'd say that."

***

MJ changed into a pair of fluffy, warm pajamas and brushed her teeth, finally ready to collapse into bed.

Knowing herself, however, collapsing into bed only meant the beginning of a toss-and-turn night. Too many things weighed on her mind.

Her gut told her that something about Millie's new relationship didn't add up. Even worse, MJ felt it connected in some way to Ira's death, though she couldn't explain how.

In consoling Shannon, MJ had almost convinced herself that she'd been telling the truth. Jefferson only focused on her because they had history.

In reality, the way he looked at her tonight . . . he might not say it, but his eyes told the truth.

She'd hurt him. That day at the beach, he'd opened up to her, dropped his guard. Whatever he planned to say, she hadn't been ready to hear it. Justin's interruption was an excuse for her and an out for Jefferson.

MJ knew she'd let her fear of vulnerability take that moment away from both of them.

And it was gone forever.

The wind howled as she let Edgar outside for the last time that night. Then she loaded the mugs from earlier into the dishwasher while she waited for the dog to finish. With this weather, he was likely to be quick about it.

After a few minutes, however, she heard barking that pierced through the rush of wind against the windows.

Edgar rarely barked at night.

No neighbors were close enough to trigger him. Only the occasional raccoon or possum could get him going.

But this bark sounded angry, something she rarely heard from her dog.

Just as she got to the door to check on him, the barking stopped. She smiled. Edgar had likely been doing his best to scare away twigs falling in the wind. Her brain was definitely in suspicion mode. She needed to relax and let Edgar take his time.

After a few more minutes, MJ opened the door, expecting to see Edgar running into the light sculpted into the darkness by the open door.

When he didn't come right away, the suspicious apprehension returned with speed.

"Edgar!" she called.

Nothing.

She stepped out onto the porch, her heart beating a little faster. What was he doing?

"Edgar!" she called again. "Edgar, come on, boy!"

The problem with a mostly black dog is that the darkness swallows him. She strained her eyes, looking for the white end of his tail.

"Edgar!" Fear clawed its way under her skin. Even if he found something intensely interesting, Edgar never failed to obey when she called him. Where was he?

Maybe Claire had taken him in for some reason that she couldn't fathom. Stepping quickly back into the house, MJ stuffed her bare feet into her rain boots. Throwing a coat over her pajamas, she closed the door and ducked her head into the wind, running around the footpath to Claire's side of the house.

She hit the door in panicked knocks. "Claire! It's MJ!"

A light flicked upstairs, and MJ's heart sank. If Claire was in bed, there was no way she had Edgar.

"Edgar!" MJ called into the wind as she waited for the older woman to open the door. Any other time, guilt would eat her up for waking Claire, but her mind had already sailed away to the worst places. Edgar was mortally wounded by a wild animal, Edgar was stolen, Edgar wandered into the surf.

"MJ?" said a sleepy Claire as she opened the door. "What's the matter?" Her spikey white pixie cut didn't look like sleep shifted it at all.

The woman stepped aside and motioned into the house. "Come in, MJ. Tell me what's going on."

"I can't." Frantic tears were freezing around MJ's eyes. "I just wondered if you had Edgar. I can't find him, and he's not coming when I call, and . . ." She turned to look behind her at the sound of something hitting the ground, realizing quickly it was just a pinecone from one of the battered fir trees.

Claire folded her arms tightly against her chest. "No, I haven't seen him. But I'm sure he's fine, MJ. Edgar's a smart dog. Here," she said, stepping back from the door. "Let me put some clothes on and I'll help you look. While you wait, take this." She reached up on a shelf and pulled down a flashlight.

MJ nodded, numb with fear and the cold.

While Claire changed, MJ used the flashlight to search for Edgar in the swath of trees and shrubs that skirted the yard.

Nothing.

Before long, Claire joined her, carrying another flashlight that cut a wedge out of the dark.

"I'm going down to the beach," said MJ.

Claire pointed her light at the gate that barred the entrance to the beach stairs. "The gate is closed, MJ. I'm not sure how he would get down there."

"I know, but . . . I just have to check." She didn't want to alarm Claire, but MJ feared that Edgar's disappearance wasn't his own doing.

Claire put a weathered hand on her shoulder. "If you must, but please be careful on those stairs, young lady. The tide is high right now. You may only have a small swath of beach, and with this wind, the water will be rough."

"I'll be careful. Can you check down the road a little way?"

"Of course. I'll call the neighbors too. Maybe he wandered too far tonight."

The two women went their separate ways. As MJ approached the gate, she tried to make out the beach below. The wind whipped her hair across her face as it moved mountains of dark clouds across the sky, offering only momentary flashes of moonlight.

She pointed the flashlight down the long, winding stairway and began a careful descent. Even in her agitated state, MJ knew better than to ignore the potential slipping hazards on the wet, mossy steps.

The flashlight created a tunnel of light that made the surrounding darkness grow in intensity. Down below, the friendly beach of her walks with Edgar had transformed into a frightening abyss ruled by the night, the wind, and the sea.

The surf crashed against the beach, eager to be heard above the insistent wind and ready to carry away anything in its path.

In her heart, she knew nothing could make Edgar come down here. The dog made scaredy cats look brave. But she pushed on. It was better than doing nothing.

"Edgar!" she called, her voice swallowed up in the competing thunder of wind and surf.

Then she heard it.

Straining her ears, she listened again.

Whining.

"Edgar! Edgar, where are you, buddy?"

Then a frantic barking came from below, somewhere on the beach.

MJ ran down the steps, the flashlight barely keeping pace with her. Just as she turned the corner to start the last few stairs, her foot slipped from underneath her, and she landed hard on her back, the flashlight falling between the stairs.

Edgar's barking, more stressed than before, pushed her to her feet. The sound of his bark told her that her dog was in danger.

"Edgar, I'm coming, boy."

As she stepped onto the beach, the icy fingers of the Puget Sound clawed at her boots as a wave came and went.

Claire was right. The tide was in and more rough than usual. And so dark.

The flashlight still beamed under the stairs where it had fallen through. Without it, MJ risked wandering too far into the sound.

She ran around and under the stairs, fighting through the dead-leaves and thorn-infested blackberry bushes that lived there. The scratches would hurt later, but now, she didn't care. Thrusting her hand in, she pulled the flashlight up, pausing twice to extricate her skin from the thorns desperate to hold her hand captive.

Finally pulling it free, she pointed the light toward the beach. She would have to stick close to the shore, where the surg would only reach her ankles.

The dog had quit barking, so she called again. "Edgar!"

Immediately, his bark filled the air.

MJ swung the flashlight around as she hugged the beach, her boots slapping against the water.

"Edgar! I'm coming."

He yelped, and to MJ's horror, it sounded as if water muffled his bark.

She pointed the flashlight toward the encroaching, foaming ocean, toward the spot where she knew the white-washed log of driftwood lay in its resting place.

Edgar stood with his front paws on the log, barking as the ocean crashed against his back.

MJ ran. Ankle deep, calf deep, thigh deep. The freezing water took her breath, but she kept going until she was at her dog's side.

Grabbing his head, she kissed his nose. He licked her and whined, trying desperately to climb up on top of the log, which was almost completely submerged in the water.

"What are you doing down here, buddy?" She tried to pull him by the collar out of the water. Every part of him was wet.

Something held him there. The flashlight soon revealed that a rope attached to Edgar's collar had been tied to one of the log's dead limbs.

The frozen claws of fear clutched her heart.

A chill cascaded over her and it had nothing to do with the wind or freezing water. Suddenly, she felt exposed. Alone and exposed.

She turned to look behind her; the flashlight casting eerie shadows on the exposed bank with its mass of tangled roots and trees.

Whoever did this could still be out here. Had to still be out here.

Edgar whined at her again, licking her face.

"Sorry buddy. Yeah, let's get out of here."

She untied the rope from Edgar's collar. The dog didn't need any more help than that. In a flash, he was bounding out of the water and toward the dryest part of the beach.

MJ unhooked the rope from the log and stuffed it in her pocket. Evidence.

She swung the flashlight up and down the beach again, looking for any movement, any sign that the person who did this evil deed still lurked in the shadows.

The churning Puget Sound and the battering wind were the only signs of life besides MJ and her dog.

Chapter Thirty

MJ could hear Claire calling from the top of the stairs. She probably feared MJ was lost at sea.

"We're coming!" she bellowed, hoping her words would make it past the wall of wind. "I found him."

Once she and Edgar made it up the stairs, Claire led the way as they all trudged back to MJ's house.

"You two are soaking wet," said the woman as she helped MJ get her coat off.

MJ pulled the rope out of her pocket, anger threatening to boil over now that they were free of the water. "Someone took him down there. Someone tied him to the driftwood log. He almost drowned." Hot tears filled her eyes, but they didn't fall, the fire in her eyes keeping them at bay.

"What?" said Claire, her eyes popping at the news. "Someone was here?"

"May still be nearby, somewhere. How else do you get Edgar down to the beach and get away without being seen?"

"That's crazy, MJ. Who would do that? We should call the police."

"Definitely. But I need to get this dog dry." She stared down at poor shivering Edgar. Then she looked closer. Something was tied to his collar.

"What the devil?" she said, pulling the paper free from the string with her cold, shaking hands.

If this was a joke, she wasn't laughing yet. With narrowed eyes, she unrolled the paper.

The words sent an immediate chill down her already frozen spine.

"Edgar was such a good boy. He followed me down to the beach with no trouble. Of course, I had to give him a treat. Good thing he likes fentanyl. Mind your own business, MJ, and keep your mouth shut."

Chapter Thirty-One

Tears blurred MJ's eyes and wind whipped at the Bronco as she flew down Cecil Bay Highway.

"I don't know," she wailed into her phone. "I just know he ate something. And there was the note. I don't know."

"Try to relax. Don't get into a wreck before getting to the hospital," said Justin, his tone calm but stern. "I'll meet you there."

After reading the note, she'd grabbed her keys and ran to the car with Edgar. Claire promised she would call the police.

As she started the drive to the emergency veterinarian hospital, she'd called Justin on speaker phone.

"Has he thrown up?" he shouted over the wind. She could hear his car starting in the background.

"No," she sniffled. Edgar stared up at her from the passenger seat. Other than still being waterlogged and stressed by her obvious distress, the dog appeared perfectly normal. She'd turned the heater on full blast to get both of them warm.

"Maybe it's a horrible joke. You teach middle school kids. They do dumb things."

She turned into the parking lot. "I don't think that's it, Justin. How would middle school kids get to my house this late? And taking Edgar down to the beach? I barely made it out of the surf." She turned off the Bronco. "I'm here. I'll see you in a few minutes."

Edgar jumped out of the car like this was a fun nighttime adventure.

MJ pulled her hood up and leaned into the wind toward the main entrance, Edgar trotting next to her on his leash, covered in a blanket she'd hastily thrown in the car.

She rang the after-hours doorbell and waited in the bright entry light, watching Edgar like he might begin gasping for breath at any second. Fentanyl was often lethal, that was the extent of MJ's knowledge of the drug. Fentanyl killed the father of one of her students. She knew it was deadly, but was it immediately deadly? Was there a safe amount you could ingest? She had no idea.

A small, dark-haired woman in mauve scrubs came to the door. "Good heavens, it's horrible out there. Come on inside, you two."

MJ's wet eyes felt frozen open. "Thank you," she said, a wobbly hitch in her voice.

The woman looked on with concerned eyes. "You two look soaked to the bone. I see Mr. Friendly here has a blanket. Let me get one for you, dear. I'm Connie."

"Thanks, I'm MJ and this is Edgar."

The woman opened a cupboard behind the reception desk and pulled out a fuzzy blanket with paws on it. "Don't worry, hon. This is my blanket for when I get cold at my desk." She smiled as she passed the blanket to MJ. "Why don't you tell me what's going on with your pup, dear? Here, sit down over here." She led MJ to a chair in the waiting room.

Fumbling in her pocket, MJ pulled out a zip-top bag with the note inside. She'd learned a few things from the police, and she didn't want anyone else's fingerprints on that paper.

"Edgar disappeared for a while. I found him down at the beach, and then and I found this note on his collar."

Connie furrowed her brow as she took the note, pulling a pair of reading glasses out of her pocket. "I'm going to check this out, but after I grab you some bandages and alcohol wipes. You're bleeding."

Sure enough, two scratches on the back of MJ's hand were covered in dried blood, with one wound still seeping.

When Connie returned, MJ cleaned and bandaged her hands as the other woman read the note. Her eyes moved across the words, her mouth silently saying each one. Then she stopped and looked over her glasses at MJ.

"How long long has it been since he may have eaten this thing?"

MJ sniffled. "About twenty or thirty minutes."

"Mm," said Connie.

The doorbell rang again. Connie wrinkled her nose. "Another one?"

"It's probably my ex-husband. I called him."

"Ah," said Connie. "Well, let's let him in."

She opened the door and Justin rushed in, looking a lot like a sniper in his all-black ensemble—pants, jacket, and beanie. Worry etched his chiseled features.

The dog started wiggling as soon as Justin entered. "Edgar, buddy," he said, falling to his knees and petting him ferociously.

"So, what do we know?" he asked, looking up at MJ and Connie.

"I think we should take him back to an exam room, and I'll fill the doctor in. He can answer all of your questions. Has Edgar been a patient here before?"

"Once," said MJ, her voice gaining strength as the initial shock of the note was wearing off. "He had a cut on his paw."

"Okay, dear. I'll just print out his record. You can mark any incorrect information rather than fill out a bunch of forms. Last name?"

"It's Brooks. Thank you," MJ said, following Connie to the exam room, Justin and Edgar behind her.

They sat down, and Connie took Edgar's temperature by inserting a thermometer into a very uncomfortable place. Justin winced and looked away. MJ petted the dog to keep him calm.

Then Connie disappeared through a door, and they waited.

"Can I see the note?" Justin asked.

She handed him the zip-top bag.

He scanned it quickly. "Mind your own business? What does that mean?"

MJ stood up and pulled a tissue from a box on the counter and blew her nose. "I don't know."

His intense blue eyes contrasted with the black of his outfit. She avoided them by grabbing another tissue, conducting a thorough wiping of her nose.

"MJ. You're not involved in one of those police investigations, are you?"

"No," she scoffed. "I mean, not really."

Justin rolled his eyes. "Here we go."

"Here we go? Were you planning to tell me about your interview with Jefferson and Rory?"

"On a first-name basis now, I see."

"Nice deflection."

"What? My interview was nothing. I hardly knew the guy they wanted to talk about."

"Ira Newman."

He gave her a questioning side-eye. "You know Ira?"

"About as well as you did," she said. "But I think it's weird that he died so suddenly."

"It is weird, but the detectives were more interested in his personal trainer. A guy named Forrest. Not the best dude. Eden, she's the owner, complained about him all the time. I think he had some questionable business going on the side. Drugs maybe."

"So that's why they were asking me if I'd heard of that Forrest guy. Do they think he could have hurt Ira?"

He shrugged his massive shoulders. "I don't see how. He didn't even train him the day he died. I did, and it wasn't cardio heavy or—" Justin stopped, staring into space with a quizzical look on his face.

"What?"

He shook his head. "It's nothing."

"Justin. That look on your face wasn't a 'nothing.'"

With a long side-eye, he finally said, "I just hope Ira wasn't stupid enough to take any drugs from Forrest."

MJ wrinkled her nose. "I don't think so. He seemed liked the type of person who was more likely to bust the guy."

"Maybe."

"Did you ever see a woman named Millie there? I saw one of their magnets on her fridge."

"Doesn't sound familiar, but I'm not there that often. Anyway, we shouldn't even be talking about this. Neither one of us needs to be involved. Especially you."

"What's that supposed to mean?"

Justin looked up at the ceiling. "MJ, the police don't need your help. All you do is put yourself, and now Edgar, in danger, running around like you can solve the case. And I think the only reason you get involved is because of that Detective Hughes." He threw his hands up. "There. I said it."

MJ fumed, staring at him with the venom of so many unsaid things rushing through her veins. Just when she thought Justin had started to change, he said something so insanely stupid.

Despite her wet clothes, angry heat fueled her next words. "You have always discounted me, made me feel like my accomplishments were only because of some male benefactor doing me a favor. It's so eighteenth century, and it makes me want to scream; I will hold off screaming for Edgar's sake. But Justin," she said, her voice calm but fierce. She was done believing this was her problem. It was his, and he needed to deal with it. "You need to fix this about yourself if you want a woman to love you like I used to."

His blue eyes seemed to fade, as if she'd stolen his life force. MJ knew a dagger to the heart wouldn't have caused him any more pain than her last words.

Pulling the paw blanket tight around her shoulders, she turned away from the train wreck she'd just caused. Her anger abated too quickly, and now she just felt sad. She didn't want to hurt Justin.

They receded into silence until the doctor walked into the room. He had to be one of the tallest men MJ had ever seen. The doorway was barely high enough for him to pass under without ducking. He had sandy hair and surely couldn't have been as young as he looked.

"Hello everyone," he said, like someone who was used to being awake at this time of night. "How is Edgar doing?"

Justin cleared his throat without looking at MJ. "He seems fine."

The doctor let Edgar smell his gloved hand before petting him on the top of the head. Then he briefly pulled each eyelid open. "Has Edgar shown any signs of weakness, blank stare, difficulty breathing, that sort of thing?"

MJ shook her head. "No. Other than being wet and cold, he seems normal."

"Do you mind if I look in your mouth, Mr. Edgar?" he said as he pulled gently on each side of Edgar's snout to glimpse inside. Satisfied, he then touched his stethoscope to the dog's chest, cocking his head toward the wall to listen.

He stood up and pulled a rolling stool over to sit in front of MJ and Justin.

"Based on Edgar's current state and the timeframe you gave us, I think you all have been the subject of a pretty nasty prank."

A relieved sob escaped MJ. Justin hesitated briefly before putting an arm around her shoulder and squeezing. She felt too grateful at the news to object.

The doctor continued. "If Edgar had indeed ingested fentanyl, I would expect to see some vomiting, staring, drowsiness, erratic heartbeat. All of those things would happen within fifteen minutes or sooner, and certainly by now. We have some Narcan here in the office for pets, but it's not risk free, and given his lack of symptoms, I wouldn't recommend it."

He reached his long arm forward and pet Edgar's head again. "I wouldn't want to put him through anything unnecessarily, but if it will make you feel better, we can send some of the Narcan home with you in case the symptoms suddenly show up. I'd like you to call me before using it, though. I can walk you through it."

"I would feel better if you did," said Justin. "MJ?"

She nodded, wiping her eyes. Her heart hadn't returned to normal yet.

"Alright. I'll send Connie in with the prescription. Of course, if you notice Edgar acting strange, like he seems dizzy or out of breath. Really, anything out of the ordinary. Call. Do the Narcan, if needed, and bring him back in."

They said they would, and the doctor wished them the best.

When the paperwork was finished and the prescription ready, Justin walked with MJ and Edgar to the Bronco.

"Listen," he said, his eyes heavy with exhaustion. "I know you're mad at me." He glanced up at the sky, mulling over his words. "You are right. I'm a work in progress. As much as I try, I keep stepping in it with you—"

"Oh, it's not just me, Justin. You'll step in it with any woman with comments like you made tonight."

He shook his head with a grimace. "I get it. I mean, kind of. Like I said, work in progress." Edgar bumped against his leg, prompting Justin to reach down and pet him. "It's just this friend thing with you. I struggle to stay in my lane." Planting his hands on his hips, he gave her a serious but surprisingly conciliatory grin. "And with all of that being said, I already know you won't like this idea, but I'd feel better if I slept on your couch tonight."

"Oh, Justin. That's not—"

"MJ, if you don't believe this was the knucklehead move of an eighth grader, then someone else knows where you live. They know you have a dog, MJ. They know his name. Whoever did this, they came prepared to terrorize you. And if this is at all related to Ira Newman, well, let me remind you that he is dead."

"Claire was going to call the police, so they may already be there. But okay, I'm sure she would appreciate having you nearby." She was too cold and too tired to put up a reasonable argument, and she still had to teach tomorrow.

"Can you stay to watch Edgar tomorrow while I'm at work, just for a while to make sure he's still okay?"

"Sure. I was just doing paperwork on base tomorrow. It can wait a few hours."

MJ had to admit she'd sleep better knowing Justin was there. She never doubted his ability or willingness to provide physical protection. But in their relationship, Justin could never recognize or admit when his need to control a situation turned into his need to control her. For his sake, MJ hoped her ex figured it out and found someone to make him happy.

"But tomorrow," Justin said, "you need to call your detective friends and give them that note. I want to know who pulled this stunt."

"So do I."

Chapter Thirty-Two

The morning briefing was short and to the point.

Larson and Mendez were already off serving the search warrant at Forrest Bernard's house. Ira's son had ironed out the legal permission for them to search the retired detective's house as well. They left early with a forensics team ready to go over each residence with a fine-toothed comb.

"Since we are likely to confiscate what could be important tech devices, I've enlisted the help of our local FBI partners for the computer forensics work," announced the chief. "I expect we'll see Jared, their tech special agent, this afternoon. And it wouldn't surprise me if Amber tagged along. She seemed very interested in the way these cases have intersected."

Jefferson welcomed this news. Amber Wells, the Special Agent in Charge of the regional West Sound FBI office, was generous with her team's resources. And she was one heck of an investigator in her own right.

He also had a personal reason for wanting to see her.

Alex, Jefferson's younger brother, would testify against a ruthless drug dealer soon. With a mix of caution and aggression, the feds were moving to dismantle the drug network, working hard to arrest criminals while protecting witnesses. The trial date was shrouded in secrecy, likely to be revealed at the last minute.

Amber usually had more of the inside scoop than anyone else. Jefferson desperately wanted to know his brother was safe, even if that meant he'd disappeared into witness protection.

But that would have to wait.

For now, Jefferson and Rory were out the door and on to their first task—meet Millie Van Buren and find out if Oloff Svensson is her mystery love interest.

The drive was a short one. She lived in a neighborhood close to the station.

The two detectives still hadn't discussed the interview at MJ's house. Rory didn't seem inclined to bring it up, and Jefferson didn't trust himself to stay calm.

They rode in silence until Jefferson's phone rang. It was MJ.

"MJ?" he said, answering. "What's up?"

Rory, who was driving, shot him a curious look.

"I only have a minute," she said. "My next class will be here soon. But you need to know what happened at my house last night."

Jefferson straightened in his seat. "I'm listening," he said, a forced calm in his tone.

She explained the scare concerning Edgar at the beach, as well as the note and the fake fentanyl poisoning.

The instant Jefferson heard the word fentanyl, he turned wide eyes to Rory, who was doing his best to watch the road while also following Jefferson's conversation.

"But he's okay?"

"Yes," she said. "The vet said he had no symptoms. We took him home with Narcan for pets, which is crazy. I can't believe they even have such a thing."

"We?"

He could hear the noise of kids laughing and chatting in the background. She didn't respond, and he wasn't sure she'd heard him.

"Uh, yeah," she said, finally. "I called Justin to meet me at the vet, since Edgar is his dog, too. He insisted on staying on the couch last night."

Of course he did, thought Jefferson. The guy just didn't give up. Justin's over-protective nature usually drove her crazy. The attack on her dog must have scared the fiercely independent MJ, otherwise she would never allow her ex to play knight in shining armor.

And knowing Justin slept at her house last night bothered Jefferson more than he wanted to admit.

"We'll need that note."

"I know. We made a police report last night, but I wanted to make sure the note got into your hands, so I held onto it. Justin is going to drop it by the station, along with the rope the person used. I'll call you later." Her voice pulled away from the phone. "Tyrone, get your notebook, please. Thank you."

Then she was back. "Gotta go."

When she hung up, Jefferson ran his hand down his face. This was not good.

Rory kept stealing quick glances at him. "You look like your dog just died."

Jefferson shook his head. Rory had no idea how close he was to the truth.

***

The detectives rolled up to Millie's house just as a workman finished installing a for-sale sign.

The wind had finally blown itself out, leaving behind a cold, leaden sky that cast a shadow over the day. It was the type of oppressive shadow the day would never escape.

The man picked up a post digger and returned it to the bed of a well-used silver pickup truck. He watched the detectives with curiosity as they climbed out of their car.

"Hello there," said Jefferson. "This is Millie Van Buren's place, correct?"

The man squinted before pulling a rumpled yellow slip from his pocket. Reading quickly, he said, "Yeah, Van Buren. That's it."

"Is she's moving?" asked Rory, his hands in his coat pockets.

"Far as I know," the man said, taking off his baseball cap and then replacing it on his balding head. "I just put the signs up. This was kind of a rush one, so I hope it's straight," he chuckled.

"Rushed?" repeated Jefferson.

"Yeah, I guess the lady just called Jasper—that's the real estate agent—this morning and said she wanted a sign up today. Like she wants to get the heck out of Dodge. So, he called me, and now it's done."

Jefferson inspected the sign from a distance. "That's quick work."

"Well, Jasper's a good guy, so I'll go out of my way for him."

Rory started walking. "We better get on up to the door."

Jefferson thanked the man and followed Rory up the walkway.

Millie answered the door after the first knock.

Pulling a gray knit cardigan close around her, she looked the detectives up and down with narrowed eyes.

"If you're here to see the house, you need to go through my real estate agent," she said in a matter-of-fact tone.

She had long gray hair pulled back from her face in a tight bun at the base of her neck. She wore an apron under her cardigan, and Jefferson guessed she'd been cleaning.

"We're not here about the house, Mrs. Van Buren. I'm Detective Hughes, and this is Detective Jackson with the West Sound Police Department. Can we come in?"

They both presented their badges for Millie's inspection.

She barely glanced at them. "Did that teacher call you?"

"Teacher?" asked Jefferson, feigning ignorance. She had to mean MJ.

"Yes. That nosy girl keeps getting into my business."

Those words. Jefferson felt his adrenaline kick in. Almost exactly the same phrase MJ used when describing the note attached to Edgar. He glanced at Rory, whose barely perceptible nod signaled he'd also noted her choice of words.

"Mrs. Van Buren," Jefferson explained calmly despite his quickened pulse, "we need to ask you some questions about Ira Newman. It shouldn't take long."

Her tightly furrowed brows relaxed by a fraction. "Oh, fine. Come in." She turned, already retreating into the house. "Take off your shoes," she ordered with her back to them.

She missed Jefferson's eye roll. He was a shoe guy, and he didn't enjoy taking them off unless he was in his own living room. Rory didn't care at all and would have slid down Millie's hardwood hall if he thought she wouldn't notice.

Once inside, Jefferson knew he'd been right. Pine scented cleaner assaulted their lungs as they followed Millie to her family room.

The woman sat on one of two recliners flanking a side table. Rory sat on the other, and Jefferson pulled over an ottoman from the corner.

"Thank you for speaking with us, Mrs. Van Buren," Jefferson began. "Are you moving out of West Sound?"

She sat on the edge of the recliner, her hands folded in her lap, as if this conversation wouldn't warrant getting comfortable. "I am, but I don't see what that has to do with Ira." Millie's sharp tone suggested she had no inclination to share details.

"No, of course it doesn't. I'm just curious. This is a beautiful home. It would take a lot to move me out of it," he said, looking around the room with the most congenial smile he could manage. "How long have you been planning to move?"

"I don't see how that's important for you to know."

Her posture may have straitened, but no further information escaped the thin line of her mouth, a sign of her barely contained impatience.

Jefferson rested his elbows on his knees, which were almost to his chin on the short ottoman. "Fair enough. And we promised you this wouldn't take long. I know you and Ira were friends. We both knew Ira," he added, motioning to Rory. "He retired when I was still a newbie. He was a well-loved detective."

"I'm sure he was," Millie said, her face softening but still guarded.

"We understand you and Ira had some kind of argument the day that he died? Can you tell us about that?"

"That Ms. Brooks has been talking to you, hasn't she?" Her eyes were dark and accusing.

"Several people saw the argument. What's important is for you to explain what the argument was about?"

"Why? What does it matter now? Ira is gone." The harshness of the last words seemed to surprise even Millie. A hand flew to her mouth as a small sob escaped.

"Can I get you a drink of water?" asked Rory.

She closed her eyes and nodded, working to compose herself.

After a slow, ragged breath, she said, "I just don't understand why I have to keep talking about it. Why are detectives even here?" She stared at Jefferson with watery eyes. "Didn't he die in his sleep from a natural cause?"

Rory returned and handed her the glass of water. She took it with her right hand, and it was then that Jefferson noticed the stiff, curled position of her left hand.

He sat back with a heavy sigh. "I'm sorry, Mrs. Van Buren, but we learned this morning that Ira may have had some lethal drugs in his system, and we're not sure yet how that came to be."

A sharp intake of breath and Millie's face lost all color. "No," she whispered, her left hand rising to cover her heart. "That can't be. Ira would never do drugs. Never."

Her wild eyes flitted between the two detectives.

"You should take a sip of that water," Rory suggested.

She did as he said, but after swallowing, her eyes still darted around the room. "I just don't understand. He loved life. He wouldn't even drink soda, much less put that poison in his body."

"That's what we are trying to figure out. We agree that it seems out of his nature to take drugs. And if that is the cause of death, then we need to know where he got the drugs and why he would suddenly start taking them."

If possible, her face went even more pale. "Could he have wanted to poison himself?" Every line on her face showed the horror of that possibility.

Jefferson looked skeptical. "It's possible, but there's nothing to suggest that is the case."

"But you're here because you think I may have pushed him to it. I rejected him, and that's . . . Oh, no."

Rory turned in his recliner and sat forward. "Mrs. Van Buren, we are not here for that reason. Because of his work, it's possible several people hold a grudge against Ira. He put a lot of bad people away."

She nodded, taking another sip of water. Jefferson wasn't sure she bought Rory's explanation, but it calmed her for the moment.

With no further prodding, Millie began explaining her argument with Ira. She told them the same story she'd shared with MJ.

"This new boyfriend you're seeing," asked Jefferson, feeling weird about the choice of words but not sure how else to ask his question. "What's his name?"

"Why?"

Rory smiled so that his eyes crinkled. "We don't want to invade your privacy, Millie, but it's important that we check anyone with a connection to Ira. It's just a simple electronic check, likely not over five minutes."

"But he's not even in the country," she said, exasperated.

She froze. Clearly, that was not something she intended on sharing.

"Where is he?" asked Jefferson.

With a glare at the ceiling, she sighed. "He's in Africa. And he's not a boyfriend. He's my fiancé."

Absorbing this information without reaction took all of Jefferson's resolve. She's selling her house, thought Jefferson. And now he is supposedly her fiancé? If MJ was right about the potential scam, this guy was in deep and had probably already fleeced Millie out of some of her money.

"Is that where you are moving to?" asked Jefferson, hardly able to keep the incredulity out of his voice.

"Look," said Millie. "I don't want a bunch of people to know. Too many of my so-called friends and relatives think I can't take care of myself. It's really tiring. You'll understand when you're my age."

"We're not here to change your mind," assured Jefferson. "But we need to check his name. It sounds like Ira may have caused some trouble with your relationship, so we'd not be doing our jobs if we didn't look into it, even if it is completely irrelevant."

Her shoulders slumped in resignation. "Fine. His name is Oloff, and he is the most amazing man in the world."

There was the confirmation they needed. If MJ's instincts were correct, the guy was a complete sham, a worthless scammer.

"If he's in Africa, how do you usually communicate with him?" Rory asked.

Millie shrugged, as if it should be common knowledge to someone so young. "Social media. You know, that KIT site. It's quite easy and convenient."

"Would you be willing to show us your computer?" Rory pressed.

This brought back the stern, uncooperative Millie. "I will not."

"That's fine," smiled Jefferson. "You've been very forthcoming, and we appreciate it." If they couldn't get Millie to trust them, convincing her of Oloff's nefarious intentions would be impossible.

"Good." She stood with a more affable smile. "Now I really must get back to work."

But Jefferson wasn't quite done. MJ had given them one other piece of information that he wanted to follow up.

"Just one more thing," he said.

Annoyance steeled Millie's face, but she waited for him to continue.

"Are you a member at Senior Strength, the gym Ira attended?"

"Oh, heavens no," scoffed Millie, with a wave of her hand. "Ira tried to get me to join. I did a tour to make him happy, but it is not my kind of thing at all."

"Did you meet a man named Forrest? He's a trainer."

After a few seconds of thinking about it, she said, "Yes. I remember him. A nice young man, but too many muscles, in my opinion. He said the workouts would help my arthritis, but I don't think that's true. And the woman I met, Eve or Eden, something like that. She just wanted me to buy her shakes and vitamins, saying that they would make me live longer." A smug press of her lips told them Millie didn't believe that either. "I told her I like to eat actual food."

"I'm with you there," Rory said.

"I know I said one more thing," Jefferson said, turning on his best crooked smile. "But this is the last one, I promise."

To his surprise, she smiled back. "Fine, detective. But this is it."

"Thank you. You've been a big help. I was just wondering when was the last time you communicated with Oloff?"

"This morning."

So not Forrest because Forrest is already dead.

He stood up. "You've been very helpful, Millie. And we appreciate you letting us take some of your time today."

As they made their way back to the car, Jefferson couldn't forget the way Millie beamed at them when she said Oloff's name. It stoked an angry fire inside of him to find out who was behind this scam. Whatever this man had pedaled, Millie bought it out of loneliness and the desire to love and to be loved.

Is there a worse kind of crime? To steal a heart just to drain it dry?

This Oloff needed to be stopped before Millie lost everything. Maybe even her life.

Chapter
Thirty-Three

A mber Wells always brought a jolt of energy to the station.
Walking into the hub, Jefferson could feel it before he saw
her. Everyone seemed more intense, more positive, and they had a
quickness to their step.

The FBI boss had a gift for leading highly efficient teams. She pulled
no punches, no politics, and showed respect for all law enforcement
officers, no matter their rank. Even if she wasn't leading the investigation, her presence brought calm and competence.

He couldn't hide a smile when he saw her sitting at his desk talking
to Jared, who had taken up residence at an empty desk next to her.

"Hello, Jefferson. Rory." Her hazel eyes twinkled behind her slim
glasses as she sat back in the chair, her legs crossed in her sensible black
pantsuit.

"Why don't you stay and take that desk permanently? I could use a
new partner. This one is ready to chuck me to the wolves," joked Rory,
jabbing a thumb toward Jefferson.

"Oh, I can't imagine that," said Amber, her face saying the opposite. "What is it this time? Did you make a joke about Italian shoes?"

"It's absolutely nothing," said Jefferson, sitting on the edge of his desk. "My partner loves to exaggerate."

Jared paid no attention to this exchange, totally engrossed in something on his computer.

Rory lowered his voice to an unnecessary whisper. "Let me just say it has something to do with the letter M and the letter J."

"Oh, does it?" asked Amber, eyeing Jefferson with a curious smile. "Are we still doing that dance?"

"I don't know what you mean."

"Ah well, never mind about that for now. Rory, lay off your partner. Jefferson, don't be so easy to needle. There, are we good?"

"Yes, Mom," said Rory glumly.

"Jefferson," she said. "Let's take a walk."

***

The cold convinced most people to stay inside, leaving the streets empty as the FBI boss and the detective toured the blocks around the station.

Tension coiled inside Jefferson when Amber mentioned a walk, an out-of-earshot stroll around downtown. This wasn't a pleasure cruise or an attempt to get steps. She likely had news about his brother, Alex, or the case Alex would testify in, against a drug trafficker named Nico.

When they'd reached a sufficient distance from the station, Amber blew out a breath, sending a cloud of steam with it.

"I think it really might snow," she said.

"That's all we need."

"Boy, you are grumpy. Who doesn't love a little snow?"

He aimed a side-eye at her. "Police officers, firefighters, paramedics . . . anyone who has to clean up the mess caused by the inevitable paralysis of good sense after snow hits people who are only used to rain."

She chuckled. "And teachers?"

He stared straight ahead, fighting the crooked smile daring to make an appearance. He could hide nothing from Amber. If he were a criminal and she was the interrogator, there'd be no hope for him.

"Now teachers," he said emphatically, working to keep MJ's face out of his mind, "they probably love a snow day, but only if it's on a weekday. Weekend snowstorms probably cut into their social lives."

"I can see that."

They walked a few more paces, each huddling further into their coats, before Amber spoke again.

"Everything is good, Jeff," she said. "No word on a trial date yet, but he's stayed clean. And according to Kota, he's been studying quite a bit."

Jefferson stopped, turning to look at her. "Studying?"

She gave him a patient smile, and then, taking his arm, said, "Let's keep walking."

They walked arm and arm as she continued. "I want you to think about why you do what you do. Remember what pushed you to become a detective. And I want you to consider the satisfaction of knowing someone truly horrible is no longer terrorizing the public because you did your job."

"Where is this going?"

This time it was Amber's turn to stop, her hazel eyes intense and yet gentle. "Jeff, you started this job because of your brother's addiction. That anger drove you to find justice for not only him, but others." Puffs of fog punctuated each word as she continued. "You're not the only one to find your purpose in the darkest moments. Your brother has, too."

He cocked his head, staring down at her. If she meant what he thought she did, there was no way he would let it happen.

"He can't be thinking of being a cop."

"Not a cop," Amber said. "Not in the way you are. He's looking at one of the intelligence agencies. DEA, HSI, maybe even CIA."

"What?" Jefferson almost shouted. "Are you crazy? He's going to have a huge target on his back. Witness protection is his only safe option."

"He doesn't want to play it safe."

Raising his eyes to the sky, Jefferson focused on the ominous gray-green clouds. Snow may be the one thing Amber was right about.

"I have to see him," he said, finally. "I have to stop this."

With a dip of her head, Amber sighed. "That's not going to happen." Lifting her head, she said, "I don't know where he is, and no one is going to risk his life to tell you. And frankly, you don't want that either."

Clenching his jaw, Jefferson turned his head to stare silently down the street.

"Look," Amber said, touching his arm until he turned to face her. "The trial isn't likely to happen for a couple more months. You'll see him then. Until that time, you need to wrap your head around this. Your brother is not a kid anymore. He's changed. You hated what he went through, but he is the one who actually went through it. Wanting to make it right . . . that's only natural."

The words made sense. They made more sense than he wanted to admit. But the fear, the worry, the need to protect, those were the feelings he associated with Alex. It would take an earthquake to shift his mind to see Alex in the same light as other agents and officers. In fact, it would take a miracle.

"Now that I have improved your mood," she said, grinning as she grabbed his arm and turned him back toward the station, "What's going on with my girl MJ?"

As much as he wasn't ready to shift subjects, he knew Amber well enough to follow her lead. She wouldn't say any more about Alex than she already had.

"It's hard to explain." It was actually easy to explain. Jefferson just didn't want to explain it. He knew now that he'd made a mess of the whole situation with MJ and Shannon. Telling Amber would only pile on the embarrassment.

"We've got about three blocks back to the station. If you slow your long legs and walk with my shorter ones, we'll have plenty of time."

He grimaced. She would not let him off the hook.

Gazing down the street, hoping to avoid her eyes, he took a breath. "I have a date—"

With a gasp, she stopped in her tracks. "With MJ?" she said, far too excited.

He shook his head and started walking again, still not looking at her. "With her friend, Shannon."

To his immense frustration, Amber stopped again. "What? Why?" She moved to stand in front of him, not allowing him to look anywhere else. "Jefferson, why would you do that?"

Despite his respect for Amber, this brought out a defensive answer.

"I did it because Shannon was interested in me. You could even say she asked me out. But MJ," he clamped his mouth shut. He had told no one how close he came to expressing his feelings to MJ. He would not start now.

They resumed walking as Amber considered his answer. "I don't pretend to know everything, but I've never seen two people so determined to ignore their feelings for each other than you and MJ."

"I don't—"

"Jeff, just don't. Heaven knows I had my share of messed up relationships before I met Jerry, but I learned a thing or two along the way. One of those things is that a woman needs to know you will fight for her. MJ is complex. That's what I like about her. But I can see how that makes her difficult to read."

They were just about at the station door, so Amber stopped again. Gazing up at him, her eyes were thoughtful and sincere.

"She is difficult to read except for a skilled FBI agent like myself," she grinned. "That girl cares about you, and she's just as scared to admit it as you are." Her hand rested on his arm with a light touch. "Don't give up, Jeff."

She let her hand fall and walked into the station, leaving him to twist in the wind of her last words.

Chapter Thirty-Four

S tacey Underhill had a shockingly grim look on her face.

It was so out of character that Jefferson stopped in his tracks as she emerged from Chief Carlson's office.

The reason for her demeanor only took seconds to discover.

Rob Newman, his tear-reddened eyes locked ahead of him, walked with his arm around a sobbing woman as the chief ushered them out of his office and toward the exit.

Poor guy. Sometimes it hurts to be right. He certainly had to prefer thinking that his dad died in his sleep rather than imagining him dying from some illicit drug. For most people, the biological evidence of drug use might make them question everything they thought they knew about their parent. Jefferson guessed that was not Rob's mind-set. He either wouldn't believe it, or he would be certain someone else was responsible. Jefferson had to admit he couldn't imagine Ira doing drugs either.

At least he'd managed to iron out the legalities of managing Ira's estate. Jefferson wondered what kinds of things Larson and Mendez were finding as they searched the two residences.

"That was torture," said Stacey, joining Jefferson and Rory at their desks. "Why do I do this job?"

Rory raised a hand in the air. "Amen."

"Seriously. And I don't have to do that half as often as you guys do. It must eat you alive." She shook her head.

"How did Newman take it?" Jefferson asked.

Stacy rocked her head side to side. "About liked you'd expect. He believes it may have been drugs. But he doesn't believe for a second that his dad knowingly took them. His sister was just devastated and couldn't even express her feelings about it, poor girl."

Jefferson's desk phone rang. He grabbed it before it could go into a second ring. "Hughes." He listened. "Fine. Send him back."

"Brooks is bringing in the note," he said, filling in Rory. "Where did Amber go?"

"To the briefing room," Jared said, unexpectantly. Jefferson had forgotten the young agent was there.

"Who's that?" said Stacey, any semblance of her former grimness having disappeared. "Oh, wait," she said, answering her own question. "That's Justin Brooks, the teacher's ex. I didn't realize . . ." her words trailed off as she touched a fingernail to her lips.

"Oh, no," said Rory, slapping his forehead. "These two in the same room may transport them to Olympus. Too much gorgeous for us mortals."

"Why thank you, Rory," said Stacey, her eyes following Justin as he made his way to Jefferson's desk. "You know if you weren't married . . . but a girl has to have boundaries."

In his right hand, Justin carried two plastic bags. Jefferson smiled, knowing MJ would have thought to preserve evidence.

"Hey, Detective Hughes. MJ asked me to drop off this note and this rope. I assume she called you." He handed the bags to Jefferson. The icy blue daggers from their last meeting had softened. Justin seemed to make an effort to be not just civil, but courteous.

"Yes, she did. Thank you. And I'm sorry for what you went through with Edgar. Even though he's fine, I know how much he means to both of you."

"Thanks. I appreciate that." He was shockingly sincere.

"Wait, who is Edgar? And what happened to him?" This was Stacey's way of inserting herself into the conversation.

Justin blessed her with his brilliant smile. "Edgar is our dog. MJ and I kind of share custody of him. I know that seems weird, but we love the guy. Someone played a prank, made MJ think they'd given him fentanyl."

With a knowing look at Jefferson, Stacey repeated, "Fentanyl, hmm?"

Jefferson raised his brows with a slight tilt of this head to indicate he'd made that connection and did not want to discuss it in front of Brooks.

"I'm sorry, but I don't think we've met," Justin said, holding out a hand, which extended from his arm of ample muscles.

"I'm Dr. Stacey Underhill, the county medical examiner." As she took his hand, Jefferson could swear he saw sparks flying between their palms.

"Doctor. Wow. I've never met such a beautiful doctor." Justin's blue eyes crinkled with his award-winning smile.

Stacey pretended to blush. If any woman knew she was beautiful, it was Stacey Underhill.

"You're so sweet. I'm on my way out. Maybe we could walk together?"

"It would be my pleasure."

With a brief goodbye to the detectives, Stacey took Justin's arm, smiling and chatting as they left the building.

Jefferson plopped down in his chair, pulling his hands down over his face. "What in the world was that?"

"That, my friend," answered Rory, pointing a pen into the air, "is Justin Brooks no longer being in the picture."

Chapter Thirty-Five

"Find anything?"

Amber pulled a chair to sit beside Jared.

He shook his mop of brown curls. "I'm not sure what I've found will help get a warrant to open up these profiles."

"Let me worry about that part," she said. "What do you think of the Oloff profile?"

Jefferson and Rory moved closer to listen in.

"MJ is right. It's a scam." He sat up and pushed his computer back so everyone could see the screen.

"This is Oloff Svensson's profile." He scrolled through the pictures of the visible posts. "And this," he said as he clicked over to a new screen, "is the profile of Scott Dixon."

It was the same man.

"So that's him? The scammer?" asked Rory.

"No," answered Jared with his usual abruptness. "Scott Dixon has a legitimate profile that has been in effect for seven years. Scammers steal photos from legitimate profiles."

"And Scott Dixon has no idea that a woman in West Sound, Washington, is madly in love with him, or at least his picture." Jefferson ran a hand under his chin. "Shouldn't this be enough to get a warrant for the profile information? Or get KIT to consider shutting it down."

"It will be enough for a warrant," said Amber, "but it may take some time and negotiation from the chief and myself. But I'm not sure we want KIT to shut down the profile just yet. That may not help your victim. Often, if the scammer senses that someone in the victim's life is on to them, they move to a new platform, like a messaging only app, and try to isolate them further. If he does that, we'll end up chasing as he jumps from log to log and still takes everything she has."

"No," she continued. "Our best bet is showing this Scott Dixon profile to Millie Van Buren and convincing her to let us take over her communications with Oloff. We'll still get a warrant. I want to know where these messages are originating."

"Likely Africa or Asia," said Jared, pulling his computer back to him.

Amber nodded, looking at the detectives to add detail to Jared's comment. "Police in the Philippines recently rescued a couple hundred people from forced labor as online scammers. It's a growing business for organized crime, much of it out of China, though they operate in less regulated areas. They use fake jobs to lure young people, kidnap them, and then force them to run fake schemes and profiles. They call the romantic scams 'pig butchering.'"

"Why pig butchering?" asked Jefferson.

"Let Farmer Rory take a crack at answering that for you." He lodged his hands beneath pretend suspenders. "Usually, you feed the pigs yummy stuff to gorge on, fattening them up before butchering time. It sounds like our scammers feed their victims what they like, build a relationship, get what they can out of them, and then take the money and run." He stroked his beard. "I'm glad my wife hasn't heard of that."

With a smirk, Jefferson waved off Rory's joke. "You'd have to have enough money to make running worth it."

"That is a problem," his partner agreed, pulling at the end of his beard.

"So, there is the potential," Jefferson said, "that the person responsible is too far out of our reach? They'll just get away with it?"

Amber pressed her lips together with an apologetic tilt of her head. "I know that's hard to hear, but we'd have to have a group of cases to get the attention of the Justice Department." She stopped, as if an idea just flashed into her mind. "Let me put a few emails up the chain. Someone else may have an iron in this fire if our case links up with theirs."

"It's worth a shot." He watched as Larson and Mendez entered the hub, Mendez carrying a plastic tub. "I'm not sure that's the case here. Something Millie Van Buren said . . . and this thing with MJ's dog. I think it's more likely that Millie's fake Oloff is closer than we think."

"Speaking of warrants," said Rory, as Larson and Mendez joined them.

"Nice to see all you knuckleheads gathered for our arrival," Larson said as Mendez set the tub down next to Jared. "Except Amber and Jared, for that knucklehead part. Hello, you two."

They both said hello. "What's in the tub?" Amber asked, standing to peek inside.

"Laptops," said Mendez. "One for Ira and one for the dead kid, Forrest Bernard. Forensics dusted them for prints and said we could take them for analysis."

Jared was already pulling the first laptop from the tub.

"They're labeled, so you know whose is whose," offered Mendez.

"I can see that," Jared said matter-of-factly as he removed the first laptop from its plastic evidence bag.

Larson looked at his phone. "Chief wants a briefing. Ten minutes."

"Why didn't he just come and tell us?" asked Mendez, looking toward the chief's office door.

Larson shrugged. "Who knows, who cares. I'm getting a coffee, though. Anyone else? Order online at Callie B's, and I'll send Meyers to make a run," he said, already headed to find the officer.

"He's going to be leaking coffee soon. He drinks so much," said Mendez.

"The beast needs his fuel," said Rory.

Chapter Thirty-Six

O fficer Meyers had never been so popular.

Loaded down with drinks and sandwiches from Callie B's, he was, for the moment, the star of the briefing.

With food dispersed to the owners, the chief called Meyers to the crime board.

"Officer Meyers here has been printing information and adding it to the board," the chief informed them. "I've asked him to take notes, adding anything relevant to what is already there."

The picture in the center of the board must have come from someone's personal photos. In it, Ira wore a white shirt and tie with his badge on a lanyard around his neck. With his hands on his hips, he smiled with a grimace beneath his bulky mustache, as if someone had just made a snarky joke.

This was how Jefferson remembered Ira. A tough, no-nonsense detective who loved his job. Ira considered his vow to protect the innocent as important as his own life. It was possible he carried that vow with him to the grave.

Underneath Ira, Meyers had pinned a picture of a bald man with tattoos covering his cheeks and neck. It was Warren Harris. Someone had drawn a red X over his face.

"What's up with Warren Harris?" asked Larson.

Meyers handed the last drink to Amber. "Dead. Looks like someone took him out in Seattle just hours after he was released."

"Live by the sword. Die by the sword," murmured Mendez, with a slow shake of his head. "I guess we don't have to worry about that guy."

Connected by a line to Ira, on the left, Forrest/Advik smiled back at them from his Senior Strength staff photo. Meyers had added the warrants against him from California and key points from the medical examiner's report.

A line straight down connected Forrest to the mug shot of Leon Albright, Forrest's couch-surfing friend. There was a list of Leon's prior arrests as well as what he revealed about his friend's drug-selling side business.

To the right of Ira hung Millie Van Buren's driver's license photo, captioned by the words "senior center altercation." To the right of Millie, Meyers had placed Oloff Svensson's profile picture. He'd listed information from the profile's bio, though there was little doubt it was all fake. A photo of Scott Dixon, the unsuspecting British man whose picture the posing Oloff had stolen, made this all too clear.

Jefferson smiled involuntarily at the last picture, connected by a line to Millie. MJ kneeled, smiling, her bright blue eyes set off by the contrast with her dark, curly hair. She had one hand on the back of a seated Edgar.

Meyers had copied the threatening note and posted it below MJ's photo. Reading the words again sent a chill through him, but it also stoked his anger. The only reason he hadn't insisted on a patrol car at MJ's house today was that she would be at work all day.

Amber sat next to the chief, who met each detective's face with his flinty eyes. "Tell me we have something to add."

Out of all the information they'd gained from their visit to Millie, there was one piece that Jefferson knew would change this investigation.

He leaned forward and motioned toward the crime board. "We believe there is a connection between whoever sent that threatening note to MJ and Millie Van Buren. After our visit to Millie today, Jackson and I believe it is also the same person posing as Oloff Svensson."

A hush fell over the room as they waited for him to connect the dots of his conclusion.

"When we first introduced ourselves at Millie's door, she complained about the nosy teacher, obviously meaning MJ."

"Haven't you used those same words?" said Larson, flipping his pen.

No one laughed, but this earned Larson a few grudging smiles.

"Maybe," Jefferson shrugged. "But not now." Did he really just say that? Admit to everyone that MJ's help was valuable? He was getting soft.

He cleared his throat and sipped his water. "Millie's words about MJ eerily echoed the note left on Edgar's collar. She told us that MJ 'should mind her own business.'"

No one said anything. Jefferson had expected a few a-has or wows. Nothing.

"That's it?" asked Larson.

"Well, yeah. Seems pretty clear to me." Jefferson glanced at Rory for support.

"I agree with Jeffy," said Rory, before taking the last bite of his bagel.

"Stunning show of support there," laughed Larson.

The chief put a hand up. "We are spit balling here." He glanced at Officer Meyers, who was hurriedly scribbling notes on a legal pad. "All theories are valid. What's yours Detective Larson?"

The senior detective pushed back from the table and stood at the crime board. Pointing to the pictures of Forrest and Leon, he began stating his case.

"I think these two created a scheme to defraud senior citizens, and possibly others, through lies and deception. We know Forrest has a record of exactly those crimes. Either Forrest or Leon began communicating with Mrs. Van Buren as Oloff." He moved to the other side of the board and pointed at Millie. "Fleecing her for cash became so easy and lucrative, Leon decided he didn't need Forrest. Why not take all the money for himself? Then he murdered Forrest, and because he has little to no knowledge of currents and tides, he dumped the body, thinking that was that." He shook his head in disappointment. "Kids these days."

He shifted to Ira's picture. "Being the tenacious investigator he was, Ira suspected something was fishy about Millie's new 'romance.' Heck, he may have even suspected Forrest was dealing drugs. Millie let it slip to 'Oloff' that Ira was asking questions. Forrest, or his buddy, or both, concocted a way to get Ira to take a lethal amount of drugs because they needed to keep him from convincing Millie to end her romance, therefore cutting off the cash cow."

Mendez clapped, and Larson took a bow.

The chief's eyes held no amusement. "Did you find evidence at either residence to support this theory?"

Mendez spoke up. "Sir, we found evidence that Leon has been living at the apartment with Forrest longer than he said in his interview. He's more than a couch-crasher. There is a bedroom full of his stuff, and . . ." He had a gleam in his eye as if his next words would seal the deal. "We found ten thousand dollars in cash stuffed between the mattresses of his bed."

Meyers glanced up from his writing. "Wait, sorry, whose bed had the cash?"

Larson nodded appreciatively. "Very pertinent question, Officer Meyers."

The young man grinned.

"Excuse me. I should have been more clear," said Mendez. "That's Leon's bed, not Forrest's."

Mendez smiled cordially at Jefferson and Rory, his teeth bright against his copper skin. "Sorry, my friends, but I think my partner is right."

"You're just now mentioning that little detail?" asked Rory.

Larson shrugged. "I had to get my coffee."

Jefferson ran a hand through his hair, blowing out a breath. "Wow. You really pulled that together. I'm impressed and truly fascinated by your new evidence." He raised his lips in a crooked smile. "If only it worked."

He glanced at Amber. Until now, she'd observed with a neutral expression. She likely already guessed where he was going.

This time it was his turn to stand. He picked up a dry-erase marker and drew a line.

"Let's do a little timeline exercise, shall we?"

Rory groaned and slid down in his seat. "Why does this feel like school?"

Jefferson ignored him. "Let's put Forrest's death here at the beginning, based on our ME's estimate of when he died." He put a dot and labeled it F.

He turned back to the group. "Now this was at least a day before Ira died."

Meyers had drawn an exact copy of the timeline on his paper and was following in rapt attention. Jefferson smiled to himself as he wondered if this what teaching felt like for MJ.

"Here," he said drawing another dot after Ira's death, "is where Rory and I arrested Leon at Forrest's apartment."

With a professorial air, he turned to Larson. "Are you following along so far."

Larson smirked. "Oh, I'm following along. I'm just wondering when you're going to blow up my theory."

"Let's see if this helps." Jefferson drew another dot after Leon was arrested. "So, at this point, Forrest is dead and Leon is here, in jail."

"Oh, crap," said Larson.

"I see you're catching on." Above the dot he wrote MJ's note. Then he drew another dot. "We have MJ's threat, and here," he said at the last dot, "here is today. This morning, to be more specific. This is when Millie Van Buren had her latest communication with Oloff."

Mendez wasn't ready to back down. "Maybe they have another partner, someone not on the board yet."

Jefferson put the marker back in the tray. "Could be. There definitely is another player. Oloff. The question is whether the man behind the persona has a connection to Forrest and Leon."

Amber sat up, joining the discussion for the first time. "And the most urgent question has to be how much danger are Millie and MJ in? If Millie is still communicating with Oloff, she's likely told him that two detectives came to visit. She blames MJ for meddling in her business."

Amber's earnest reminder that lives were a stake immediately squelched the sarcasm and banter. And she wasn't done.

"If a connection exists between all these pieces, in some twisted way, then we know this Oloff person, or group, will kill to stay hidden. And as you all know, desperate criminals will escalate. In this case, ramping up the financial demands on Millie, getting as much money as possible before they cut her off. We need to get Millie on our side. Now."

The chief mulled all this over. "I agree with everything SAC Wells has said. I am also troubled by the possibility we are dealing with multiple people, unknowns that have so far escaped our notice."

He turned to Meyers, whose hand must have been cramping by now. "Grab another officer. Someone with computer skills. Research whether we've had local reports of suspicious online activity or scam complaints, especially from older folks, as they seem to be a favorite target."

"Chief, we should add Senior Strength to the board," suggested Jefferson. "I'm not sure it's related, but we know that Ira, Millie, and Forrest all have ties to the place."

"Good thinking. Larson, you and I will take another crack at Leon. Mendez do a dive on the owner and the other employees. See what you come up with."

Rory tutted. "Will that be an interview or an interrogation? Where is our state-appointed instructor, anyway?"

"Jackson, that line is getting old," warned the chief. "The truth is we can all do better in that area, but for the time being, I've suggested Valencia adjust his schedule, take a break until we wrap up this investigation."

No one rejoiced out loud, but satisfaction showed on every detective's face

"Good call," said Rory.

The chief stared at him. "Would I make the call if it wasn't a good one?"

"Of course not, sir."

Shaking his head in annoyance, the chief continued. "Jefferson and Rory, you need to get Millie to cooperate. Perhaps Amber could be some help there."

She nodded. "Of course."

"And Jefferson," the chief added. "For heaven's sake, make sure MJ is safe and not getting herself into any more danger than she already is."

Chapter
Thirty-Seven

M illie's hands shook as she read Oloff's latest message. Tonight, the fingers of her left hand were unusually stiff as she tried to stretch them apart.

"What did you tell them?"

He'd told her in the past not to give people too much information about him. According to Oloff, the government in Zimbabwe would yank his permits if they sensed anything corrupt about his clinics. Having other people ask questions might make them suspicious, even if the questions were innocent.

Had she said too much? What if the police started digging around Oloff's business? She could ruin everything for him.

"Your name. I'm sorry. I didn't know what to do."

"Why did they come? Did your kids call them?"

What? Why did he keep blaming her kids? "No," she typed. "It's still about Ira."

"With your house for sale. Kids might know."

She didn't think that was it. None of her kids had called to ask about the sale. She hadn't told them a thing, and she couldn't think of anyone else who might tell them?

"My daughter lives in Virginia and my son is in the army, stationed in Germany. I don't think they know."

"We can't be sure. Sorry, love. They should call you more."

A pang speared her heart. Millie never admitted how much her children's lack of attention hurt her. They were busy with their own lives, their own children. That was the lie she used to comfort herself. There was truth to that statement, but it was a dishonest truth. They would make time to visit if she were an important part of their lives.

But Oloff knew the truth. He knew her heart in ways no one else ever had. Even her husband.

Before she could respond, Oloff had typed a new message.

"Are police watching you? Your house?"

What a strange question. Why would the police spend their time watching her?

"I don't think so. Why do you ask?"

"Do they blame you for Ira?"

Blinking, she read the question again, her hand clutching her shirt collar. The dramatic shift in subjects had her mind reeling. Was there a chance Oloff could be right again? The police said they suspected a criminal from Ira's detective days. What if they were lying?

The hair on her arm stood up at the thought of being watched. She had to know.

Slowly, she got to her feet, taking a second to stretch her hips and calves before walking stiffly to the dining room at the front of the house. Once there, she pulled aside the lace curtain and peered into the street. As usual, it was quiet in front of her house. One block down, a parked black car seemed to stare at her with its dead headlights. It appeared empty, but she couldn't be sure in the gray day's shadowy light.

Stepping back, she dropped the curtain, her pulse racing. With a thump, her heart warned her to calm down. She closed her eyes and took a series of deep breaths. When the beats slowed to normal, she slowly worked her way back to the office.

"Millie?"

"Are you still there?"

"Millie?"

She'd forgotten to tell Oloff before stepping away from the computer. Guilt pushed into her already overcrowded emotional space. He was so busy, and here she was wasting his time.

"Sorry. I was checking the street. I don't see anyone watching."

"I'm worried. About you and my clinics. I don't want our plans to fail."

Millie bit her thumbnail. What did he expect her to do?

An acrid juice churned up in her stomach, replacing the elation that so recently bubbled there. How could she have been so happy just an hour ago? Now that her plans were in motion, Millie couldn't imagine not being with Oloff.

"What should I do?"

"It will be fine, my love. Just move money now. I will get you a plane ticket and set up accounts here. Then no one will stop you."

"How?"

"Hired an international money security expert. In West Sound."

Shocked, Millie stared at the screen. She'd never heard of such a thing, but then she'd never traveled or lived outside of the United States.

Surely this had to prove how much Oloff wanted this to work. He wasn't waiting for her to take care of everything. He knew this part would be hard for her.

"That makes me feel better."

"He needs an initial cash deposit to start. Is that a problem, my love?"

"No, of course not. How much should I have?"

"$10,000."

Millie sucked in a breath. She wasn't even sure the bank would let her take out that much money.

"Bank will allow it," wrote Oloff, reading her mind. "His name is Jessie. Will contact you later for a meeting. Get the cash today."

Chapter Thirty-Eight

The sight of Edgar floating in the raging waters of the sound haunted MJ throughout the night.

It wasn't real, but it had come too close to real.

Her mind replayed the vision during the school day, every minute that wasn't consumed by students. Being busy kept the anger at bay.

But it was Friday before winter break, a half day at school. By lunchtime, MJ was free to grow angrier each time the memory of last night resurfaced, which was too often.

Someone came into her yard. That same person touched her dog, led him to the beach where he almost drowned. They threatened Edgar's life trying to scare her.

Earlier, Shannon had tried to calm her down as she relayed the story, but it was a halfhearted attempt. Of course, she'd been sympathetic and worried, but her friend's mind had its own all-consuming distraction: her impending date with Jefferson. She'd made MJ promise to go shopping with her tonight. It felt sort of like being asked to dig your own grave, but MJ had agreed. At least she would have a few hours to prepare with school getting out early.

For now, MJ pushed thoughts of Jefferson and Shannon away, focusing instead on her next steps to discover who left that note. No matter what it took, she would figure it out. Whoever threatened her dog had made a big mistake.

In the daylight, Justin had done a full search of her yard and the beach. Any footprints in the sand had been washed away by the tide scrubbing the beach has it had for thousands of years. A few broken branches near the house could have been a hiding place, but with the wind sending twigs and boughs flying all night, Justin couldn't be sure. None of the neighbors saw anything unusual, but none of them were looking, most having already gone to bed. The homes near MJ were set back far enough from the road that a random car could drive in and out without being seen from a window.

MJ guessed that whoever tied up Edgar escaped by walking farther down the beach to the access stairs at a neighbor's house. With the wind howling, they could easily sneak into someone's yard and out to the road without being heard or seen. What she couldn't fathom was someone waiting outside, in the freezing wind, for her to let Edgar out. That was some dedication. And how did they avoid being seen by the detectives or Shannon?

Those were questions for another day. Today, the only question she wanted answered was who.

And it all started with Millie and Ira. Someone didn't like her checking on Millie Van Buren. Someone obviously thought MJ was onto their scam. That someone knew Ira, who also suspected or knew that Oloff was a predator.

By the time she left school, MJ knew where she would start.

***

When she pulled up to the strip mall, MJ questioned whether the maps program on her phone had misdirected her. This did not look like a gym.

Sure enough, though, a small sign with the words "Senior Strength" hung above a set of glass doors tinted too dark for her to see through.

This was it, and it looked shady. Why the small sign and tinted doors? It reminded her of the massage parlors down by the Shopside Docks. Everyone knew they weren't really massage parlors.

She prepared herself to leave the warm Bronco. The cold persisted, taking a toll on her skin. Her hands and feet felt like sandpaper, all the moisture being sapped by the wind outside and the heaters running inside.

This morning, she'd almost woken Justin to grill him about this place, but he was dead to the world. After their long night with Edgar, she let him sleep in peace. He was the only reason she felt comfortable going inside this place. Justin wouldn't volunteer at a shady organization. Not knowingly, anyway.

She reached for the door handle, pausing briefly to plan what she would say. Nothing came to mind. But she was well-trained to fly by the seat of her pants. Every teacher had days where even the best-laid plans flew out the window, requiring the ability to think on your feet. She was good at that. At least with eighth graders.

Taking a deep breath of her festering anger for strength and inspiration, she opened the door. Now or never.

A young man looked up from his task of folding towels to greet MJ as she walked in.

"Good afternoon," he said, with a mystified smile. "Are you here for tickets to the ball?"

MJ wrinkled her brow until she noticed the poster for the Christmas Ball on the counter. It was the same ad posted at the senior center.

"No, I already have my ticket."

"Oh, cool. Senior Strength is one of the major sponsors." He pushed his pile of towels to the side while giving her a sneaky once over.

Pretending she didn't notice, MJ glanced around the foyer. On the left side of the desk, a wall of windows showed the workout room. Someone must have opened a door she couldn't see as strains of a Beach Boy's song grew loud and then soft again. The area to the right had a line of closed doors.

"I'm Shane, by the way," he said with too much hope. "I love your sweater."

MJ turned back to him, unable to hide her bemused smile. This kid had to be at least ten years younger than her, but he was determined to try. He had his arms folded on top of the counter, as if she'd just stopped by for a flirty chat.

She gave her sweater a tug and the enormous Christmas tree on the front lit up and started playing "Deck the Halls."

"I'm a middle school teacher," she explained. "Today was ugly sweater day. And my name's MJ. I'd like to see Forrest."

Had she imagined that quick clench of his jaw? Or the change in his eyes. They were looking at her, but they lost focus, like a deer in the headlights.

"Forrest?" his cheerful smile was still there, but she detected a tad more distance in his voice.

Or had she imagined all of it?

"I think he's a trainer here," she said.

This time, there was no mistaking the disappearing smile or the shadow that passed over Shane's face.

He cleared his throat. "I better get my manager."

She cocked her head. "Okay. If you think that's necessary."

Shane offered a pinched smile as he picked up the phone. "Sorry Eden, can you come out here? Someone named MJ is here to talk to Forrest. Thanks."

"She'll be right out," he said, hanging up the phone.

Within seconds, MJ heard a door close and a pony-tailed redhead in leggings and a Senior Strength sweatshirt came into the foyer, her head down as she finished something on her phone.

Stuffing it in the side pocket of her leggings, the woman approached MJ. "Sorry," she said with a sigh. "Vendor issues for our latest shake mix. It's never ending." A friendly smile broke out on her face, but her eyes didn't follow. "I'm Eden. You must be MJ."

The woman had shocking green eyes, and they were taking in MJ as if appraising a car on the sales lot.

"Yep, that's me," MJ smiled. "I wanted to talk to Forrest?"

"Follow me," said Eden, still scrutinizing MJ. "Let's go to my office."

MJ was more confused than ever as she sat across from the manager in her strangely empty office. Not one for decorating, apparently.

"So, MJ," said Eden. "Do you mind if I ask why you want to see Forrest?"

"Is he here?" MJ asked, not ready to share her reason for coming.

Eden pursed her lips and shook her head. "No. Forrest has been missing for a few days. He hasn't shown up for work. The police are involved. It's a whole mess. We've had to shift his clients to other trainers." She watched MJ like she expected her to suddenly burst into flames.

"You mean Justin."

A slow smile crept up her face. Then she openly gave MJ the same once over treatment Shane had. Except this was more like three times over. It was then that MJ remembered Justin mentioning Eden's name. Was there more than friendship there? She guessed Eden would like that.

"Yes, like Justin. And I remember him telling me about an MJ causing trouble." She steepled her hands on the desk. "I guess that's you."

"Um, you could say that. He's my ex-husband."

Eden eyes flew open like this was a revelation, but MJ didn't believe it. Obviously Justin had told Eden about her. "No kidding? Wow. That must have been hard."

"I think divorce is always hard."

"No, I mean having *him* divorce you. He's such a god."

MJ tried to maintain a straight face. "Oh. Yes. Very hard."

"Yeah. I thought so."

Trying to clear the air of Justin worship, MJ returned to Forrest. "I know Forrest was training a man named Ira Newman."

"Oh yes, poor Ira. We loved that guy here."

"Of course," MJ continued. "Do you know if Forrest ever trained a woman named Millie Van Buren?"

Eden touched a finger to her chin. "Millie . . . I think I remember meeting a Millie, but she never joined. Why do you ask?"

"Millie and Ira were friends. Ira seems to have found some information about Millie that it would be good to know, that's all. I hoped to ask Forrest about it."

"Are you with the police?"

"Not officially."

Eden smiled and stood, pulling out her phone and swiping up the screen. "I wouldn't worry about it too much, MJ. As a gym owner, I don't get into other people's drama. There's way too much, if you know what I mean. I just stick to minding my own business."

A chill froze MJ to the spot. She stared at Eden, her pulse pounding in her ears.

"What did you say?"

"What? Oh, I said, it's time to mind my business. Get back to work. I'm sorry I couldn't help more."

***

MJ pulled out of the parking lot, her mind swirling with questions.

How much of that was her imagination?

Eden obviously had her sights set on Justin. She wondered exactly what Justin had said about her. Did Eden see her as a threat?

And then Eden's comment. Had she said "mind her own business" or "mind her business?"

"I'm going nuts," MJ said to herself as she turned left.

It was then that she noticed the black Honda making the turn with her. Hadn't that car been behind her when she left Senior Strength?

If the day wasn't so oppressively dark with clouds, she could see the driver. However, her frequent glances in the rearview and side mirrors only revealed a shadow in the driver's seat.

Looking ahead, MJ saw a Safeway on the next corner. When she reached it, she cranked the wheel and took a random right turn. The Honda stayed with her.

She wasn't officially worried yet. There were hundreds of reasons for the Honda to go this direction and following her wasn't even in the top ten. No need to worry, she told herself. Just breathe.

The road she turned onto was four lanes. MJ slowed to an annoying speed to see if the other driver would pass her. With the speed limit of the road posted as thirty-five, the Bronco putted along at thirty miles per hour. The black car devotedly trailed behind her, not any closer and not any farther away.

Other cars flew past them, one driver even honked, jerking his head back to hurl a string of words she thankfully couldn't hear.

Twenty-five miles per hour. The car still followed.

Swallowing her fear, MJ switched into the other lane. The Honda switched with her.

Gritting her teeth, MJ realized she wasn't afraid. Now she was just mad. No one would terrorize her like this. She refused to let them have that power.

Jerking the wheel, MJ switched back to the other lane and hit the gas. The black car tried to follow, but she'd caught him off guard. At the next intersection, she took a hard right. Looking in her rearview, she could see that the Honda had not yet appeared. It wouldn't take long for him to be right behind her. She took a quick left.

This was closer to downtown. The long strips of shops offered several dark alleyways to get lost in. Before the Honda caught up to her, MJ picked one, turning right and pulling behind a dumpster. She turned off the Bronco and jumped out of the car.

Still not seeing the Honda, she ran to a dumpster a few shops down. There, she wedged herself between the dumpster and the brick wall.

Breathing hard, she gagged as the smell of rotting food combined with old urine assaulted her lungs. She pulled her sweater over her nose, which only blocked the foul odor enough to keep her from throwing up.

As she waited, the cold seeped into her bones. She hoped the Honda driver would show up soon. Pulling out her phone, she prepared to snap some pictures of the jerk. Was there a chance the guy wasn't actually following her? Perhaps. More likely, whoever was behind the wheel of that car was the same person who threatened Edgar, and by proxy, her. She'd be ready to make sure he didn't get away with it.

Chapter Thirty-Nine

"So, Jeffy, where are you taking Shannon on your first date?" asked Rory as he drove to Millie's house.

Jefferson looked out the window, ignoring him. Every time he remembered his scheduled date tomorrow, he pushed it out of his mind. He didn't have time to think about it. This is the reason he'd been single for so long. Romance was so much work.

Amber, in the passenger seat, shook her head at Rory.

"Okay, forget that question. I have a better one. How do you plan to keep MJ out of trouble as the chief so indelicately ordered today?"

"She can't get into too much trouble while she's teaching. I'll worry about that later."

Rory shot him a look in the rearview mirror. "Dude. You don't know, do you?"

"What?" Involuntary alarm bells sounded in his head.

"It's the last day before Christmas Break. It's a half day. She's probably been out of school for hours."

Amber shot Jefferson a stern look. "Millie has to be our priority right now. I'm sure MJ is fine."

"I know. I'll just call her to check in." He flashed her a crooked smile, though his pulse was not in smile mode. "Chief's orders."

He opened MJ's contact information and hit call. Holding the phone to his ear, he willed her to answer.

She didn't. The call went to voicemail.

He tried again. Voicemail again.

"She's not answering," he said, staring at his phone. "I'll send a text."

"She's fine, Jeff. MJ can take care of herself," assured Amber.

"I know."

He wrote, "MJ, please call me."

MJ can take care of herself, but she was also fantastic at getting herself into trouble. Someone threatened her dog. Edgar meant the world to her. When MJ cared about someone, that's when she could be the most reckless with her own safety. Unfortunately, he couldn't imagine the MJ he knew sitting idly by, waiting for the perpetrator to do more than make threats.

***

Jefferson's mind was nowhere near Millie's house as Rory knocked on the door.

MJ still hadn't texted him back, and his danger senses were going berserk, stealing his focus from the task at hand.

They stood on the massive porch, insulated slightly from the cold. Amber held a computer case in her gloved hands.

So far, no Millie. Rory rang the doorbell.

Jefferson stepped around to one of the lace-curtained windows.

"Can't see much," he said, "but I don't see any lights."

"She could be hiding in there," suggested Rory. "We're not her best friends."

"Could this be her?" asked Amber.

Jefferson and Rory followed her gaze to see a silver Mercedes sedan moving down the road toward the house.

Sure enough, as the car got closer, the garage door opened. The sedan pulled into the driveway with an annoyed Millie at the wheel.

The three of them left the porch, following the walkway down to the garage. There, they waited for Millie to disembark.

She met them with hostile eyes as she clutched her purse close to her chest. If he didn't know any better, Jefferson would think she'd mistaken them for muggers.

"What do you all want?" she glowered.

"Hello, again, Millie. We brought an associate with us today," said Jefferson. "This is Special Agent Amber Wells."

Millie scrunched up her face. "Special agent? The FBI?"

Amber nodded. "Yes, Mrs. Van Buren. It's a pleasure to meet you. Can we go inside?"

"I can't." She shook her head. "I promised. I can't talk to you anymore." She pulled her purse even closer to her body.

"Mrs. Van Buren, I assure you that what we need to show you is important. I wouldn't have joined the detectives if I didn't believe you could be in real danger."

The woman turned and looked down the street, a look of fear on her face. "Do you have people watching me?"

There were no people or cars to be seen.

The three looked at each other. "No," replied Rory. "Has someone been watching you?"

"Maybe . . ." Her eyes skittered down the street again. "Fine. A few minutes."

Once in the house, Amber opened her laptop case. Millie sat in a recliner, still clutching her purse. Jefferson wondered what she had in there. It clearly made her nervous.

Then he realized that he was the nervous one. MJ needed to call him back or he would be useless in this interview. It wasn't that he didn't trust MJ to take care of herself. He just wasn't sure she was fully aware of the danger. She didn't know that Forrest, someone too closely connected to Millie and Ira, was dead. The stakes were higher than MJ knew.

"I don't know what's going on," complained Millie. "But this all started when that school teacher started getting in my business. We were just fine before that."

"She has a name," said Jefferson quietly, surprising himself.

Millie stared at him. So did Rory and Amber, eyes wide.

"Jeff, maybe now—" Amber started before he cut her off.

"Her name is MJ. And do you know why MJ came to see you?"

Millie remained silently frozen in place.

He plowed ahead, not waiting for an answer. "She came to see you because one of her students was worried about you. That young girl worried you would be alone when you heard the news about Ira Newman."

"I . . . I didn't know that," faltered Millie.

Jefferson didn't know what was happening to him, but he felt something like a fever overtaking him. Sweat broke out across his forehead and his tie suddenly felt like a noose. He loosened it and then ran a hand through his hair.

"Jeff," Amber said, touching his hand. "Are you okay?"

Rory grinned. "Maybe I pushed him a little too hard," he whispered to Amber.

"Then," Jefferson said, standing up and thrusting his finger into the air. "Then MJ came over here on her own time, of her own free will to check on a woman she barely knows. And do you know why?"

Millie shook her head, her face a mask of either fear or intense interest.

"Because MJ Brooks, as stubborn and frustrating as she can be, cares about you. She cares about her students. She just cares. MJ is one of the best people I know. In the entire world. She would never try to hurt you."

"Or you."

Amber said it so quietly, he almost missed it. His wild eyes landed on her, the truth of her words hitting the center of his hidden hopes, lighting them with new life.

He stared at Amber, but his eyes saw MJ. "I have to cancel that date."

Amber grinned as Rory chuckled. "About time, partner."

With a raised palm, Amber signaled for Jefferson to put the brakes on his revelation. "But not right now. You can sort it out later. I'm sure MJ will wait, because we need to get to work."

Jefferson nodded with what he knew was a crazy, unfocused grin. He was a caged animal, suddenly set free.

Chapter Forty

MJ's feet were close to numb and her lunch close to regurgitating when the Honda finally appeared.

She stood just enough to watch as the Honda crept up on the Bronco. The driver seemed to be a man, but MJ still couldn't get a clear view of the person, and it didn't help that he wore a beanie and sunglasses. When the Honda pulled up beside the Bronco, she shrank back to stay hidden behind the dumpster If she were still in the Bronco, he would have trapped her inside.

MJ held her breath as the driver's door opened. She couldn't see him, but she could hear him.

"She's not here. Just the ugly beast of a car she drives."

That voice. She knew it.

"I'll look around, but I'm not freezing my tush off out here for anyone, even you, sweetie. I already did that once. Why do you even care so much about this annoying wench? This is stupid."

MJ stuffed her hands under her armpits. He must be on the phone. No one else had been in the car.

Now she knew for sure that this man had been following her. Was it possible he'd followed her to Senior Strength? Did he follow her to work and home? Watch her house? She wanted to believe that couldn't happen without her noticing, but was it true? A potential stalker of some kind should scare her, and it did, to an extent. But the overwhelming emotion fueling her at the moment was still anger.

He was still talking. "Oh come on. You know grandma, the old bag, called everyone a wench. And I've done what you asked, so back off."

Suddenly, MJ's phone buzzed in her hand.

Jefferson's name flashed on the screen. She silenced it, praying the man hadn't heard it buzzing. Luckily, he seemed too engaged in his phone conversation.

"Should I take a crowbar to her car. That'd be more fun than drowning a dog. That was just wrong, hon."

MJ covered her mouth, forcing herself to stay quiet. What she wanted to do was run out from behind this putrid dumpster and . . . and what? That was the problem.

No, she needed to stay quiet and wait for an opportunity to get a picture.

Her phone buzzed again.

Jefferson.

Leave it to the detective to give away her position.

But the man had moved away from her car now, walking down the alley. She had a clear view of his back.

Her phone buzzed a third time, this time with a text. And this time, the man turned. But before MJ saw him or could snap a picture, the door directly in front of her opened. A heavy-set man in an apron covered in what she hoped was red sauce stood there holding a bag of trash.

"Hey—"

MJ put her finger to her mouth and motioned with her head toward the man walking down the alley.

The big man's eyes narrowed as he watched the Honda man coming nearer, probably thinking he was some kind of abusive boyfriend. "What are you doing back here, man?"

"What? It's a free country, friend," replied the Honda man.

Bad choice of words.

The aproned man glanced down at MJ with a glint in his eye.

MJ made a picture taking motion at him, and the man, quickly understanding, winked at her.

He set down his bag of trash to take out his own phone. Then he yelled, "Smile, before I throw you in this dumpster, you piece of trash."

Shrinking back to stay out of view, MJ almost laughed out loud at this line.

"What? Hey, you can't take my picture."

"Just did. Now, if anyone reports trouble in this alley, I'll be sending it to the cops."

"Hey hon, no need to do that. I was just leaving."

"Don't 'hon' me, you freaking weirdo," said the big man as he picked up his bag of trash and threw it away. "Now get outta here before I throw you through your windshield."

"Going," the man said as he opened the car door. After a few seconds, the engine started, and he drove away.

MJ slowly stood up. "Thank you."

"Are you in some kind of trouble?" the man asked.

"Not anymore," she said.

"Here's your picture," he said, holding up his phone.

MJ studied it for a moment before letting out a gasp.

"What?"

She shook her head. "Nothing. It's just not who I expected." She opened her camera and took a picture of his phone. "Thank you, again. You saved me."

A gigantic smile spread across his face. "Well, that made my day, miss. Is that your rig?"

She nodded. "Pretty, huh?"

"It's a beaut."

"What's the name of your place here?"

"Danny's Pasta Palace." He stuck his chest out. "I'm the owner."

"I'll have to try it out sometime. You're Danny?"

"Yep, Danny Morreti."

"I'm MJ. And this was a weird way to meet, but it's been a pleasure."

He smiled shyly. "I'll keep watch while you get in your car."

"Thanks, Danny."

As she climbed inside the Bronco, MJ took a second to read Jefferson's text. "MJ, please call me."

Chapter Forty-One

Faced with all the evidence, Millie crumbled in front of their eyes. It was the profile of Scott Dixon that did it. The differences between his real profile and Oloff's fake one were obvious.

She cried as Amber held her hand. Jefferson looked on, his anger growing by the second. This could be his own mother. Like Millie, she was a widow, having lost his father, the love of her life, a year ago. These scammers were so insidious in the way they studied the lives of their victims to make their connections feel real. Jefferson's mother wasn't stupid, and neither was Millie, but under the right circumstances, lies and deception could cloud anyone's judgement.

"I feel like such a fool. Poor Ira. He knew." She buried her head in her hands. "He knew."

"That's why we need your help, Millie," said Amber. "We need to stop this person before they can hurt anyone else."

The woman lifted her head. "How? How can I help?"

Amber smiled gently. "How do you feel about scamming the scammer?"

Through the tears, a glint shone in Millie's eyes. "I'd like that very much."

***

"I have the money," she typed.

"My love! Our plans can finally happen."

Amber, her hands on the keyboard, said, "What's the courier's name?"

"Jessie," said Millie.

Amber typed her next message. "I just need to give it to Jessie? Is he going to call?"

Oloff's response followed almost instantly. "He got tied up. Asked me to set up meeting."

Jefferson and Rory looked on. "This should be interesting," said Rory, taking a sip of coffee he'd made in the kitchen.

Jefferson took out his phone as it buzzed in his pocket.

"MJ" flashed across the screen, sending a flood of relief through him.

When he clicked the message, a picture came up of a man walking in an alley. He looked vaguely familiar, but he wore a black beanie large sunglasses that partially concealed his face.

He showed it to Rory. "Where did we see this guy?"

Rory inspected the photo with narrowed eyes. Then he grinned, his eyes relaxing. "How could you forget, sweetie?" he said in the worst southern accent ever.

Millie shot a look at Rory. "You mean Ned at the senior center? That man is annoying. I'm not his honey or sweetie. He always gave me the creeps."

"Me too," said Rory. "Why are you carrying pictures of Ned on your phone, Jeffy?"

Ignoring his partner's latest attempt at humor, Jefferson opened the next message from MJ.

"This guy followed me. I think he's the one who tried to hurt Edgar. He's working with someone else."

"Where are you now?" he texted back.

"Shannon's house. Edgar is with Justin. We're all okay."

Jefferson smiled at the phone.

"Can we focus here?" chided Amber.

"Sorry," said Jefferson. "What do you have?"

"Oloff says the courier doesn't want to meet at his office or at Millie's because he fears the police are watching. All of this is under a guise, created by Oloff, that Millie's children are behind a plot to stop her from moving and taking their inheritance to Africa." Amber shook her head. "This is almost enough to make me swear."

"That would be awesome. I think it's about time you buy us all dinner," Rory said.

"I said almost." She stared at the screen. "Okay, here it is. He says the courier wants to meet at the Christmas Ball." She turned to Millie. "That's the one at the senior center, right? Jerry and I went a couple of years ago."

"Yes," said Millie. "It's a big deal. Hundreds of people will be there. It's tomorrow night."

Jefferson read the screen over Amber's shoulder. "So he wants it public. Easy to get lost in the crowd once he has the cash."

"That'd be my guess," agreed Amber.

Rory set his coffee down on the desk.

Millie stood up and grabbed a cork-centered coaster and handed it to him.

"Oh, sorry," he said, placing it under his mug. "Doesn't this seem like a lot of work for ten thousand dollars?"

Amber turned to Millie. "How much are you asking for this house?"

"Well, I won't be selling it now."

"But when you were selling it, what was the list price?"

"One and a half million."

"Oh," said Rory. "Wow."

Jefferson whistled. "That's a pretty penny. And they were in it for the long haul."

"Until MJ stuck her nose in it," Millie said with a smile at Jefferson.

For a heartbeat, the room went silent. Then they all burst out laughing.

Chapter Forty-Two

M eyers and Evie Hanson had been busy.

"We've found at least three hundred and fifty complaints of online scams just this year," said Meyers.

Evie nodded. "Some were for products that were defective or had misleading advertising. Others were false links designed to get the victims' bank information. And some are just fake messages meant to infect computers with malware."

"The most relevant are the ten cases of seniors defrauded by fake accounts," continued Meyers. "Of those, seven were at one time members of Senior Strength. And even more horrifying, six have since passed away from 'natural causes.'"

"What? How have these not come to our attention until now?" asked Jefferson.

"Most cases get reported months or years after a death," said Evie. "Families try to recover lost money, but the trail goes cold. Often the money gets stolen in fake cryptocurrency apps or exchanges. The scammers get the money and then the app or exchange disappears."

"If Millie had sold her house," said Amber, "Oloff likely planned to have her drop the proceeds into a fake crypto account."

The chief glanced around the briefing room. "Is Jared joining us?"

Amber raised a hand. "He asked that I share his report."

No more needed to be said. They all knew how much Jared hated the spotlight.

"Of course," said the chief, turning to face her. "Please go ahead."

Referencing a paper report, she began. "Forrest Bernard's computer held documents consistent with online fraud activities, including image searches, copying of images from legitimate profiles, and KIT profiles for several users open on his computer. One of those was Oloff. Until his death, Forrest had been operating online in that persona, as well as others. Jared has outlined all those names here in the report, so I won't go through them all. He also found email exchanges with the username paradisered. This person may be orchestrating the schemes."

Meyers jumped up and wrote the username on the whiteboard.

Amber continued. "There is an exchange in which Forrest expresses a loss of interest in the scheme. He suggests the client is asking too many questions. This may refer to Ira, Jared believes, based on what he found on Ira's computer. Paradisered clarifies that there is no backing out. Make of that what you will." Amber smiled. "That's Jared's note."

"Sounds like Forrest grew a conscience," said Larson.

"Probably what got him murdered," added Jefferson.

The chief rubbed his chin, a sheen on his eyes. "Still investigating, to the end."

The room fell quiet. The chief cleared his throat. "Please, continue."

"Jared found nothing to show Leon Albright knew anything about the scams. No one has logged onto Forrest's computer since he went missing."

"That jives with our interview with him," said Larson. "But he's deeper into the drug trade than he led us to believe, so he's not going anywhere."

Amber took a sip of water. "Ira's computer showed extensive searches about online scamming and searches directly related to Oloff Svensson. It also showed a search for Advik Peterson. So, Ira somehow found Forrest's real name. And there was an article about Advik's illegal activities while working with Hampton and Cole Care International."

"Sounds like he connected Forrest to Millie's scam boyfriend. I wonder if he planned to confront him," said Jefferson. "Justin said he seemed distracted and upset that Forrest wasn't at the gym."

"Someone beat him to it," said Mendez.

Larson, chewing on a straw, said it for all of them. "Paradisered."

"And that is the report as of today," Amber said, dropping the paper on the table.

The chief looked around the table. "Who else do we need to add to our board?"

"The owner of the gym checks out," said Larson. "We found nothing on any of the other employees either. Just a few complaints about the shakes and supplements being a rip-off, but hey, what's new?"

"I've got something." Jefferson had printed out the picture sent by MJ. He slid it across the table to Meyers, who put it up with a magnet.

"This is Ned," said Jefferson. "We don't have a last name yet, and it's possible Ned is not his real name. These guys seem to like aliases. He works at the senior center." He took a deep breath. "This guy followed MJ today after she visited Senior Strength."

He put his hand up before anyone could ask the obvious question. "Don't ask me why she went to Senior Strength. We all know MJ."

He put his hand down. "She also heard this man on the phone with someone who sounded like the boss. Ned specifically mentioned the attempt to harm MJ's dog."

Larson threw his hands up. "So why don't we just arrest this guy now? Squeeze all the info out of him. That'd be fun. I hate people who are mean to dogs."

"I think we all do," said Amber. "But we don't want to spook the head of the snake. Plus, we have a much better case if we catch them taking cash from a victim in the flesh. Digital trails are too easy to lose. Arresting Ned would alert the rest of the actors and send them scurrying."

Mendez held his head to the side, staring at Jefferson with a curious squint to his eyes. "Is this Ned's interest in MJ for certain connected to Ira and Millie?"

Amber jumped in before he could give a reply. "I can answer that. When MJ visited Millie, she popped up on the scammers radar as someone who might mess up their scheme. I've read Millie's previous chats with Oloff. She mentions the 'nosy teacher,' which caused Oloff to ask questions. Through his conversations with Millie, Oloff obtained MJ's name and information about where she lives."

Larson let out a whistle. "Dang. This is all so messed up. So if we can't start arresting people, what's the plan?"

Amber grinned, somewhat wickedly, Jefferson thought. Then she glanced at the chief, who gave her a stiff nod.

"Ladies and gentlemen, cancel your Saturday plans and call up your fairy godmothers. You're all going to the ball."

***

At home, showered and in his sweats, Jefferson sat in front of the TV. The first round game of the College Football Playoffs ran on the screen. He didn't follow either team, and his mind was not on football.

After Amber outlined the plan, the chief sent them all home with permission to sleep in. Tomorrow would be a late night. But before then, he had to do an unpleasant, uncomfortable task.

His phone stared back at him. Not the blank screen. He'd at least gotten as far as entering his pin and getting to the home screen where his niece and nephew, his brother George's kids, smiled at him They were both holding small fish they'd caught during a family camping trip last summer.

He could stare at it all night, but the phone wouldn't do it for him. Jefferson had to find her contact information and hit the call button. Putting it off wouldn't make it easier.

He had a good excuse. A major operation. The chief ordered them to cancel their plans. He was sure she'd understand.

But then there was the real reason he had to cancel.

He'd learned something from this case. People's hearts should be treated with care. Using them for your own gain, or as a stand-in for someone else, was wrong and cruel.

Dating Shannon would only lead to heartache, because the person Jefferson really wanted was too close to both of them.

He picked up the remote and muted the TV. Time to make the call.

Chapter Forty-Three

S hannon dropped the phone in her lap.

"What's the matter?" asked MJ.

Tears welled in her friend's eyes. "He canceled. They have a big operation happening for some case," she sniffled.

MJ grabbed her shoulders. "But he'll reschedule. I know they've been working on this case with Millie. It's probab—"

"MJ. I know you're trying to help, and I love you for it, but no, he won't reschedule." She wiped under her eyes with her sweatshirt sleeve. "He said it isn't going to work. He thinks I'm beautiful and smart, but he didn't think it would be fair to me. His heart is somewhere else."

MJ sat back against the couch. "He said that? I wonder what he meant?"

"Do you?"

She looked up to see Shannon's teary, gently accusing smile. "Come on, MJ. I didn't see it before, but the more I think about that interview . . ." She shook her head. "He couldn't keep his eyes off you."

An intense hammering started in MJ's chest. "No. I don't think so. It's got to be someone else. He thinks I'm annoying and that I just cause trouble."

"And you do, but I think that's exactly what he loves about you."

"Oh, don't say that word."

"Love."

"Stop."

"Love, love, love, love." Shannon laughed as she grabbed MJ in a tight hug. "I hate it. He's too good looking. So you have to find me one, okay?"

"One what?"

"A detective, of course."

"Stop it. Listen, no more guy talk, okay?"

Shannon let her go. "I was looking forward to shopping."

"Let's go then. In fact . . . let's go to the ball tomorrow. We both have tickets. Why not?"

With a finger on her lips, Shannon considered this proposal. "Yes! Let's do it. Dresses, heels, nails, up-dos, the whole deal." She jumped off the couch. "I'm going to change."

MJ had already changed out of her loud sweater. "Alright. I'll be ready."

When Shannon was gone, MJ rested her head against the back of the couch.

She knew her friend had put on a brave face for her. Jefferson's call had to be crushing.

But did he really mean MJ when he said his heart was somewhere else? She wanted to believe it, but then she didn't. The prospect scared her as much as it thrilled her. Opening her heart again meant accepting the possibility that it could get broken. Was she ready for that?

Chapter Forty-Four

J efferson adjusted his bow tie as he and Rory sat in the car watching the entrance to the senior center. That was when he saw the first snowflake. Then two, then three. He stuck his hand out of the widow to catch one, watching as it touched his skin, his heat melting it instantly.

"Here it comes," said Rory. "The snowstorm they've been promising. Too late for a snow day. The kids lost out again."

Larson and Mendez were already on their way into the building. Millie would enter just in front of them.

She wore a sparkling black shawl over her long black dress, her silver hair twisted into a bun at the base of her neck. On her head, she'd pinned a black hat with red feathers, an easy identifier as the detectives kept watch over her in the ballroom.

Millie had been nervous, but also determined to see this through. Jefferson couldn't believe how fast she went from heartbroken to resilient, or perhaps vengeful was the right word. Millie Van Buren was out for justice.

If everything went as planned, she would get it.

Larson would send them a signal when it was clear to enter. Since Jefferson and Rory had visited both the senior center and Millie previously, specifically to ask questions about Ira, they had to steer clear of Millie. If those conducting the scam suspected their target had involved the detectives, the whole deal would go south and put Millie in greater danger.

The chief was already inside the ball with his wife. He'd worn his dress uniform and made a show of professing police support for the senior center when he talked with the greeter, who was Ned.

Ned, the man who had followed MJ, was unaware the police had him on their radar. To keep him from suspecting anything to the contrary, the detectives needed to make their presence as unremarkable as possible. As far as the other guests knew, the police in attendance were there to show their support for the community.

The snowflakes had already doubled in size and speed. "Larson should have called by now," said Jefferson, closing the window and brushing snow from the arm of his tuxedo.

"Relax and enjoy the snow, Jeffy—Wait a second. Is that who I think it is? Uh-oh."

Jefferson looked up to see two women gingerly making their way through the snow to the entrance, both in impossibly high heels.

Jefferson slapped his forehead. "What are they doing here? Ned is right at the front entrance. She can't be in there with him."

She had to know Ned would be here What was MJ up to? "That's it. I'm going in." He opened the door and got out before Rory could stop him.

Rory huffed, but opened his door to join him. "Look, Jeffy," he said, holding out his phone.

It was a text from Larson. "Your turn, gents."

"Let's go." Jefferson only got one step in before Rory grabbed his arm.

"Look," he said. "I understand your concern for MJ, and you should look out for her, but don't forget why we're here."

"I won't."

Rory didn't let go. "I'm serious, Jefferson. Like really serious, not joking that I'm serious, but actually serious. We have to keep our heads in there."

"I get it," he said, removing Rory's hand from his arm. "Now let's go."

He sprinted toward the entrance, snowflakes plastering his face.

When Jefferson ran through the door, Ned immediately looked away from the couple he'd been welcoming. MJ was nowhere to be seen.

Ned surveyed Jefferson from head to toe with a strange combination of derision and awe.

Rory came in right on his partner's heels.

When the couple moved on, Ned fixed his full attention on the detectives.

"Do you have your tickets, gentlemen?"

"We're on the WSPD list. The department bought our tickets and then made us come to this, uh, party. As if I didn't have better things to do," complained Jefferson with his finest acting skills.

Ned glared. "Well, now that's just rude."

"I apologize for my partner," said Rory. "His girlfriend just broke up with him. You get it, right?"

"I get why she'd break up with such a grump." Ned rolled his eyes dismissively. "What are your names? I don't remember."

"Hughes and Jackson," answered Rory.

"Sounds like a country band," joked Ned as he marked their names on his list. "Which one are you?" he asked, his eyes on Rory.

"I'm Detective Jackson."

"Detective Jackson. You try to have fun with this crabby pants. Find him a new girl in there."

Rory sighed. "I'll try."

When they finally made it into the ballroom, normally the senior center cafeteria, Jefferson swore he could smell the lingering scent of boiled carrots.

"Do you see her?" asked Rory.

Jefferson scanned the dimly lit room. "Yes. Over there by the ice sculpture."

Rory followed his eyes to where MJ and Shannon were getting drinks. "Not them," Rory said in a biting whisper. "Millie. Have you seen Millie? Put your height to use and find her."

"Oh, wow."

"What? What's the matter?" asked Rory, searching the crowd.

"Justin and Stacey Underhill. Here together."

"Told you. But focus. Find Millie. If I find her first, God wasted those inches on you."

"There she is," Jefferson said. "Not now, but in a minute, look toward the Christmas tree in the back right corner. She's there talking to two women."

"An hour until drop time. Why didn't Amber, posing as online Millie, negotiate for an earlier time with Oloff? An hour in here might kill me," groaned Rory. "My wife was baking snickerdoodles."

"Hey, at least the music isn't bad." A live jazz band played Christmas tunes on a small stage nearby. Round tables outfitted in white tablecloths and cream candle centerpieces surrounded the dance floor in a semicircle. Three couples moved in slow circles to the band's rendition of "White Christmas."

On the wall farthest from them, guests waited in line along a table of food and drinks. White Christmas trees adorned with twinkling white lights reached for the ceiling in each corner of the room.

Jefferson looked out over the crowd. "Keep your eyes on Millie. I'm going to see who else is here."

As much as he tried to move his eyes around, they kept floating back to MJ. She wore a gold dress that had the perfect combination of glamor and class. It skimmed her figure perfectly, stopping just above her knees. Her hair was up, with sexy dark tendrils curling around her face and neck.

She hadn't seen him, and he almost didn't want her to. The next time they spoke, things would be different. He knew it. As much as he wanted it, he feared it at the same time. There was no bottling his feelings for her again.

"Hey partner," said Rory. "Have you seen anyone else? I mean, besides MJ. If I'd known Jefferson in love would be so annoying . . ."

"Hey now," said Jefferson. "Let's not jump the gun."

Rory just shook his head. "We should move around or we look weird or like we're on a date together, and you are definitely not my type. I'd say split up, but I don't trust you not to run off with MJ."

"You're being dramatic."

"You're being a Hallmark movie."

Jefferson scanned the crowd, ignoring Rory's last barb. "Hey, I see Eden from Senior Strength. She's sitting at a table eyeing Stacey Underhill with evil intent."

"Good. Let's say hi. Millie hasn't moved, by the way."

They made their way across the room to a round table near the food tables where Eden sat alone, looking at her phone.

Rory and Jefferson took seats on either side of her.

She looked up, confused, not recognizing them at first. "Oh, the detectives. You two scared me."

"Sorry, how's your night so far?" asked Rory.

She watched with narrowed eyes as Justin and Stacey moved to the dance floor.

"Horrible. And I was just looking at the snow forecast. It's really coming down. They say parts of I-5 up north are already closed. My night is not turning out how I'd hoped, so I might just go home."

If they weren't on this job, Jefferson would be right behind her. The only place he liked to see snow was on a mountain with a ski lift.

He glanced at his watch. They still had forty-five minutes before the drop. His seat was such that he could still watch Millie without making it obvious. She'd moved on from her conversation with the two ladies and now stood at the food table filling a plate.

Larson stood nearby, drinking a bottle of water and pretending to look at his phone.

"What kind of car do you have?" asked Rory.

Jefferson felt his phone buzz just as Eden and Rory started a discussion about the best cars for snow travel.

He pulled it out and saw it was a text from MJ.

"Got the entire crew here," she'd typed.

"Working."

"I guessed that. I don't think Ned knows I saw him yesterday."

"That's good. But stay away from him."

"I think I should stay away from you."

He smirked to himself. "Why is that?"

"Don't want to distract you from work."

Was that a flirty text? He stared at the screen, trying to imagine MJ saying those words in person. Would she emphasize the word distract, or would each word carry the same weight? There was only one way to find out.

"Appreciated. That dress is distracting."

She sent back a blushing emoji.

So it was flirting. His world tilted on its axis, and it felt good. But MJ was right. She'd already distracted him.

"And still. Say away from Ned."

"I won't talk to him. Promise."

"Talking isn't the only way to get into trouble."

"Just keeping my eyes open. Professional habit."

It couldn't hurt for MJ to be aware of Ned's movements. He had threatened her, after all. But if she engaged with him, it could compromise the WSPD plan.

"Please do not talk to him. Sensitive investigation underway."

"Got it."

He shook his head. It would be better for everyone if MJ was not here, but she had a mind of her own. He didn't trust her to be careful. She never was. But he did trust her to be smart. At least that much he could count on.

Chapter Forty-Five

A fter the brief text exchanged with MJ, Jefferson spent his time watching Millie and the surrounding people while his partner chatted up Eden.

It didn't surprise Jefferson to see Millie sidle up to MJ and Shannon. The ballroom appeared crowded, but it was a small room, making it hard to avoid rubbing shoulders with everyone eventually. He hadn't seen Ned in the crowd. Perhaps he would just greet people at the door all night. When it came time for the drop, they would know just how far Ned's involvement went.

The three women could be mistaken for longtime friends. MJ talked excitedly with active hands. Shannon put a gentle hand on Millie's shoulder. He wondered what they said.

Soon, Millie moved to a converse with an older couple, who greeted her with hugs. Jefferson marveled at how relaxed she appeared, knowing the scammers were somewhere in the building, moving through the crowd, potentially watching her as closely as Jefferson and the other detectives.

He let his eyes move quickly back to MJ.

Big mistake.

Their eyes connected across the dim room. The strains of a single saxophone wove through the air, each note pulling him deeper into her gaze. The world didn't just melt away—it dissolved like the snowflake had when it hit his warm skin.

Gone was the sparkling humor in her deep blue eyes. Now they were so soft, so vulnerable. The honesty in her expression made his chest tighten.

This wasn't one more moment they could file away and pretend to forget. It was the truth they were finally willing to share. It was electric and dangerous and beautiful.

He flinched at a punch to his arm.

"Earth to Detective Hughes," said Rory.

"Ow, was that necessary?"

Eden laughed. "You should just go ask her out. MJ, right? Justin's ex-wife? I thought he might still carry a torch for her, but . . . he's clearly smitten with someone else." She flung a hand toward the dancing pair of Justin and Stacey. For a brief second, Jefferson saw intense malevolence in those green eyes. Just as quickly, however, she wiped it away with a sigh. "That's life, I guess."

"We should go get a drink," Rory suggested. "Eden, do you want anything?"

"Nah," she said, standing. "I am going to head out. I have to do inventory tomorrow. Boring but must be done. And getting snowed in here sounds horrible."

The three of them stood, and Eden excused herself. "Have a good night, fellas."

They wished her well on her drive home.

Once she was out of earshot, Rory whistled, "Man, that girl has it bad for Justin Brooks. And she's pretty, but it doesn't surprise me it would take someone like our Dr. Underhill to get MJ off his brain." He gazed out at the dance floor where the two of them had just ended a dance.

Stacey stepped back from Justin, her face suddenly serious. With a flick of her head toward the detectives, Justin nodded, and the couple walked in their direction.

"What's this about?" Rory said in a low voice.

Jefferson shrugged, looking around to spot Millie again. "Looks like your drink will have to wait." He found Millie. She was sitting at a nearby table, chatting with the two women she'd conversed with earlier.

"Hey, guys," said Stacey as they approached. "Justin here," she said, sliding her arm through his, "has remembered something that could be very important to Ira's case. It answers a lot of questions for me, and I think you will agree."

"Okay," said Jefferson. "Let's hear it."

Justin nodded. "I don't know why I didn't think of it before, but with everyone saying Ira died from natural causes . . . It was just an offhand comment, and I didn't give it much thought until tonight."

The two detectives said nothing, but they watched him expectantly.

Justin hurried on. "Anyway, Ira liked the supplements and shakes they sell at the gym, Senior Strength. That's not unusual, but I remember him saying that he got a new one, one to help him continue to build muscle in his sleep. I told him he didn't need anything like that. The dude was already making serious muscle gains. Ira agreed, but said he was trying it out as a favor."

"A favor to who?" asked Rory.

Justin shrugged. "He didn't say. And I didn't ask because we were short on time."

The two detectives looked at each other.

"You thinking what I'm thinking?" asked Jefferson.

"Probably not exactly what you're thinking, given your distracted state, but about this? Yes. I think I am."

"Paradisered."

Rory shook his head. "Dang. My Bible-reading mama would be so disappointed in me for not getting it before now."

Chapter Forty-Six

M J hadn't told Shannon her real reason for coming to the
Christmas Ball because her friend would certainly disap-
prove.

Ned.

MJ had a feeling he would be there, completely clueless that she had
listened in on him in the alley. Now she just had to find out what he
was up to.

When she saw Millie and all the detectives in the room, MJ'd known
the big "operation" was happening at the ball. Ned may be their target
too, but she couldn't be sure. Whatever it was, she didn't want to mess
it up. And she wouldn't. Listening and watching. That's all she would
do. And if she found out something to help the detectives, then all the
better. More than anything, she wanted to know why Ned had tried to
hurt Edgar and to make sure he didn't get the chance to hurt anyone
else.

When Jefferson's attention turned to Rory, MJ made her move.

"I'm going to go find the ladies' room," she told Shannon. "You
want to go grab us a couple of drinks? I'll just take a soda of some kind,
if they have it.

"Sure. Meet me back here?"

"Yep."

Shannon eyed her briefly. "Are you going to ditch me and run off with Jefferson?"

MJ flung an arm around her and squeezed. Shannon glowed tonight, her beauty on full display. Her blonde hair, arranged in a partial top knot, cascaded down her back in a sea of ringlets. The dress she'd chosen was a floor-length, figure-hugging, red berry velvet with a sweetheart neckline and slit up to her thigh. MJ's own dress was alluring in a classy way. She knew that, but Shannon pulled off the glamourous and sexy look much better than she did. It wouldn't surprise MJ if Jefferson changed his mind about that date.

"Of course not," she assured her friend. "I wouldn't do that. And, remember, they are on a secret operation right now. That's why he had to cancel." She put her finger to her lips. "Shh."

"You mean that's one reason he canceled on me. But I promise not to bring that up again. Water under the bridge. Now go." She stepped away, making a shooing motion at MJ.

With Shannon off getting drinks, MJ checked to see that Jefferson's attention was elsewhere. Sure enough, he and Rory were in a discussion with Justin and Stacey Underhill. Seeing those two together didn't shock MJ as much as it seemed all too perfect. If she'd known Stacey better, she might have set them up herself.

First MJ would try the reception desk at the entrance. If Ned was still there greeting guests, he wasn't likely to spill any secrets.

With her head on a swivel, MJ crept past several groups of people having pleasant chats, so engaged with each other that she slipped by unnoticed. When she reached the entrance, no one was there. The foyer was dim with only the Christmas tree and reception desk lights giving off any illumination. No one came in or went out. She paused for a moment at the entrance door to watch the snow falling in thick, healthy chunks under the parking lot lights. Every car already had an inch of snow on its hood. Any other time, she'd step outside to catch a few flakes on her tongue. As a Las Vegas kid, MJ considered snow a magical experience to be savored.

A sudden, muffled sound from the classroom hallway made a breath catch in her throat. Someone was down there, and they weren't alone.

With her heart thumping in her ears, MJ slipped off her heels, moved past the desk, and took a few quiet steps down the hallway. One door sat slightly ajar, a sliver of light cutting into the dark hall.

"She's only bringing ten thousand? That's hardly worth all this trouble, hon."

"Quit calling me that." It was a woman who hissed the words. "It's because you're too soft. I have to do all the dirty work. 'I don't want to hurt anybody, sweetie,'" she said in a mocking whine. "Grandma was right. You are the idiot of the family. All you had to do was take care of that teacher, and all you could manage was pretending to hurt her dog. You're pathetic."

MJ moved a little closer to the door. Ned was one speaker, but she also recognized the woman's voice, but she couldn't quite pin it down.

"Look cuz, the teacher isn't even important," said Ned. "You just wanted me to hurt her because you were jealous. Forrest told me about your little crush. So, you can insult me all you want, but it was Ira that got the police on our tail. And that was all you, *hon*." The last word held a derisive emphasis.

"Who cares? What's one more dead old fart? They're all like grandma. Keep all their money and then leave it to some stupid church when they die. The way I see it, they don't need it, anyway. We might as well get some use out of it."

"Now *that* I can agree with."

"So it's only ten thousand now, but I have other irons in the fire. We'll be collecting more. I've got another lady about to put fifty thousand in my bitcoin wallet."

"Woohoo, cuz. You're such a lady charmer."

"Ew, gross. Don't even say that. It's just acting, and I'm a star," the woman replied with a lilt to her voice. Then her harsh tone returned. "So don't go screwing this up tonight. Just leave it to me. I'll just get the money and disappear before anyone's glass slipper comes off. If Millie's smart, she won't make a fuss. I'd hate to have a senior heart attack right here at the ball."

"You're so cold. In fact, hon, you might be a little psycho."

"Shut up, Ned. Now get—"

That was all MJ needed to hear to start a sprint back to the entrance before Ned could catch her in the hallway. Without looking behind her, she continued into the ballroom, stopping momentarily to put her shoes back on and calm her breathing. She should have kept going.

Chapter Forty-Seven

Jefferson looked to the last spot he'd seen MJ. She was gone. Shannon, however, stood in the space holding two drinks, looking around her in confusion.

"Something's happened," Jefferson said.

"What?"

"MJ. She's gone."

"I'm sure she's just gone to the bathroom or something." Rory turned him toward the drinks. "Stay with me Hughes. We have fifteen minutes to drop."

"But . . ."

"We have to see this through. You have a job to do."

Jefferson swallowed. His partner was right. Running after MJ would not only compromise the mission, it would signal to MJ that he didn't trust her ability to handle her own life. That's what drove her away from Justin, and it would drive her away from him.

And he *did* trust her. More than he trusted anyone. Yes, her curiosity often led her into dangerous paths, but if anyone could think their way out of a mess, it was MJ."

"Now, remember," said Rory. "You're having fun, or you're at least relaxed and not looking like a frantic detective. Grumpy, we can do. Frantic or suspicious, no. Let's walk around."

As they picked their way through the crowd, Jefferson searched for that gold dress. She was nowhere.

He stopped when he felt a hand on his shoulder. Hoping it was MJ, he turned with a relieved smile already working its way up his face. Instead of MJ, Shannon stood in front of him, looking beautiful and flustered.

"I'm going to go get that drink," said Rory, with a brief smile at Shannon, before walking away.

"Hi," she said, her face almost as red as her dress as she tried to avoid eye contact with Jefferson. "I don't want to bother you. I know you're on an operation thing," she said, lowering her voice. "It's just—"

"It's MJ."

"Yeah. I don't know where she went. She said the bathroom, but I checked. I'm worried. That Ned guy is here, and she told me what he did. Following her as well as that weird stuff with Edgar. What if he found her here?"

Jefferson smirked. "More like she found him."

She let a small smile escape. "You're probably right about that."

He watched her with something like amazement. Her willingness to talk to him attested to how much she cared about MJ. Such friends were scarce. A shock of guilt hit Jefferson as he realized how close he came to potentially putting a wedge between them. Thankfully, their friendship was stronger than his weakness.

"I know it's hard not to worry. MJ likes to walk into trouble, but she's also smart. Definitely smarter than that knucklehead Ned. But I'll keep my eyes open for her. We have a lot of police here tonight, even more than you realize. I think MJ will be fine, but if you see her, please tell me." The words carried more confidence than he felt, but it wouldn't help to let Shannon know the extent of his own worry.

She nodded, her eyes suddenly stern. "Fine. I'm trusting you to keep her from getting hurt."

The intensity of her gaze, her brown eyes locked on his, told him this statement extended beyond tonight.

He returned a gentle smile. "I take that charge very seriously."

"Good," she said, her eyes relaxing as her lips turned up to reveal her winning smile. "Then together, we'll keep our girl from getting into too much trouble."

"Deal," he agreed, hoping he could keep that promise tonight.

Chapter Forty-Eight

One minute MJ was slipping her shoes on, and the next she had a knife in her back.

"Walk," said Ned, pushing her forward.

"Where are we going?"

"Don't you worry about that, sweetie."

He pushed her roughly back toward the dark hall, causing her to stumble repeatedly on her too tall heels.

"Can I at least take these shoes off?" asked MJ.

"Fine. But hurry."

Reaching down, she slipped the straps off each foot, holding both shoes dangling from one hand.

Ned tutted. "Nuh-uh Miss Too Clever For Your Own Good. I know why you women wear them spikey heels. Weapons on your feet. You just drop those things right here in the garbage can."

"But they were expensive."

He shrugged as he pushed her forward again. "If you're lucky, you can come back for them. If you're not so lucky, you won't be needing shoes anymore. How much did you hear?"

"I don't know what you mean."

Ned clicked his tongue. "Don't go treating me like I'm stupid, sweetie. I know you were down here spying on us."

MJ chuckled. "Don't be silly, Ned. Why would I want to listen to you? I was just heading to the bathroom. I know there's one down this hall."

"Sure, Ms. Smartypants, but there's also one in the cafeteria."

"It was full."

"You shouldn't lie," he hissed. "I'm going to have to punish you for butting in our business again."

These words should have made MJ tremble with fear, but they didn't. After overhearing the earlier conversation down this hall, she knew Ned talked a big game, but actually hurting people, or dogs, was beyond his threshold for criminality. His partner in crime, like the boss on the phone in the alley and the woman in the room . . . that person scared her.

He resumed pushing her down the hall, eventually stopping at the same door Ned had just left.

"Ned. You don't have to do whatever you are planning to do," said MJ, as he pushed her into the room. It was dark as night but for one streetlight streaming in through a row of narrow windows. It seemed to be empty, and MJ wondered where the woman had gone.

"We're going to sit in the corner over there and be very quiet. Understand?"

"Whatever you say, Ned."

"Stop that."

"Stop what?"

"Being so mouthy, as if you're not scared at all. You're really annoying, you know that."

MJ sighed. "So I've been told."

"I guess you get to be our insurance policy. If the police get any ideas tonight, it's off with your pretty head."

"Our?"

Ned pushed her onto the floor in the corner. "Don't make a sound."

"Where's Danny when I need him?"

"Who's Danny?"

MJ laughed. "Only the giant man who scared you into leaving the alley. I almost laughed out loud when you tried calling him 'hon.'"

"Shut up."

"Sorry, it was funny."

"You were there the whole time?"

"Saw the whole thing. That picture. Yeah, the police already have it."

Ned pushed the knife so the point just broke through the fabric of her dress.

"Ned, don't do that. You don't have to push the knife into my skin. I know it's there," MJ said, her voice much more controlled than she felt.

The door opened, and someone else walked into the room.

"Ned," she whispered. "You in here?"

"Over here," he said.

As the woman approached, there was just enough light for MJ to make out her long red hair. It was Eden from Senior Strength.

She stopped short when she saw MJ kneeling on the floor. "What? Ned, what have you done?"

"She was listening," he hissed. "Heard everything we said."

MJ sighed. "Actually, that's not true. I was just—"

"Shut up," Ned hissed.

Eden shook her head. "Ned, you're such an idiot. Now all those cops are going to be looking for her. That blond detective has the hots for her." She turned away, her hand on her forehead. "If you screw this up, you are not getting anything. Do you hear me? Nothing. It's bad enough I have to do everything that even mildly upsets you. This one is on you, and you have to take care of it."

"I was just trying to help," he said weakly.

"Just sit there and be quiet. That old bag will be here any minute." She glared at MJ. "If you make a sound, I'll take that knife and cut you myself."

A gasp caught in MJ's throat. Not for the threat Eden made against her, but because she realized they were waiting for Millie. This had to be the police operation, but how could they let Millie walk into this trap? Eden was dangerous. Ned was right; she was psycho.

Before she could make it make sense, the door opened again. A woman shuffled forward and sat in a chair in the middle of the room. The lights were still off, but the red feather in Millie's hat made it obvious that's who it was.

MJ realized the older woman couldn't see her or Ned. They hunched in the darkest corner of the room, and Millie had her head down. If MJ dared make a sound to warn the woman, unhinged Ned would put a knife in her back.

"Hi, Millie," said Eden, moving toward the older woman. "Do you have the cash for Oloff?"

Millie nodded, saying nothing.

"Ned," said Eden, her voice sounding tight and suspicious. "Go lock the door and turn on the light."

Ned stood up, pulling MJ with him. "Move," he said. "Quit dragging your feet."

"Just leave her and lock it, you idiot. She's not going anywhere. Are you MJ? You want to stay and protect Millie, don't you?"

Ned released her arm long enough to step to the door, turn the lock, and flip on the lights.

The sudden brightness blinded them all, and MJ put her hand up to shield her eyes. "I can stay. Although, Millie's pretty tough on her own. I'd say she's tougher than you."

Ned returned to holding MJ by the arm. "She's our insurance policy. To make sure we get out of here alive. Plus, she has a Bronco. Have you seen the snow out there?"

"I told you I wanted to sneak out of here, not drag some annoying teacher along with me, and then fire up her obnoxiously loud car. How can I possibly share blood with such a moron? I should have kept Forrest around," lamented Eden.

MJ glanced at Millie. She had her head down and didn't say a word, just sat with a large handbag on her lap. She must be so frightened.

"Well, you're the one who put that fifteen pounder through his head," pointed out Ned.

"Shut up, Ned!"

MJ took the chance to break in. "Wait, so one of you must be Oloff?"

"I didn't say you could talk," hissed Ned.

Eden put her hands on her hips. She'd changed out of her evening gown and into leggings and a zipped-up parka. "Ned, you have control issues. Yes, I am Oloff, at least since Forrest flaked out. I guess we can quit with the act since you'll be Ned's problem once this is all over."

"What do you mean?" asked Ned.

Eden huffed. "What do you think I mean? You'll have to kill her, dump her somewhere. Maybe run that lousy car into the sound."

This pronouncement caused a slight ripple of fear through MJ, but she held a shard of hope that Ned, tasked with such a thing, could never do it.

"So you killed Ira," whispered MJ.

"Well," said Eden. "Technically Ira killed Ira. I just gave him the sample Night Builder supplements filled with enough fentanyl and ketamine to do the trick. He didn't know what was really in them, but no one forced him to take them before bed. He was all alone. If he hadn't, I suppose I would have just found another way to kill him."

She moved closer to Millie. "Give me the cash?"

Without a word, Millie picked up the handbag and held it out.

Eden almost reached out to grab it, but then she changed her mind.

"Ned, bring your friend up here. Let's have her get the cash and make sure it's all there."

"See, I told you she'd come in handy," said Ned as he pushed MJ toward Millie, the tip of his knife still pressed to her back.

Millie kept her head down, but she held the bag out, gripped with her left hand.

And that's when MJ knew. The woman in the black dress was not Millie.

She should have known that Jefferson and the rest of the West Sound PD would never put Millie in that kind of danger. They were probably listening to this entire conversation. But she would bet her Bronco that the police did not plan on her being in that room. They didn't plan on Ned having a knife to her back. And as long as she was in danger from that knife, the police couldn't make a move without putting her life at stake.

She had to get away from Ned.

Chapter Forty-Nine

"We can't go in yet," said Mendez quietly, momentarily removing one side of his headphones.

Earlier in the day, Mendez and a small surveillance team posed as part of the catering team in order to get in prior to the ball and set up microphones in Oloff's designated meet-up room. In a different room, across the hall, they established the listening station, which Mendez had the responsibility of monitoring all night.

"Why not," whispered Larson. "We need to make this quick. It's a blizzard out there."

With a grim sigh, Mendez said, "Ned has MJ."

"What!" Jefferson hissed. He ran his hands down his face. "I knew something was wrong. I knew it."

"And MJ must know we are listening," continued Mendez. He turned his serious eyes to Jefferson. "I'm sorry, man, but she made it clear that Ned is holding her with a knife. If we go barging in there . . ." He shook his head.

How could everything be so right and then, in a flash, go so wrong? Jefferson dropped into a chair, his hands cupping the back of his neck. He had to do something. Leaving her in there at the mercy of those perps wasn't an option. No matter what he had to do, he would get her out of there.

His head shot up. "I can go in. I'll offer to take her place."

Larson shook his head. "They'll never trust you or us. I say let's give it a few minutes to see if our Millie can make a move."

"I bet MJ has already figured something out," said Rory.

"Yeah," agreed Mendez. "She's a lot smarter than the criminals in there. Forrest must have been the brains of the group. In fact, MJ already got the woman to confess, on tape, to murdering both Forrest and Ira."

"Wowza," said Larson. "See? Smart cookie you got there."

For once in his life, Jefferson didn't shrink from the insinuation that MJ and he were an item. Instead, he resolved to waste no more time pretending he didn't care about MJ. That he didn't love her. He prayed they would get through this night and he would finally get the chance to tell her.

***

Taking the money bag from Millie, MJ looked up at Eden. "What now?"

"Count it."

"Really, shouldn't you just take it and go? You have your money," said MJ.

"Count it. When I want advice on being a thief, I won't be asking self-righteous teachers."

"Fine."

"She so mouthy, ain't she," said Ned.

MJ opened the bag. It was chock full of money. "This is going to take all night to count."

"Ned, help her."

"What?" Ned asked, holding up the knife. "But I've got the weapon."

"Give it to me."

Ned screwed up his face, tightening his grip on the knife. "No."

"What?" asked Eden, her face suddenly full of fury. "Did you just tell me no?"

Ned stepped back, his bravery wiped away by a flash of fear so sudden that MJ had to wonder what Eden had done to instill such terror in the man.

"Sorry, Eden. Here, you can have it," Ned said, his voice weak and panicky, like a child begging for forgiveness from an abusive parent.

"That's right, you'll give it to me," said Eden, stomping over to him. "I should have known you were the most worthless cousin. All those years at Grandma's house, I did everything. Tried to take care of you when she left us nothing. And this is how you show gratitude?" Her green eyes were wild with fury, but her words cut through the air with a seething calm. "Give it to me now."

Before he could obey, Eden snatched the knife from his hand. "I never wanted to share the money with you anyway," she seethed. Then, without warning, she plunged the blade into his stomach with a sickening sound.

MJ screamed as Ned crumpled to the floor. But she didn't have time to indulge her fear. Eden turned, holding the bloody knife at her waist with it pointed at MJ. Her green eyes glinted as her lips curled into an evil grin. "So now it's just the old lady, me, and Justin's ex. He found someone new. How does that make you feel, MJ? Because it makes me feel very, very angry."

Eden had her back to Millie, facing MJ. And that's when the Millie, who wasn't Millie at all, quietly stood. MJ didn't dare look, but somehow she knew it was Amber.

Meeting Eden's eyes with a grin of her own, she said. "I feel like . . . I feel like it's over, Eden."

"Freeze!" Amber shouted, her weapon held in front of her with both hands.

Eden turned and tried to run for the exit, but before she could take more than a step, a crash echoed through the room as the door splintered off its hinges. A flurry of uniformed officers ran through, shouting commands with their weapons raised, followed by Jefferson and two other tuxedoed detectives.

Chapter Fifty

"We need an ambulance," shouted MJ, kneeling over Ned. Blood had already soaked through his white shirt and was pooling on the floor.

"Mendez is on it," Larson said.

"MJ," Jefferson called, rushing to her side.

She looked up, but the paleness of her skin sent a shock through his heart.

"We have to help him," she said, her blue eyes so intense against her skin. "Give me your suit jacket."

He did as she said, but all he really wanted was to get her out of this room. "Here," he said, giving her the jacket.

Without a word, she turned and used it to apply pressure to Ned's wound. "You're going to be fine," she said. "Just try to relax."

"He deserves to die for being such an idiot," sneered Eden as the officers pulled her up from the ground where they'd cuffed her.

"Not helping your case, sweetheart," said Larson. "Get her out of here."

Ned's already fair skin now had a gray tinge as his breath came in shallow puffs. "You're so sweet," he wheezed at MJ. "But I'm a . . ." he sucked in a wet breath. "I'm a bad . . . guy. I could . . . have hurt . . . you."

Jefferson noticed tremors in MJ's arms from the effort of trying to apply pressure to the wound. "Let me do that," he said. "You just keep him talking."

She reluctantly let go of the jacket and moved to the other side. The blood on her hands created a red record of her movement across Ned's body, the floor, and the bottom of her gold dress.

"You wouldn't have hurt me, Ned," she said. "I knew you wouldn't."

The man closed his eyes. "You're right," he whispered. "But Eden would. She's crazy."

A firm hand grabbed Jefferson's shoulder. It was Rory, holding out towels and a first aid kit.

"Thanks, man."

His partner nodded, before turning his attention to MJ. "I just saw Shannon on her way out with Justin and Stacey. They're taking her home."

MJ nodded, her attention clearly not focused on anything outside of Ned.

Rory took off his suit coat. "Here, MJ. Put this on. We can't have you going into shock."

Just then, Amber appeared. Her Millie disguise was gone, and she now wore an all-black pull-over and leggings combination. She took Rory's jacket and helped MJ into it.

Jefferson removed his tuxedo coat from Ned's wound and replaced it with towels. Then Rory was on his knees beside him. "Let me do this, Jeffy. You take care of MJ."

MJ shook her head. "No. I don't want to leave."

Rory gave her a stern look. "MJ. Ned has passed out. There's nothing you can do here. I have some medic experience. I will do everything I can until the paramedics get here. But you are in danger of going into shock, which can be life-threatening if not taken seriously. Do you understand?"

She stared at Ned's ashen face without responding.

To Jefferson, Rory said, "Get her out of here, even if you have to carry her. Make sure she gets warm."

Jefferson nodded. "Thanks, man."

Amber squatted down with a hand on Jefferson's shoulder. Her grim expression told him she had bad news. "The paramedics are delayed. A multiple-vehicle accident not only has the paramedics busy but has blocked at least one station from getting down Cecil Bay Highway. They've put a call out to neighboring cities and the county. I've asked for a life flight, but we'll see if they can get through this storm."

Jefferson almost ran his hand through his hair, but stopped himself. Both were covered in Ned's blood. He should've worn gloves, but protocol abandoned him when he saw MJ on the floor, the injured man's blood already staining her dress.

"Here," said Rory, throwing him a pack of alcohol wipes. "Clean yourselves up."

"Come on, Jeff. I've got some clothes MJ can change into," said Amber.

He stood, wiping his hands, then stuffed the pack of wipes into his pocket. He stepped around Ned to help MJ up.

As she took his hand, her eyes met his with an intense glare. "Don't you even think of carrying me out here."

With a flash of his crooked smile, he said, "Then I suggest you come willingly."

Chapter Fifty-One

MJ exited the senior center's bathroom wearing a black zip-up pullover, black leggings, and running shoes that were just a tad too small. All of this came from Amber's store of workout gear she kept in her trunk. It didn't fit perfectly, but well enough, and MJ was grateful to get out of her blood-soaked dress, which now hung at her side in an evidence bag.

"You already have more color in your cheeks," Amber said, smiling at MJ as she approached her in the hall.

MJ handed her the bagged garment. "Thanks. I don't know what happened to me. Even in other dangerous situations, I've never seen someone get hurt like that, right in front of me." Another shiver hit her, a little smaller this time.

"Shock like that is pretty common. It happened to me when I first became an agent, after my first shoot out. You're strong. You'll be fine," Amber assured her. "But take it seriously by watching for other symptoms, like dizziness, shivering, clammy skin, that sort of thing."

"I will," MJ said.

Just then, a door opened, and Eden's angry voice spilled into the hall as Chief Carlson emerged with Jefferson behind him.

"You can't hold me here," she sneered. "I want my lawyer."

Closing the door, Jefferson rolled his eyes. "She's a nasty one. The sooner we get her to the station, the better. The officers in there are taking some serious abuse."

"Nothing they can't handle," said Chief Carlson. "I just got word that life flight is on the way. They should be able to land in the empty parking lot next door in the next ten minutes. How's the victim?"

Amber shot a glance at MJ and then back to the chief. She tilted her head toward the end of the hall. "Can we—"

"No," broke in MJ. "Please. I'd like to know how he is."

With a deep breath, Amber nodded reluctantly. "Fine. But you have to know that it's not looking good. His pulse is weak, and he's still unconscious. Rory is doing his best to stem the flow of blood, but he needs to get to a hospital soon, or he's not going to make it."

MJ nodded as if she had expected such news. "I know I should hate him for what he did to Edgar, but seeing him with Eden . . . I can't help feeling like he's one of my students. The ones beaten down by horrible people. Ned and Eden must have grown up together. As cousins?"

"She's not saying," said Jefferson, "but based on what we heard her say to you, that's probably the case."

"It's not an excuse for what he did, but I think he's endured a lot of abuse from her," said MJ.

"Grandma doesn't sound like much of a peach, either," added Amber.

"Well," said the chief, "that chopper will be here any minute. Unfortunately, because of the snow, most of the guests are still here. I've told Larson and Mendez and any free officers to keep the crowd in the ballroom while we get the victim transported."

"Millie?" asked MJ, her eyes wide as she remembered the older woman was here. Did she know what happened? Did she know about Ned and Eden?

"Yes, Millie is still here," the chief responded, a rare, gentle smile on his lips. "And she's been asking about you."

"You two should go find her," said Amber, a twinkle in her eyes. "We'll get Ned off. In case I don't get to tell her myself, let Millie know how much we appreciate her help tonight."

"We can do that," agreed Jefferson. "Shall we go?" He gazed down at MJ, his eyes not smiling, but different. Less guarded? The blue shone bright in a way she'd never seen before.

MJ stiffened, suddenly awkward as she remembered her earlier flirtatious texts.

"Um, yes, let's go," she said, eager to be around other people, unsure of how to look at or talk to Jefferson. It was so much easier to be vulnerable when he was far away, across the room. Butterflies erupted in her stomach, and she realized she had buried those feelings for a long time.

As they began walking, Jefferson didn't touch her, but the heat of his body next to her prickled her skin, sending warmth through her entire being. She let out a slow breath.

He glanced down. "Are you okay? Are you sure you're up for this?"

She licked her lips, and nodded, afraid any words might come out as unintelligible sounds.

You're being ridiculous, she thought. Get ahold of yourself, MJ. It's not like you've never stood next to this man before. She tried to convince herself that she was indeed experiencing shock, but she knew it wasn't true.

About half of the crowd remained in the ballroom, and it only took moments to spot Millie. She found them at the same time, rushing as fast as her legs could carry her to meet them near the dance floor.

The band still played, attempting to keep the atmosphere lively with the strains of "Let It Snow." It was clear, however, from the anxious faces in the crowd that the attendees knew something had gone awry. If nothing else, they knew closed roads and police activity hindered their chances of getting home soon.

Millie clutched MJ's hands, her eyes full of relief. "I'm so glad to see you. The other detectives told me what happened to Ned. I'm just glad he didn't hurt you or anyone else. And to think I came so close to giving them everything." She let go and grasped Jefferson's hand. "And you. Thank you so much for setting me straight about this young lady."

MJ wrinkled her brow in confusion. "Setting you straight?"

Jefferson cleared his throat. "It's nothing. I was just—"

"Oh now, don't you even try to deny it." She winked at MJ. "I daresay this young man is your biggest fan. What was it you said, 'best person you know in the world?'" Her eyes twinkled in merriment as she was clearly causing Jefferson discomfort.

"Best person in the world, eh?" repeated MJ. "So much for reckless."

Jefferson chuckled. "Oh, you're still reckless. I think it might be your middle name. MJ 'reckless' Brooks."

"Reckless maybe," said Millie with a soft smile. "But also brave. I think I need to be more brave. So, I've decided to sell that ole house after all. I want to travel and see the world. I don't need a scam man, or a real one, to do that." Millie beamed at them.

"But before all of that," she continued, still holding Jefferson's hand. She grabbed one of MJ's. "Do me this one last favor," she said as she joined their hands together. "Dance."

Jefferson's hand in hers sent a shiver down MJ's spine that she couldn't write off as any kind of shock. She kept her eyes on Millie as the band shifted to the slow, saxophone-heavy "Have Yourself a

Merry Little Christmas." With legs that already felt like Jello, MJ knew dancing with Jefferson would embarrassingly melt her completely.

She shook her head. "Detective Hughes is technically working, so—"

"I think that's a fine idea," Jefferson said, cutting off her excuse. "Shall we?" He gazed down at her, his blue eyes sparkling like the Puget Sound on a sunny day. A smile lingered on his lips, but there was tension there, too. He was taking a risk. Taking her hand again and asking her to come with him. Studying the contours of his face, she felt the urge to stroke his cheek, his chin and mess up that perfect blond hair. She wanted to tell him the risk would be worth it.

A breathless "Yes," escaped her lips, and his smile, crooked and beautiful, filled his face. Then he took the hand given to him by Millie and led MJ to the middle of the empty dance floor.

Every eye in the room watched them, but MJ didn't care. When Jefferson encircled her waist, she put her arms around his neck. The music lulled them into the mirage of being alone, and their eyes connected like the sea and the sky.

"I guess we have a lot to talk about," Jefferson said, his breath warm on her face.

She closed her eyes briefly, letting the heat of his closeness course through her. "No talking right now," she whispered. "Later."

He nodded. His eyes held a quiet fire—warm but restrained as he watched every subtle movement of her face with tenderness. Then he leaned in so that they danced cheek to cheek, his lips brushing her ear.

The saxophone wailed with longing and a promise. MJ heard the words in her head. "From now on, our troubles will be out of sight." She closed her eyes, almost swooning from happiness, wanting it to be true.

His whisper tickled her ear. "Are you warm now? No shock?"

She swallowed. That was so unfair. "I'm fine," she said when she could finally trust herself to speak. "Better than fine."

He pulled back, raising his hand and brushing her cheek. "I don't know exactly when you stole my heart, MJ Brooks, but I don't think I'll ever get it back."

As his hand traced her chin, she enclosed it with her own. "I'm keeping it forever."

Chapter Fifty-Two

MJ messed with her curls for the fiftieth time. They were being crazy today, but at least her makeup worked. MJ didn't wear it often, and even when she did it was subtle and natural. Today it helped her eyes pop against the white cashmere sweater her mom gave her for Christmas last year.

Jefferson would be here any minute, and the nerves were making her crazy.

She decided to take a quick jaunt on the beach to clear her head. If Jefferson showed up before she returned, the detective would quickly realize where to find her.

The grass still had a blanket of snow, but the sand of the beach was clear as she took each step down with care, watching for ice on the wooden stairs.

No Edgar today. He was already enjoying his outdoor adventure with Justin. No, not just Justin. Stacey Underhill tagged along. MJ shivered for her. Stacey was a trooper.

Now, there was a surprise. MJ was pretty sure Justin and Stacey hadn't spent a free minute apart since they met. Justin glowed more than he usually did, and MJ loved to see it. He hadn't been truly happy since their divorce. That wasn't the case anymore.

She took a breath to calm her heart. The last thing she wanted to do was act like some freak version of herself. Jefferson knew her. All she had to do was be herself. He liked her for her . . . and her ability to help him solve cases.

Surprisingly, Ned survived. Rory must have had some amazing medic skills. Unfortunately, Ned's involvement with Eden would land him significant jail time once he recovered fully. After Eden's arrest, the detectives discovered more disturbing information about her past. Eden and Ned were cousins. Their grandmother raised both of them after all four parents died in a car accident. Eden was twelve and Ned was ten. Their grandma was a moderately wealthy Richmond, Virginia woman, and when she died from a "fall" down the stairs three years ago, no one thought of it as anything other than a horrible accident. The Richmond police were reexamining her death based on Eden's assumption, revealed during Millie's case, that her grandmother would leave the estate to Eden and Ned. That disappointment and her unsteady mental state seemed to have hurled the woman into a revenge scheme targeting elderly victims.

It was clear Eden had some deep-seated psychological problems, probably brought on by multiple traumas in her life. MJ was just grateful they stopped her before anyone else got hurt.

Today, there would be no talk of crime. A spark of excitement hit her as she thought about seeing Jefferson again. A lunch date wasn't the ideal first date, but MJ had a flight to Las Vegas tonight. She was excited to spend time with her parents, but now, well . . . she had more reason to stick around.

A part of her hated feeling so happy. Like being so full of joy invited the negative forces of the universe to come balance it out.

She shook her head. "Stupid. Just don't think that way," she told herself.

"Don't think what way?" she heard behind her.

She turned to see Jefferson standing there, his blond hair sleek and casual at the same time. He wore a navy wool coat that made the blue of his eyes deep and powerful. He raised his lips in the crooked smile she loved, the one just for her.

"Don't think Jefferson will wear his best shoes on the beach," she said in a half-hearted attempt to explain her monologue.

Picking up a foot, he wiggled it for her inspection.

"Boots," she said, her own mouth unable to turn off the smile. "Very nice."

"If I want to walk here with you, I need the proper gear."

She took his arm and began walking. "I think we need to break in those boots."

They took a few steps, the cold air unable to penetrate the space between them.

"So, where do you want to go to lunch? You said you had a place in mind."

"I do," she grinned. "I think you'll like it, but you might not love it."

"Not exactly the best recommendation," he chuckled.

"I promised the owner, Danny, I'd come try out his place. He did me a favor. I'll tell you all about it on the way."

"I'm intrigued."

"Good."

They faced the water for a second. The breeze had just enough power to bite at their cheeks and noses. MJ's mind returned to the last time they stood here. Maybe that memory would never go away, but she closed her eyes against the cowardice it represented. They hadn't spoken of it, but she felt the injury she caused Jefferson as if she'd cut herself.

She slipped her hand into his.

Small ripples disturbed the surface of the mostly calm sound. The surf gently pressed its lips to the sand before sliding away again. There was contentment in the land and contentment in their hearts.

Jefferson looked down at their hands, switching their grip so their fingers intertwined. There was a hint of tension in his touch, a hesitancy she hated. She felt it in herself. How long does it take to completely trust someone with your heart? MJ didn't know, but she was willing to try, and she knew he felt the same, even if it took time to remove every brick from the walls they'd built around themselves.

He watched her, the beach reflected in his eyes, as she raised his hand to her mouth. Her lips coasted across his knuckles, a promise on her breath that, like the sound, she'd always return.

He raised his other hand to brush her cheek, tucking a wayward curl behind her ear. She pressed her cheek against his palm, and he saw it for the invitation it was. When he brought his lips to hers, the sweet warmth of his kiss stole every doubt from her heart.

* * *

Next from Gemma Christina

Nowhere on the Sound

On the Sound Book Four

The echoes were deep and short, quickly swallowed up into silence.

Though her legs were bound, she'd wrenched onto her back to send both feet slamming into the metal wall. The material didn't clatter like something thin or cheap. It was thick and unyielding, not likely to make much noise on the other side.

It didn't matter. MJ Brooks had been kicking at it for at least an hour. Maybe longer. Her legs ached from the jarring movement and the unrelenting cold of the stale air.

Light? She couldn't tell because they'd left the blindfold over her eyes. The material smelled of motor oil. It rubbed at her skin like a cheap hand towel.

Dropping her head back to breathe, she maneuvered onto her side to avoid lying on her hands, which were bound behind her. They were already numb, the zip tie cutting deep into her skin.

A blanket lay beneath her, but with her cheek to the floor, she breathed in the fine particles of dust that seemed to ride on every molecule of air. Snot already caked her nose from sneezing with no hands, much less a tissue.

Wind roiled outside. She could hear the high-pitched whistle of it as it battered this place, whatever this place was. She heard no other sounds. No birds. No cars. No people talking. No chance to get someone's attention.

A tear rolled out of her eye, trailing across the bridge of her nose and onto the opposite cheek before hitting the dirty cloth around her eyes.

In her mind, she saw her mom, blood trickling down her face as she fell against the car.

No, she screamed inside her head, squeezing her eyes shut. Don't think about it. Keep your wits.

But grief and fear gripped her heart in a way she'd never experienced.

Squeaking hinges whined as a rush of cold air ran over her body like a curious animal. Someone had opened a door.

MJ sat up and scurried back, pushing with her feet until she felt the freezing metal wall assault her skin through the back of her t-shirt.

Feet shuffled and then something clanked as if the person were setting things down on the floor. MJ's heart thrummed in her ears and she breathed in short, panicked spurts.

Rough hands gripped her own, causing her to yelp in pain. There was a snip, and then a sudden release of blood as it flowed back into her hands.

"Do not take off the blindfold until you hear the door close," said a man's deep voice. "Otherwise, I will shoot you."

A waft of body odor reached her nose. She held still, afraid to move away from the offending smell.

"Do you understand?"

MJ gave a slow nod, holding every other part of herself still.

"There's a good girl," the man said. His voice held no humor at the irony of his remark. The words were dead and cold. She knew this man would shoot her. He may even want to shoot her.

And this man was not the only one. There were at least two. When they took her, one held her from behind. She'd kicked back, catching his shins with the cowboy boots her dad gave her for Christmas. The man swore, but it made no difference. He held tight as the other one threw a bag over her head. Her mom was the last thing she saw before everything went dark.

"And you can kick that wall all day long. We are nowhere, and no one will hear you."

He stepped away. The hinges squeaked like a dying animal. Then a click as the door closed again.

Afterword

While this novel is fictional, online pig-butchering scams are real and drain the accounts of unsuspecting victims worldwide. If you believe that you or someone you know may be the victim of online scammers, visit the FDIC Inspector General information site to learn more. If you are in immediate danger, call 911 (United States) for your local law enforcement. You can also file a complaint with the FBI's Internet Crime Complaint Centerhttps://www.ic3.gov.

A Letter from the Author

Book One   Book Two   Book Three

Visit My Website at GemmaCBooks.com

Thank you for reading the On the Sound Series! Writing fiction means very little without readers. It's fun and fulfilling to put the words on the page, but the real thrill comes from readers enjoying the plot, characters, and setting of each novel.

MJ's teaching experience is very much a reflection of my own years as a classroom teacher in a rural Washington middle school. These are very general experiences that other teachers will likely find extremely relatable. The crime side comes from my innate curiosity about the origins and consequences of the real-life crime that plagues our communities, or simply asking "what if?" My family will tell you that my imagination gets away from me quite often, taking seemingly innocent events and mulling over the criminal possibilities. As much as the crime side intrigues me, however, I do love the good guys and gals, those who go into the dark places and shine a light.

There is more to come from the On the Sound crime-solving team. You may even see a new series or two involving familiar characters (think Amber Wells as a young FBI agent in Northern Nevada). More to come on that! Visit my website at GemmaCBooks.com where you can sign up for my newsletter for updates.

Happy Reading!

Gemma

Made in United States
Troutdale, OR
02/21/2025